The Ember War

by

Richard Fox

ISBN: 1515071758
ISBN-13: 978-1515071754

For Mom

CHAPTER 1

THE NEAR FUTURE

Humanity's only hope of survival entered the solar system at nearly the speed of light. The probe slowed as the sun's heliosphere disrupted the graviton wave it rode in on from the abyss of deep space. Awakened by the sudden deceleration, the probe absorbed the electromagnetic spectrum utilized by its target species and assessed the technological sophistication of the sole sentient species on Earth.

The probe adjusted its course to take it into the system's star. If the humans couldn't survive—

with its help—what was to come, then the probe would annihilate itself. There would be no trace of it for the enemy, and no chance of humanity's existence beyond the time it had until the enemy arrived. The probe analyzed filed patents, military expenditures, birth rates, mathematical advancement and space exploration.

The first assessment fell within the margin of error of survival and extinction for humanity. The probe's programming allowed for limited autonomous decision making (choice being a rare luxury for the probe's class of artificial intelligence). The probe found itself in a position to choose between ending its mission in the sun's fire and a mathematically improbable defense of humanity—and the potential compromise of its much larger mission.

Given the rare opportunity to make its own decision, the probe opted to dither. In the week it took to pass into Jupiter's orbit, the probe took in more data. It scoured the Internet for factors to add to the assessment, but the assessment remained the same: unlikely, but possible. By the time it shot past Mars, the probe still hadn't made a decision.

As the time to adjust course for Earth or continue into the sun approached, the probe conducted a final scan of cloud storage servers for any new information…and found something interesting.

While the new information made only a negligible impact on the assessment, the probe adjusted course to Earth. It hadn't traveled all this way for nothing.

In the desert south of Phoenix, Arizona, it landed with no more fanfare than a slight thump and a few startled cows. Then it broke into the local cell network and made a call.

****

Marc Ibarra awoke to his phone ringing at max volume, playing a pop ditty that he hated with vehemence. He rolled off the mattress that lay on the floor and crawled on his hands and knees to where his cell was recharging. His roommate, who paid the majority of their rent and got to sleep on an actual bed, grumbled and let off a slew of slurred insults.

Marc reached his cell and slapped at it until the offending music ended. He blinked sleep from his eyes and tried to focus on the caller's name on the screen. The only people who'd call at this ungodly hour were his family in Basque country…or maybe Jessica in his applied robotics course wanted a late-night study break.

The name on the screen was "ANSWER ME".

He closed an eye and reread the name. It was way too early—or too late, depending on one's point of view—for this nonsense. He turned the ringer off and went back to bed. Sleep was about to claim him when the phone rang again, just as loudly as last time but now with a disco anthem.

"Seriously?" his roommate slurred.

Marc declined the call and powered the phone off. He flopped back on his bed and curled into his blanket. *To hell with my first class,* he thought. Arizona State University had a lax attendance policy, one which he'd abuse for nights like this.

The cell erupted with big-band music. Marc took his head out from beneath the covers and looked at his phone like it was a thing possessed. The phone vibrated so hard that it practically danced a jig on the floor and the screen flashed "ANSWER ME" over and over again as music blared.

"Dude?" said his roommate, now sitting up in his bed.

Marc swiped the phone off the charging cord and the music stopped. The caller's name undulated with a rainbow of colors and an arrow appeared on the screen pointing to the button he had to press to answer the call. *When did I get this app?* he thought.

Marc sighed and left the bedroom, meandering into the hallway bathroom with the grace of a zombie. The battered mattress he slept on played hell with his back and left him stiff every morning. Dropping his boxers, he took a seat on the toilet and answered the call, determined to return this caller's civility with some interesting background noise.

"What?" he murmured.

"Marc Ibarra. I need to see you." The voice was mechanical, asexual in its monotone.

"Do you have any frigging idea what time it is? Wait, who the hell is this?"

"You must come to me immediately. We must discuss the mathematical proof you have stored in document title 'thiscantberight.doc.'"

Marc shot to his feet. The boxers around his ankles tripped him up and he stumbled out of the bathroom and fell against the wall. His elbow punched a hole in the drywall and the cell clattered to the floor.

He scooped the phone back up and struggled to breathe as a sudden asthma attack came over him.

"How…how…?" He couldn't finish his question until he found his inhaler in the kitchen, mere steps away in the tiny apartment. He took a deep breath from the inhaler and felt the tightness leave his lungs.

That someone knew of his proof was impossible. He'd finished it earlier that night and had encrypted it several times before loading it into a cloud file that shouldn't have been linked to him in any way.

"How do you know about that?" he asked.

"You must come to me immediately. There is little time. Look at your screen," the robotic voice said. His screen changed to a map program, displaying a pin in an open field just off the highway connecting Phoenix to the suburb of Maricopa.

"Come. Now."

Marc grabbed his keys.

****

An hour later, his jeans ripped from scaling a barbed-wire fence, Marc was surrounded by desert scrub. The blue of the morning rose behind him, where his beat-up Honda waited on the side of the highway.

With his cell to his ear, Marc stopped and looked around before deciding how to continue. Spiked ocotillo plants looked a lot like benign mesquite trees in the darkness. A Native American casino in the distance served as his North Star, helping him keep his bearings.

"You're not out here, are you? I'm being punked, aren't I?" he asked the mysterious caller.

"You are nine point two six meters to my east south east. Punk: decayed wood, used as tinder. Are you on fire?" the caller said.

Marc rolled his eyes. This wasn't the first time the caller had used the nonstandard meanings of words during what passed as conversation between the two. Marc had tried to get the caller to explain how he knew about his theorem and why they had to meet in the middle of the desert. The caller had refused to say anything. He would only reiterate that Marc had to come quickly to see him, chiding him every time Marc deviated from the provided driving directions.

"If you're so close, why can't I see you?" he asked. He took a few steps in what he thought was a northwesterly direction and squished into a cow patty.

"Continue," the caller said.

Marc shook his foot loose and tried to kick the cow leavings from his sneakers.

"You know what this is? This is exactly what's all over my shoes, you monotone bastard. Forget it!" Marc shoved his phone into his back pocket and limped back toward his car, his right foot squishing with each step.

The route back to his car was comparatively easy; he just had to walk toward his headlights. That was the plan, anyway, until the lights on his car shut off.

"Marc, this is important." The muffled words came from his pocketed cell.

"How are you doing this?" Marc shouted into the night.

"Turn around, please."

Marc did as asked and a silver light like the snap of a reflection from a fish twisting just beneath the water flared on the ground ahead of him. No one was there a moment ago and Marc hadn't heard any movement.

"I swear if I get my kidneys cut out I will be so pissed about this," Marc said as he made his way to where he saw the light. He stood for a moment, then flopped his arms against his sides. "I'm here."

"You're standing on me." The voice came from beneath Marc's feet.

Marc skipped aside like he'd just heard a rattlesnake's warning.

"Holy—did someone bury you? Why didn't you tell me to bring a shovel?" Marc went to his knees and poked at the ground, which felt solid. "How deep are you? Do you have enough air?" Marc asked, using both hands to shove earth aside.

"Two inches ahead and three down."

Marc's face contorted in confusion as he kept digging. He moved a mound of gray dirt and pebbles aside and a silver light washed over his face.

A silver needle no more than three inches long rested in the dirt. Tiny filaments of lambent energy crept from the needle and undulated through the air like a snake in the ocean. Marc was frozen in place, his jaw slack as the filaments extended away from the needle, shades of white swimming in and around it.

"We don't have much time." The words came from the needle in the same mechanical voice as his mysterious caller. A point of light appeared in the air above the needle, sparked, and then lit into a flame no bigger than he'd seen on a match head. The white flame, which gave off no heat, rose and grew in size. A flame the size of Marc's head came to a stop a few feet in the air.

Marc, transfixed by the flame until now, got to his feet. The filaments from the needle had extended past him and formed a perimeter ten yards in diameter. Tendrils of energy writhed against each other and against an invisible boundary. His heart pounded in his ears and his innate fight-or-flight instinct made a decision.

"This is a different experience for you. Let me—"

Marc turned and ran away. He got to where the tendrils had stopped and ran into what felt like a wall of water. Air thickened around him as he tried to push through and find purchase on the ground ahead. It felt like he was moving through clay.

"Marc, you're being ridiculous." The air hardened and spat him back toward the flame. Marc tripped over his own feet and tumbled to the ground. He snapped back to his feet and looked for a way, anyway, to put some distance between him and the flame.

The flame, white on silver or silver on white—Marc couldn't tell as it morphed in the air—floated toward him slowly.

Marc made the sign of the cross with two fingers and looked away. He heard a sigh.

"Look at me." The flame, again.

Marc opened an eye. The flame was a few

inches from his hands but he still felt no heat.

"I'm not here to hurt you. I'm here to help you. Understand?" The flame bobbed in the air gently until Marc nodded. "I am an emissary from an alien intelligence sent to save your species from extinction and I need your help to do it."

Marc pointed a finger at the flame and tried to touch it. His fingertip passed into the flame's surface without sensation.

"I thought unsolicited physical contact was against your species' norms," said the flame, the tendrils rustling with the words.

Marc snapped his hand back.

"Did you say something about…extinction?" The flame bobbed in the air. "How? Why?"

"An armada is coming." The flame morphed into an oblong shape with a half dozen tendrils sticking from it, like a misshapen spider. "They are the Xaros and they will annihilate your species with ease. Unless you and I work together, your extinction is assured," the flame said, floating closer to Marc, who stood dumbfounded. The flame came so close that he could see his reflection on it. Deep blue motes of light sprang from the flame and evaporated in the air.

"Why me? What am I supposed to do about an alien armada? I'm a B-minus grad student with a mountain of student loans, not some…some world leader!"

The probe returned to flames and a hologram of a white paper popped into the air next to it. Pages flipped open from the book, the mathematical proof he'd finished the night before.

"We expected that your species would have progressed to the edge of your solar system by now. To see such potential squandered on wars and Internet cat videos was disheartening, but this is well beyond what you should be capable of. The advancements you discovered in material science and energy storage are a springboard to technological advancement that will give you a 27 percent chance of survival, provided everything goes as planned. We can start here." The proof stopped with the picture of a lattice of carbon atoms. The last page had the words "No way!!!!" scrawled next to the diagram.

"I don't understand," Marc said.

"You will, but we need to get started right away."

"How much time do we have?"

"Sixty years."

CHAPTER 2

SIX DECADES LATER

Lieutenant Ken Hale of the Atlantic Union Marine Corps felt blood rush to his head as the pilot swung their drop ship through a breaking maneuver and g-forces pressed him against the restraints of his acceleration bed. A glance out a porthole offered nothing but swirling stars against the deep void. A holo appeared against his visor showing the drop ship relative to their target.

"In position. Go for hard dock or umbilicals?" the pilot asked through his helmet comms.

There were no unusual energy readings from

their target. There were no readings at all, which was why he was there in the first place. The Ibarra Corporation asteroid mining outpost had gone dark hours ago, with no warning or explanations. All attempts to contact the miners had been met with silence, leaving many unanswered questions to this mission. He wouldn't trust a standard docking assault, which meant a riskier boarding maneuver.

"Go for umbilicals," he said as he tapped a flat screen on the back of his left hand to open a channel to his team.

"We're going in on the wire. Hang tight and use your secondary clamps. Anyone goes Flying Dutchman and you're on Gunny's shit list for the whole trip to Saturn," he said. Six icons on his visor display went green as his Marines acknowledged. One icon pulsed as it broadcast.

"I swear he does this just to scare me," Lance Corporal Standish said over the squad net.

"Standish!" Gunnery Sergeant Cortaro's icon pulsed.

Hale fought a grin. Cortaro's icon kept

20

pulsing as Cortaro and Standish went into a private channel. As the officer in charge, he could cut into any channel, but he had a pretty good idea what his head enlisted Marine was saying to the junior Marine—mostly four-letter words and a series of promises of what would happen to Standish if he screwed up his radio discipline again.

The infrared, IR, net used by the Marines and the rest of the military under combat conditions was limited to a few tens of meters in range. Transmissions with extended range, such as radio, could be detected, triangulated and targeted. Staying off a potential enemy's radar was the surest way to survive the 21st century battlefield, on Earth or in the void of space.

A vibration shuddered through the drop ship followed by a sudden jerk. Hale felt the deck lurch as the umbilical latched onto their target and the speed between the two objects almost matched. The drop ship would maintain a bit more relative speed to keep the line taut.

The restraints on the acceleration bed

popped open silently as there was no atmosphere in the bay to carry sound. Hale activated the magnetic plating in his boots and let it pull him to the deck. He shrugged his gauss rifle off his shoulder and locked the weapon into his right hand with the mag plates in his palm and the rifle's grip.

Sliding his feet against the deck lessened the grav plating's hold, keeping him attached but not immobile. Moving across the deck was more akin to ice skating for him than walking. The ramp at the end of the bay opened, the final traces of gas in the hold venting around the widening gap in wisps of fog.

Two of his Marines—Torni and Franklin, according to the labels his visor projected on their armor—stood at the edge of the hull and the remaining four stood in line behind them. All his Marines looked nearly identical in their armor; only the vagaries of height and musculature would set them apart to an outsider. After enough drops and exercises, the men and woman of his team could pick each other out by gait and silhouette.

Franklin's Gustav heavy gauss rifle, a beast of a weapon with three rotating barrels, slung ready from his hip, braced against his body by a harness. Franklin lowered the barrel in time with the descending ramp, ready to engage any targets that appeared.

Torni stood against the bulkhead, scanning their target with the cameras of the heavy gauss guns slung underneath the drop ship. Hale peeked around her and saw that the surface of their target was nothing but craters and dust.

"Nothing on the scope. No transmissions," she said. Her words came into Hale's helmet through shortwave infra-red transmissions and adjusted for distance and location. Despite being in a near total vacuum, the commo tech in their helmets allowed the team to speak naturally and without radio transmissions that would betray their location to an enemy.

"I don't like this," Franklin said. The heavy gunner tried to shift his footing, a useless gesture as the grav plating in his feet held him fast. The recoil from his Gustav would pitch him against the hull like a pinball if he fired the cannon without being held in place.

The asteroid factory, an oblong rock seven hundred yards long marred by billions of years' worth of impacts, came into view. The asteroid, its name nothing but a series of letters and numbers assigned by the prospectors that cataloged it decades ago, bore a man-made superstructure in its middle. The blocky structure made the asteroid look like one of the old cargo ships that plied the Earth's oceans at the beginning of the century before anti-grav blimps replaced them.

Beyond the factory was the void, the black abyss punctuated by stars far beyond humanity's reach. Hale swallowed hard as his eyes followed the cable running from the hull just above the open ramp to where it tethered onto the factory.

"Bad feeling about this one, yeah," Franklin said.

"You always say that. Some drunk miner probably broke their commo," Torni said. She closed up the control panel, took a D-ring from her utility belt and pulled some slack from the carbon-fiber cord linking her to the D-ring.

"You first, sir? As always?" she asked Hale.

"As always," he said as he pulled his own D-ring out and attached it to the tether wire. He grabbed the wire with his left hand and activated the grav plating to latch him to it. Then he looked over his shoulder to his team. The five Marines were weapons ready, fidgeting in place like well-trained hunting dogs raring to be let off the leash. Franklin would stay on over watch until the rest of the team was safely across the tether.

"Treat this as a combat drop until we know otherwise," he said to his Marines. Some nodded their understanding; others clicked their tongues twice to send their affirmative. Hale stepped into the void, swinging his legs forward momentum to push himself along the tether. A few yards from the drop ship, he brought his body parallel to the tether.

"Let's go!" He activated the anti-grav lining on the soles of his boots and used the push to accelerate down the tether, pushing his speed to a hair's breadth below the safety threshold, where any faster would cause friction damage between his hand and the tether and then cut the anti-grav. The asteroid closed as his speed remained constant, no atmospheric drag to slow him. The location mini-map on his visor showed the rest of his Marines on the tether behind him.

Hale's focus went back to the approaching asteroid factory. Location beacons flashed from the superstructure, but there were no signs of life or power from the bridge. He saw no obvious signs of damage from an attack by Luna extremists or from a collision. Four gigantic spikes attached the mining superstructure to the asteroid, pylons of steel that bit into the rock like fangs.

A hundred yards from the asteroid, Hale swung the soles of his feet into his direction of travel and triggered the anti-grav. The rapid deceleration robbed blood from his head and grayed out his vision despite the automatic pressure his suit squeezed onto his core and thighs to keep his blood in his brain where he needed it most.

A distance meter on his visor ran to zero and the mag plating in his hand automatically cut out. The tether to his D-ring detached and the carbon wire zipped back into the spool on his belt. Now in free fall, Hale toggled his grav/anti-grav plates to bring him to the surface at a manageable speed—too fast and he'd end up as a smear on the asteroid, too slow and he'd be an obstacle for the Marines coming in behind him.

He hit the asteroid hard enough that he had to crouch into his landing. Fine dust spat from beneath his boots. He trained his weapon on the metal structure just ahead of him but saw no sign of a welcoming party, hostile or otherwise, to greet him. Hale took leaping strides toward the structure, using his boots to compensate for the microgravity.

The tether was anchored against the hull, triple grounding spikes dug into the deep blue metal. Atmosphere leaked from where the tether punctured the hull; ambient moisture from the air in the factory shot out into the near-absolute-zero vacuum as tiny flecks of ice. The outgassing told Hale that the station still had atmosphere, but no one was reacting to the hull breach.

Hale stopped next to an access door on the superstructure and slapped a hand against the metal to anchor himself, magnets in his fingertips securing him to the metal hull. The lamprey superstructure was the only man-made thing on the asteroid; the actual mining work happened deep within the rock.

Five of his Marines were on the ground and Franklin would land in another minute.

The access panel was unpowered. If Torni couldn't get in, then Standish would have to cut their way in. A hard breach was noisy enough to alert any defenders and kept the team exposed in a vacuum far too long for comfort.

Torni loped over and knelt next to the air-lock door. She took a void-hardened Ubi—the ubiquitous mini-tablet that had replaced every cell phone and personal computer on the planet within a few years of their introduction by the Ibarra Corporation—and ran a cable into an access port.

Her military grade Ubi came with backdoor keys into every computer system on the factory, courtesy of the Ibarra Corporation.

The screen on the access port blinked to life, the Ibarra corporate logo spinning in place as the access port booted up.

Hale looked up at the life pods attached to the superstructure. The standard complement of six were still in place. If the miners were gone, that wasn't how they'd left the station.

"Someone cut the power line. Batteries died...twenty hours ago. Give me four minutes to get us in," Torni said. As the team's dedicated cyber hacker, Torni had proved her expertise on nearly every mission they undertook. Hale had no need to doubt or quiz her further.

"Gunny Cortaro, get that hull breach under control," Hale ordered.

Cortaro and Corpsman Walsh, their team medic, crouched and launched themselves off the asteroid with an anti-grav–assisted jump. Using their boots to pull them against the hull, Cortaro stood perpendicular to the wall. No matter how many low-G ops Hale went on, watching men and women walk on walls always struck him as unnatural. Walsh jabbed a nozzle into the hull breaches around where the tether gripped into the hull and injected quick foam around the spikes. The foam expanded instantly and solidified in a half second; the graphene and titanium lattice within the foam went rigid to seal the hull breaches with ease.

One less thing to worry about.

Hale felt a sudden vibration through the soles of his feet. Franklin had reached the asteroid.

"Sir, there's still atmo and gravity inside. A little cold, but nothing else out of the ordinary," Torni said, reading from her Ubi.

"Can you get the station logs?" he asked.

"No, whatever cut the hardline power cut the data lines, too. I've got the sensors on the other side of the air lock and that's it," Torni said.

Red warning lights pulsed around the air lock as the door slid aside, revealing the interior compartment, a small space with just enough room for three miners in EVA suits.

"Standish, with me. Torni, get the interior doors open soon as we're clear," Hale ordered. He stepped into the air lock and glanced into an inner porthole. Emergency lighting strips ran along where the walls met, ceiling-mounted warning lights flashed "PRESSURE," most likely from the damage done by the tether.

Standish's footfalls thumped against the hull as he ran down the wall to join his platoon leader. Gripping the lip of the doorway, he swung himself into the air lock with a gymnast's grace. Standish banged a fist against the bulkhead twice to signal his arrival and the air-lock door slid shut. Gravity returned as the station's plating kicked in. Hale felt lightheaded for a moment as his heart brought his blood pressure back to where evolution and Mother Nature intended.

"You think it's aliens, sir?" Standish asked.

A yellow light pulsated on the ceiling and gouts of atmosphere burst into their air lock.

"There's no such thing as aliens, Marine.

Everyone knows that," Hale said. He brought his rifle to his shoulder and aimed it at the door.

"One of these days, it *will* be aliens and then everyone will be all, 'Wow, Standish, how'd you know?'"

"Team, go low velocity or scatter shot with your weapons. Punching a hole through the side of the asteroid would be very, very bad," Hale said over the IR. Their gauss rifles could fire the cobalt-jacketed rounds as a shotgun blast of small bullets, low-velocity single slugs for armored targets and high velocity for use as anti-materiel munitions. The high-energy setting wasn't recommended for boarding operations, both for the collateral damage the rounds would cause and for the slow rate of fire—the capacitors on their weapons had to build up charge and would suck the batteries dry after a few shots.

The sensors on Hale's suit read a standard atmosphere of pressure and ambient temperature over freezing. He could remove his helmet and be just fine but his face had limited ballistic protection.

Hale tapped a green button to open the inner door, which slid aside without fanfare.

Silence greeted them. Standish and Hale stood stock-still, ready for whatever might come around the many corners in the passageway. Hale triggered the megaphones built into his helmet.

"North Atlantic Union Forces boarding party, come forward and be recognized," his voice boomed through the station with the subtleness of a thunderclap. The command echoed, then died away. No response. For the first time on this mission, Hale felt unease. There was no obvious reason for the station to be empty. Where was everyone?

Cortaro and Franklin were the next Marines to enter. Hale took his top sergeant aside while Standish and Franklin pulled security.

"What do you think?" Hale asked Cortaro.

"No one here. Only other place they could be is in the factory. Maybe there was an industrial accident and they're held up in a life pod," Cortaro said.

"Yeah, that's what I'm thinking," Hale said.

He pulled up schematics for the station on his forearm display and programmed a route to the factory within the asteroid. Direction arrows lit up on his and the rest of the team's visors.

The Ibarra Corporation's Lamprey class factories arrived on asteroids with little more than a life-support facility, 3-D printers and minimal crew. The printers used the asteroid's own mass to create the mining robots and smelters that hollowed out the asteroid. After a few months, an asteroid the size of the Martian moon Phobos could be changed from just another space rock to megatons of rare earth minerals needed for terrestrial manufacturing.

In the decades since the Ibarra Corp harvested the first asteroid near Ceres, space mining had advanced almost to the point where the human crews could be replaced by robots. The work came with enough danger from rogue impacts, cosmic rays and the occasional industrial accident that the crews earned enough to retire from the workforce after a few years on the job. A whole crew hadn't been lost in years, which was why this mission made Hale's skin crawl.

Because his job was command and control now, and not to pull the trigger, Hale fell behind his Marines as they made their way through the station.

Vincenti, the team's communications specialist, came up to an open hatch and stuck his rifle barrel around the entrance. The camera attached to the muzzle fed into his visor, which he fed to Hale through their shortwave infra-red network.

Vincenti's camera focused on the unmanned bunkroom: beds with rumpled blankets, Ubis with paused video screens and clothing left all over the room as if a pack of teenagers slept in there, not grown professionals known for their strict attention to detail.

"Someone left-a in a hurry," Vincenti said, his Italian accent adding vowels to the ends of words that didn't need it.

"Where'd they go? Air locks haven't been opened in weeks, no life pods jettisoned," Franklin said. The big Marine, one of the few Hale had ever met that could lift and fire a Gustav gun without augmented armor, sounded more worried than Hale had ever heard.

Standish ran ahead, sweeping the corners at the end of the passageway with fluid grace. The wall beyond the hallway was raw asteroid, the jagged craters and hard angles of its formation never smoothed by the touch of air and water like the mountains of Earth. Yellow and black chevrons bordered a shiny metal door that led into the asteroid proper.

Standish tapped at the blank control panel, then signaled for Torni to come forward when there was no response.

"Lieutenant Hale?" an icon for their drop ship popped on his visor.

"Hale, go."

"The *Breitenfeld* is burning back to the fleet. Our recovery window got cut to thirty minutes. What's your status?" the drop ship pilot asked.

Hale grit his teeth in frustration as he considered a series of replies, each less diplomatic than the last. The *Breitenfeld*, the escort carrier he and his Marines operated out of, was supposed to stay within support range until this mission was complete. Even if Torni opened the door to the mine in the next ten seconds and they found the crew conducting business as usual, they'd be hard-pressed to make it back in time.

"No sign of the crew. No idea what happened to them yet either," Hale said. He set a timer countdown on his visor and looked at the mine entrance. Torni was hard at work as the rest of his Marines looked at him with anticipation. The call to the drop ship was private, but every Marine out of boot camp could tell when the lieutenant was on the channel with higher headquarters. A new set of orders in the field was rarely a cause for celebration.

"I'm not going to leave you here, but if we miss the *Breitenfeld*, we'll be out here for weeks waiting for pickup *and* we'll miss our ticket to the colonies. So…hurry the hell up," the pilot said.

"We're working on it," Hale said. "Why the

sudden change in plans?"

"Admiral Garrett wants the entire fleet together ahead of schedule. You want me to patch you through to him?" the pilot said, half-joking.

"No grav on the other side," Torni said as she backed away from the door and tucked the butt of her rifle into her shoulder. Franklin moved to stand in front of the door, his Gustav at his hip and ready. A scanning laser speared out from his helmet and ran up and down the door, ready to touch whatever lay beyond. Torni and Standish were on either side of him, weapons ready.

The quad barrels on Franklin's machine gun whirled to life.

Warning lights flashed around the air lock and a buzzer sounded.

"Remember, low-velocity rounds," Hale said.

The access door slid open with the hiss of a blade leaving its scabbard. A single figure in a heavy mining suit, bands of reinforced graphene plates on top of heavy graphene weave, stood beyond the doorway. The miner had one foot mag locked to the deck while the rest of his body floated in the air like a doll hung out to dry. A red and black veneer on the inside of his faceplate hid his countenance. A rent in his suit ran from his backbone through his side and light from deep in the factory shown through the gash. Old blood floated in the air in amorphous blobs before flowing through the air lock and falling to the grav plating with soft splashes.

"Oh boy," Standish said.

"No life signs," Franklin said. The heavy gunner moved forward, Standish and Torni on his flanks. Franklin, using his grav linings to keep him on the deck, stepped around the dead miner and locked his feet into place a few steps later. Standish and Torni pushed off the deck and went airborne.

Hale grav-stepped past the body. A quick glance at the wound made him think it was the result of some sort of blade, not a projectile. He stopped next to Franklin and the view took his breath away.

The interior of the asteroid was hollow. The entire rock was nothing but an eggshell around a vast cavern of…some sort of machinery. Gleaming silver columns ran down the spine of the cavern from top to bottom. Robot arms peppered each column, frozen in whatever routine they were running. Ammunition crates were stacked along the flanks of the cavern, grav-locked to each other and the deck.

There had to have been tens of thousands of crates, some large enough to hold the rail gun shells used by the fleet's cruisers. Forklift robots, little more than two giant pairs of calipers attached to a gravity drive, were stationary in the air. Standby beacon lights flashed from their metal cores.

"Sir, what the hell is this?" Cortaro asked.

"Not a mining operation, that's for sure," Hale said. He tried to open a channel to the drop ship, to no avail. "Vincenti, what's blocking our commo?"

Vincenti grabbed his Ubi from his hip and sank back to the deck. Walsh took his place on the asteroid wall.

"Got a floater…two, make that four," Standish said. Gun camera pics of four separate bodies hanging in the air or rolling against the rock walls popped onto Hale's visor. Two of the bodies floated amidst black blobs of blood; one lacked legs and the last was split from shoulder to hip.

"Crew complement is six. Where's the last miner?" Cortaro asked.

The forklift bots' blue lights went yellow, then started flashing. The bots rose into the air, their grav drives resonating from a slight thrum into a heartbeat pulse of static. The bots swung toward the Marines and accelerated.

"Um, sir," Standish said.

"Open fire!" Hale shouted. The Marines' gauss rifles snapped as the electromagnets in their weapons shot bolts at the new threats. The bolts sliced through the air and smashed into the forklift bots. The bots were void hardened, designed to take micro-meteorite hits and keep functioning. Bolts ricocheted off mandibles and sent the bots spinning through the air. A careful shot from Torni to the grav drive of the closest bot shattered it into pieces. Another disintegrated with the force of a grenade.

Franklin's Gustav smashed two bots into fragments and stitched a line of bullets across the nearest silver column before it annihilated the last of the bots. Spent bolts ricocheted off the far walls and sent off sparks where they collided against the bare rock.

A bolt warbled past Hale's head and smacked into someone's armor with a thump. He whirled around and found Walsh with a hand over his forearm. His icon didn't register any serious injury, but Walsh was wincing.

"You alright?" Hale asked.

"Armor took it, just stings like hell." Walsh shook his hand out and opened and closed his fist.

"One of the bots is still functional. Want me to get it?" Torni asked. She pointed into the expanding clouds of debris where a red light pulsed on the spinning thorax body of the robot, its mandibles shot off and grav drive wrecked.

Hale checked the timer. There wasn't much time to recover the forklift bot's computer core, which should have code logs of what caused their malfunction. Hale knew what his Marines could and couldn't do—there was only one person for this job.

"I've got this. Cover me," Hale said. He stepped onto a railing and launched himself into the air. As a former champion high diver, Hale's kinesthetic senses were second to none. He made micro adjustments to his course with bursts of anti-grav from his boot emitters, flotsam of robot fragments bouncing off his helmet as he neared the robot core.

Hale held his arms out and snagged the core as he sped past. He flipped over and used his boots to pull him to the cavern wall. Bullet rents scarred the core, but the central processor looked intact. If there was some new malicious code inside it, there was no way he could risk tapping into it outside a firewalled lab on the *Breitenfeld*.

"Sir, you feel that?" Cortaro asked. Hale put a hand against the cavern but felt nothing out of the ordinary.

"Like…footsteps," Cortaro said.

"This rock doesn't have engines. What is that?" Torni said. Hale finally felt what Torni was talking about as a vibration shimmered through his feet.

"Sergeant Cortaro, I think it's time for us to go," Hale said. He squatted against the cavern wall and prepared to disengage his boots. He felt the vibration again, then another one.

"No objections here, sir," Cortaro said.

At the end of the cavern, one of the larger ammunition crates spun into the air and a shrill keen filled the space. Franklin popped his ammo can loose from his Gustav and fumbled for the spare he had hanging from his lower back.

"I told you it was aliens!" Standish cried.

A beast climbed on top of the far ammo boxes. Black segmented legs gripped into the boxes and a dual-segmented body the color of bruised flesh hovered in the air. A red laser swept over Hale's team and the thing skittered toward them, its half-dozen limbs pulling it forward faster and faster. Hale recognized it instantly and almost wished Standish had been right about aliens.

"It's a heavy construction bot! Suppression fire, now!" Hale shouted. He tossed the forklift bot core away and switched his rifle's energy setting from personnel to anti-materiel. The rifle showed a forty-second countdown before the capacitors could provide the power for the shot. This would be over in twenty.

Gauss rifles snapped as they sent bolts into the construction robot. Half of the robot's arms folded into a shield in front of it, deflecting rounds from its key systems but robbing it of forward momentum.

The construction robots were designed for punishment and the massed gauss shots his team could put out were a child's touch compared to the hammer blow needed to put the machine down. Franklin slammed a fresh ammo can home and Hale came up with a very bad idea.

"Franklin, let it get another ten feet closer

then let loose. Be ready to lift fire on my command," Hale said as he touched his control screen and a knife shot out of his right gauntlet, extending six inches beyond his fingertips. The blade glowed red as the laser field around it activated.

"*Closer?*" Franklin asked.

"Yes! Ready—loose!" Hale ordered.

`Franklin's Gustav roared and the construction bot brought all its limbs forward to shield it. Hale leapt off the wall and steered himself toward the bot. The bot's arms were canted forward, deflecting Franklin's bolts away from Hale as he approached.

Hale swung his legs forward and crouched to put his blade between his feet.

"Cease fire!" Hale yelled. The fusillade ended and Hale activated his grav boots to full power. He shot to the construction bot like one of Franklin's bullets and his blade slammed into the forward segment of the robot's body. The impact drove the blade deep into the bot and ended when

Hale's fist met the robot's armor.

Bones snapped from his knuckles to his shoulder. His scream of pain was lost as the bot's trill overloaded his helmet's audio safeties. Hale used his left hand to drag the impaled blade across the bot's body, hoping that the blade would damage something vital.

One of the construction robot's limbs hit his side like a jackhammer. The force of the blow sent him flying, removing the impaled blade from the side of the machine.

Hale tumbled end over end through the air, his world full of pain as he wondered what would kill him first, smashing into the cavern or the construction robot.

Something tugged at his boot, then at his arms. He slowed to a stop and found himself at rest in the air, an arm's length from the wall...oddly alive.

"Got you, sir!" Cortaro said. The sergeant spun Hale around, his big face beaming with a smile.

"We need to—ah, shit! This hurts," Hale pulled his broken arm against his body.

"Move. Let me see him," Walsh, the team medic pulled Hale to the deck and ran a laser scanner over Hale's right arm.

Hale's world shrank to the deck plating beneath his feet. At the edge of his hearing, Cortaro was barking orders. There was a slight hiss and the pain subsided. Hale swallowed hard and tasted blood.

Looking up, he saw flecks of blood floating inside his helmet. The armor around his broken arm tightened into a vice and he lost feeling in it.

"Blood…there's blood in my suit," Hale said.

"You've got an open fracture on your ulna. I've got you patched up best I can until we get you to sick bay on *Breitenfeld*. You've got quite the contusion on your sternum, but no internal bleeding," Walsh said.

"I'm…fuzzy," Hale said. He looked up, his eyes struggling to focus on Walsh's face in front of him.

"That's the pain meds. Give it a few seconds and you'll be right as rain." Walsh helped Hale to his feet.

The construction bot lay on top of an ammo crate, bobbing against the limbs fastened to the crates. Whatever Hale's knife had severed, it had done the trick. Torni held the forklift bot core up for Hale to see it.

Standish gave Hale a quick salute. "Damn, sir. That was some—"

The side of a nearby crate popped ajar. Gauss rifles swung to bear down on the sudden noise.

"God dammit! Don't shoot me!" came from inside the crate.

Cortaro yanked the crate open and revealed a miner in a light vacuum suit. The miner held his hands up and turned his head away from the bright lights on the ends of the Marines' rifles. A coffin would have had more space than the crate offered the miner.

"I'm so glad you aren't dead!" the miner said. He glanced at the Marines, his face filthy and hair matted behind his helmet glass.

"Who are you and what happened here?" Hale asked.

"I'm John Thorsson, Ibarra Corp miner second class. The damn bots went nuts two days ago, killed the hell out of everyone. I got in this crate right before Garten bought it, figured someone from the fleet would come," Thorsson said.

"Any idea what caused the malfunction?" Cortaro asked.

Thorsson stretched his arms over his head, groaning.

"I'm not positive but they're running new sub routines for the..." Thorsson caught himself and sighed. "For what you see here," he waved an arm at the silver columns. "Corporate espionage, maybe. The Chinese trying to damage the corporation, more likely."

"And what are those? And why didn't we pick up your life sign when we scanned the room?"

Torni asked. She looked hard at the ammo crate, her fingers touching a lining made up of silver fractals between the graphene and carbon-fiber composite of the crate.

"I'm not at liberty to discuss that information," Thorson said.

"We just saved you from being torn apart and/or starving to death and you're going to stonewall us?" Standish asked.

Thorsson looked at the column marred by Franklin's bullets and clicked his tongue.

"The Ibarra Corporation has some very strict nondisclosure policies. I'm going to need you all to sign a series of agreements before you leave," Thorsson said.

Standish mag-locked his rifle to his leg, freeing his hands, and grabbed Thorsson by the shoulders. "Buddy, why don't I throw you back in that crate and wait until you're ready to show a bit of gratitude for—"

"We're leaving. Now," Hale said. The timer on his visor to catch up to the *Breitenfeld* was running dangerously low. "Come on," he said to Thorsson.

"No thanks." Thorsson looked at the mess of robot parts and deformed gauss bolts floating through the air. "I have to clean up."

"You're a witness to several deaths," Hale said.

"And you're military and I'm Ibarra Corp. The treaty between the Union and my employer is pretty clear here: I don't have to do a damned thing you say until my superiors tell me to. I do thank you for your help. There are stale cookies in the mess if you'd like some on the way out," Thorsson said.

Hale glanced at the timer again and turned away from Thorsson.

"Let's go," Hale said.

Thorsson saw the bot core in Torni's hands and reached for it.

"That's Ibarra property!"

Torni slapped his hand away. "It's salvage, Ibarra boy. Have fun cleaning up."

Hale's broken arm stayed mag-locked to his

side as he led his Marines from the factory cavern. They had a drop ship to catch.

****

Captain Isaac Valdar, United States Space Navy, thumbed through the *Breitenfeld*'s manning roster for the umpteenth time since he left Armstrong space dock hours ago. His Ubi held detailed personnel records for the entire crew; whatever more he could learn in the little time he had left would be useful.

Normally, a ship's captain had a great deal of say when it came to selecting his executive officer and senior staff officers but this situation was anything but normal. The last captain of the *Breitenfeld*, a venal career chaser named Riggs that Valdar had known of but never met in person, had been arrested for passing secrets to Chinese military intelligence three days ago. The arrest had been kept under wraps until her accomplices, if any, were swept up. The real reason Riggs was off the

Breitenfeld and Valdar had suddenly been assigned to the escort carrier wasn't common knowledge. Valdar would make due with whatever crew Riggs had left behind.

As such, Valdar couldn't tell his family why he'd had to pack up and make orbit. His wife, who was used to his many sea and void tours and who understood their finances best, had taken it well. His sons, who'd graduate from high school during the mission to Saturn, not so much.

He closed out the record on the chief engineer and opened a picture folder: he, his wife and two sons at the Grand Canyon, the entire family at his father's seventieth birthday party, an old photo of his wife on the beach during their honeymoon. He sighed, regretting the decision that put him on this drop ship—not that he had a choice to take the assignment.

Valdar stood up and shuffled from his seat to the aisle way. The mag soles on his feet would take some getting used to. He grew up in the wet navy, where the deck rocked but at least you knew it would catch you when you fell. Transitioning to the void fleet hadn't broken him of his sea legs. He glanced at the Ubi on his forearm sheath and saw they should be there soon.

A crewman floated up to him, a big smile on his face. "Sir, we're coming up on *Breitenfeld*. Pilot's got room for you in the cockpit if you'd like a look."

"Read my mind. Show me the way," Valdar said.

The cockpit looked like it was surrounded by glass, the illusion of floating in space provided by three-dimensional perspective screens over graphene lattice steel around the cockpit. Valdar's hand shot out, reflexively gripping a handle on the wall. The ability to look around outside the drop ship by turning one's head was invaluable in combat and the fleet paid an enormous expense to give that edge to their pilots. A loss of power to the screens would cut their line of sight to only a few view panels to their fore. Valdar knew he was cocooned in the best armor the fleet could provide, but the illusion of floating in empty space was too strong to shake.

"Got me the first time too, sir," the crewman said. He unlatched a panel from the wall and snapped it into a seat for Valdar.

The pilot, co-pilot and systems officer sat one behind the other, belted to their seats. The pilot craned her neck around and motioned to Valdar. The captain used the handrails behind each seat to get parallel with the pilot.

"Sir, I'm Ensign Jenkins, pleasure to meet you," the pilot said.

"Jenkins…first void tour out of pilot school. Good marks at Annapolis. Implicated in an attempt to capture the mule from that other academy in New York back in '73," Valdar said from memory.

"That's in my file?" Jenkins said, her eyes wide behind her void helmet.

"All but the last part. I had to call in a few favors to get those Rangers to let you all go," he said.

"Sir, I can neither confirm nor deny my

involvement in those activities," she said.

"First rule of any spirit mission, 'Don't get caught.'" Valdar patted her on the shoulder. "You're on the roster as a fighter pilot. Why are you flying a Mule?" Valdar asked.

"The flight controls are almost identical between the fighters, bombers and this flying brick. Air boss wants us cross-rated on more than one plane. He tells stories about flying evac missions out of Okinawa and he didn't exactly know how to pilot the Mule he used."

Valdar's lips twisted in a half smile. He'd been on Okinawa when the Chinese broke through the Kadena defense lines. Nightmares of civilians begging him to take them away on his overloaded patrol boat still dogged his sleep.

"How far out are we?"

Jenkins grabbed a holo screen visible only to her and tossed it at Valdar. The screen popped to life on the perspective screen and a wire diagram of the *Breitenfeld* came to life. A distance meter and alert information filled the space around the diagram. Valdar reached out and tweaked the display with his fingertips.

"Why is she running so hot?" Valdar asked.

Jenkins gave Valdar a double take. "How do you know that?"

"The engineers always hide a status feed in the sub routines, just have to know where to look. Do you know why?"

"Right, sir. *Breitenfeld* went out to investigate a mining operation that went dark. Then Admiral Garrett decided he wanted to get to Saturn a little bit earlier than planned. *Breitenfeld* had to burn hot to rejoin the fleet. Looks like the orbital strike team they sent to investigate just made it back," Jenkins said.

Valdar chewed on the inside of his lip, an old habit his mother claimed he'd had since he was a baby. There was one of two reasons the *Breitenfeld* would join the fleet anchorage above Luna—one good for his executive officer, one very bad. He hoped it was the former as the *Breitenfeld* had had enough leadership turnover in the past few days.

"There she is," Jenkins said, pointing to a red light twinkling in space. In a vacuum, starlight was constant; a ship's engine burn flickered.

"*Breitenfeld* control, this is Mule Zero-Two on approach with the ash and trash and the precious cargo," Jenkins said, the mic on her throat transmitting her words to the approaching *Breitenfeld*.

"Precious cargo?" Valdar asked.

Jenkins shrugged. "You…and we've got the alcohol ration in the cargo hold."

"Don't tell me which is more precious," Valdar said. He leaned forward as the drop ship came around the *Breitenfeld*.

By the standards of the void navy, ten years of service made the *Breitenfeld* an old maid. Most of the fleet above Luna had been built in the last five years by Ibarra Corp to accompany the Saturn colony mission, and if the navy was to keep up with Ibarra's ships, it would need their new slip coil engines integrated in their construction. The

Breitenfeld spent a year in dry dock before the new engines were installed but none of the cash-strapped governments of the combined NAU militaries complained so long as Ibarra foot the bill.

The drop ship came up on the *Breitenfeld* from behind, Valdar's first look at her clouded by the exhaust of her ion engines, two banks of three engines apiece flaring with garnet-red light. The rear launch bay's blast door was closed. The rear point defense emplacements, quad-barreled gauss guns designed to shoot down incoming torpedoes and attacking fighters, tracked the drop ship as it approached. *Good,* Valdar thought. *Take every chance to train.*

The drop ship nudged closer to the escort carrier as it cleared the engines. The ship had a long rectangular hull painted a deep blue with gold trim. Four-point defense turrets surrounded the super castle housing the bridge. Two batteries of rail cannons, their bifurcated rails crackling with electricity, filled the space from the forecastle to the prow. The forward launch bay entrance, flanked by gauss cannon banks, was open, bright guide lights around the entrance making the fore of the ship look like an open maw.

Not for the first time, the *Breitenfeld* reminded Valdar of the twentieth-century battleship *Alabama* he'd visited as a child. *Breitenfeld* measured more than five hundred yards from stem to stern and displaced over a hundred thousand tons of the finest technology the Ibarra Corporation's engineers could muster, all of it surrounded by graphene-reinforced composite steel armor. Modern ships of the line had to take a punch and keep fighting.

Three thousand sailors and Marines made the ship live and breathe, all his responsibility once he stepped aboard.

A motto in gold lettering beneath the fore rail cannon caught Valdar's eye.

"*Gott Mit Uns?*" Valdar said aloud.

"'God is with us,'" Jenkins translated. "She was built in a joint Swedish-German venture and most of the crew is from central and northern

Europe. The motto's tied to the battle she's named for, somehow. I'm from the States. Can't say I understand their passion for all things religion or know much about European history."

"You didn't live through a Crusade. Did they lower the rear blast shield yet?" Valdar asked.

"Actually, sir, Commander Albrecht, the wing commander, has the ship on intake recovery until she's with the fleet. No slowing down just to make the pilots lives easier. You may want to buckle up," Jenkins said.

"*May*, she says."

Valdar pulled against the handle aside her seat and flew to the seat against the wall the crewman prepared. He strapped himself in and pulled his helmet from the pouch on his thigh. In carry mode, the helmet was barely bigger than an Ubi tablet. With the helmet between his palms, he gave it a quick twist and the helmet popped into wear mode—a rounded cylinder with a loose plastic front. He slid the helmet over his head and it automatically fastened to his high-collared suit. The loose plastic went rigid and pressurized. The drop ship's control feed popped onto his visor.

The drop ship went clear of the *Breitenfeld*'s bow and Valdar braced himself. The stars ahead morphed into streaks as the drop ship performed an inline Immelmann turn, turning around and over without losing any speed in their direction of travel away from the *Breitenfeld*. Some maneuvers could be done in the void that would result in a quick and messy death in atmosphere and Jenkins had just performed one elegantly.

Valdar held his breath for the next part. Still moving away from the *Breitenfeld*, Jenkins gunned the afterburners and Valdar felt the crush of g-forces against his body. The ship stopped shrinking, then grew larger on the screens ahead of them. Valdar looked to the port side and saw the wire outline of the wing engines swing 180 degrees and pulse. Instinct brought his gaze to the starboard side, where the matching engine had shifted as well.

The drop ship pitched beneath the gun deck and approached the hangar entrance. Crewmen evacuated the flight deck, where another drop ship was on the deck, steam and coolant streams puffing from the ship like the outer edge of a geyser.

"Speed disparity achieved, going to anti-gravs," Jenkins said. Valdar felt the thrum of the engines die away and the drop ship hung in space before the *Breitenfeld*'s hangar entrance. The drop ship wouldn't fly in and land; it would let the *Breitenfeld* overtake it, like krill swallowed by a whale shark.

The *Breitenfeld* moved around the drop ship and Jenkins used the anti-gravity emitters to guide it to the deck. The drop ship lowered, a bit too fast by Valdar's estimation, and hit the deck hard enough that it bounced once.

"Oops," Jenkins said.

All-clear icons popped onto his visor and Valdar removed his helmet. The upper and lower blast doors over the forward hangar entrance clamped together and amber lights warbled as atmosphere returned to the hangar.

Valdar felt weight return to his body with

increasing pressure as the deck grav plating activated. He closed his eyes and took a deep breath. The weight of command waited for him once he disembarked from this drop ship.

This wasn't what he'd planned. This wasn't what he wanted but this was his duty.

Valdar collapsed his helmet with a twist and slipped it back into his thigh pouch. He unsnapped his restraints and strode from the cockpit, doing his best not to wobble on legs that hadn't felt gravity for hours.

The Mule crew chief had the rear hatch lowered. A dozen naval officers and sailors stood in two even lines at the base of the ramp, all in their blue underway uniforms: coveralls over vacuum-rated skin suits. The men and women waiting for him had serious faces, all except one who bore a beaming smile. The smiler had dusky skin and her hair in a tight bun behind her head. He recognized his executive officer from her personnel file.

Valdar made his way down the ramp on rubbery legs. *This is not the time to fall down*, he told himself.

A boson held a music box to his lips and played three notes to pipe aboard the new captain.

"*Breitenfeld*, arriving," boomed from the ship's intercom system. The navy kept the traditional greeting of a ship's commander as it evolved beyond the waterways to the void.

Across the hangar, a team of corpsmen ran up to another drop ship, a stretcher held between them. Valdar lost sight of the other drop ship as he came to a stop in front of his XO and exchanged salutes. Eyeballs from the assembled officers and sailors lingered on the ribbon racks sewn over the left breast of his uniform. Valdar had most of the ribbons one would expect of an officer with as many years served as he: The Defense of Australia, The Ryukyu Evacuation, a Purple Heart and a fruit salad of service ribbons. He knew they were staring at his Naval Cross and the Silver Star, the second and third highest awards for valor in the navy.

"Captain Valdar, I'm Commander Janessa Ericson. Welcome to the *Breitenfeld*. I have the department heads assembled and ready to brief you at your convenience. I understand you had a long flight and—Sir? Where are you going?"

Valdar had stepped around her and was running to the other drop ship where the medics carried a Marine from the bay on their stretcher.

Ericson, barely over five feet tall, struggled to catch up to her much longer-limbed commander as he trotted across the hangar bay.

A half-dozen Marines, their tan void armor stained in soot and blotches of blood, formed a semicircle around the medics and the Marine on their stretcher. A Marine in spotless armor and captain's rank on his shoulder and chest plates saluted as Valdar came to a stop next to him.

"I told you I can walk just fine," came a voice from the stretcher.

"What happened?" Valdar asked the Marine captain.

"The L-T took out a berserk Ibarra construction bot with his bare-fricking-hands, that's what happened," came a voice from the back of the

Marines disembarking from the drop ship.

"Standish! Shut the hell up! That's the new skipper," said a panicked whisper.

Marines parted to let Valdar pass. Lieutenant Hale was on the stretcher, his right arm mag-locked to his side. The active camouflage on his injured arm flashed red to alert attending medics to his injuries as his vitals pulsed on his chest plate.

"That true, Marine?" Valdar asked, guiding the stretcher toward the air lock leading to sick bay.

Hale's face flushed red and he looked down at his injured wrist where the jagged remnants of his gauntlet dagger still jutted from its sheath.

"Wasn't barehanded, sir. Besides, I couldn't have done it without my team distracting the bot," Hale said.

Valdar nodded and let the stretcher and the Marines escorting it continue on without him. He turned around and locked eyes with the Marine captain.

"Sir, I'm Major Acera, commander of the joint army-marine task force on the *Breitenfeld*,"

Acera said. He hadn't promoted himself by accident. There was room for only a single captain on a ship; as such, those with the rank of captain from the other services were called the next higher rank as a matter of courtesy. The tanned Marine had pockmarked scars on the right side of his face and a sewn-up socket where his right eye should have been. Bionics were forbidden in combat areas and his injury would have been the end of Acera's career if his armor's systems weren't able to make up for his lack of depth perception.

"Berserk Ibarra robots?" Valdar asked Acera.

"One of Ibarra's asteroid factories went dark and the company asked us to investigate. There was some sort of malfunction with a new programming language. And whatever Ibarra was doing in that rock, it sure wasn't mining. We've got one of the bot cores for analysis," Acera said.

"Don't touch it on this ship. If there's some new Chinese malware running loose, the last thing we need to do is touch it and put the whole fleet at risk before we step off for Saturn," Valdar said.

"All our systems are decentralized, firewalled and properly shielded, sir," Ericson said, stepping on her toe tips to talk over Acera's shoulder.

"I heard that right before the Chinese turned my ship's computers to slag," Valdar said. "When was the last ship-wide analog drill?"

Ericson pursed her lips and whipped out her Ubi.

"Too long," Valdar answered for her. "What's our burn time to the rest of the fleet?"

"Eighteen hours and twelve minutes," she said.

"That's enough for a level two analog drill. Let me get situated and we'll get it knocked out before we have to decelerate." Valdar walked away and came to a sudden stop in the middle of the hangar.

He looked over his shoulder and said, "XO, where are my quarters?"

"Follow me, sir," she said.

As captain of the *Breitenfeld*, a marvel of human engineering and capable of leveling entire cities from beyond the moon's orbit, Valdar's quarters were just large enough to hold his arms out without touching the walls and boasted a desk that folded down from the bulkhead.

His duffle bag was waiting on the bed for him. Some enterprising crewman had the courtesy to bring it up for him while he was otherwise engaged on the flight deck. Valdar pressed his hand against the bag and his palm print unlocked the flaps.

A framed picture tumbled from the bag and landed facedown. Valdar picked up the frame, a picture of his family on a Florida beach from years ago: him, his wife and two boys, all sunburned and caked in sand—his idea to turn everyone into a sugar cookie through a combination of surf and beach. The physical picture was something of an anachronism; most people kept photos in an online cloud or on their Ubis, but Valdar had little trust in ephemeral ones and zeroes dependent on a host of technical factors. The photo would remain intact and at his side, as subject to the passage of time as he was.

The photo went on a shelf above his bunk, a bunk he'd probably use less than four hours per day cycle if he was lucky. He looked at the display on the back of his left hand. There was enough time to run the analog drill and maybe a call to his family before the *Breitenfeld* joined the rest of the fleet.

A screen on the wall came to life and showed the face of one of his bridge crewman over a flashing bar of text alerting him that his video feed was off. Wouldn't do to have the crew see the captain in any state of undress.

"Sir, sorry to bother you. Admiral Garrett on the line," the crewman said.

"Patch him through," Valdar said. He wiped his hand over his face and steeled himself for what could be a very angry call.

The face of Admiral Garrett, deep-set dark eyes over a square jaw and gray hair cut perfectly high and tight, came up. A red and yellow border around the screen marked this call as classified top secret.

"Isaac, good to see you. How's the *Breitenfeld*?" the admiral asked.

"Just got in, sir. About to run an analog drill then have a sit-down with the department heads. Thank you for the opportunity to helm a ship one last time," Valdar said.

"Don't shit me, Isaac. I had to drag you kicking and screaming from your cozy little shore duty in Norfolk," Garrett said, shaking his head slightly.

"I got to Norfolk two months ago...This new assignment was rather sudden."

"Indeed. You'll get to ride out your retirement tour back at Norfolk as soon as the Titan orbital is up and running. Four months if nothing goes wrong, so probably seven months before you're home. Just like I promised. I didn't call just to chitchat though. I called you because you're a man I know I can trust.

"Captain Riggs broke under interrogation, spilled everything about what the Chinese are after with the colony fleet and its capabilities. Given what we've learned elsewhere about the Chinese strike force at the Hainan orbital, the intelligence types have 'high confidence' that they'll try to disrupt the launch to Saturn."

"'High confidence'? Is that a *yes* or *no* that the Chinese will attack?" Valdar asked. He glanced down at his forearm display and plotted out intercept courses from the Chinese space station to where the fleet massed over the north pole of the moon. If the Chinese came around the Earth at full burn…the largest space battle in the last two decades could be hours away.

"The secret squirrels never give a definitive answer. They got their pee-pees slapped for screwing up the Iraq invasion way back when and haven't forgotten that lesson. The fleet will step off once the *Breitenfeld* has linked up with us at the L4.

You're tail-end Charlie on this so don't skimp on the burn to get here. Understand?"

Valdar swallowed hard. He knew what was coming next.

"Yes, sir."

"I'm putting the *Breitenfeld* on a communication blackout immediately. The rest of the fleet will go dark soon as I shoo away the civilian reporters. Can't tip our hands to the Chinese just yet," Garrett said.

There went Valdar's last chance to speak to his family.

"We'll be ready, sir."

CHAPTER 3

Marc Ibarra stopped to examine his first creation: a single sheet of graphene suspended in a glass case. Graphene, a lattice of carbon one atom thick, had been around for a few years before he cracked the code on mass producing the material in a commercially viable manner. After that discovery (and with some help) he developed super dense batteries that—when combined with Ibarra's highly efficient solar panel—ended the world's dependence on fossil and nuclear fuels. That radical shift in the energy economy had resulted in several failed states and wars across Europe and the Middle East, but such was the cost of humanity's survival.

He leaned away from the display before his back could knot up. He'd been a young man when he made his first breakthrough. *His* only breakthrough. At seventy-nine, the breakthroughs kept coming, but he was little more than a conduit. That's what his life had come to, laundering ideas for the human race.

Ibarra sighed and looked down the corridor. More glass cases commemorating "his" inventions: the first robot control core, the man-machine neuro-cowl interface, a lung 3-D printed from a bio reactor, the Ubi, the first sheet of grav plating, the gauss rifle and a mockup of his final invention—the slip-coil Alcubierre drive that could take a spaceship up to a decent percentage of the speed of light. At least, that's what everyone was supposed to believe about the slip-coil drive.

He grabbed his walking cane by the platinum and gold handle and tottered down the hallway. A small entourage followed in his wake, all trained not to speak until spoken to. The heavy footfalls of two bodyguards in exo-armor drowned

77

out the sound of Ibarra's cane striking the marble floor that had once been in the Vatican.

Drones zipped past the windows flanking the hallway, all controlled by Ibarra's proprietary software that guaranteed a safe drone work environment. Every drone accident in the last decade was directly attributed to human error, a fact he used to keep his insurance claims low and to drive marketing efforts.

His view from the bottom floor of Euskal Tower's ninety-nine stories wasn't much. The city that grew up around his company headquarters just south of Phoenix, Arizona, had crept north into the suburbs of the metropolis. His city boasted solar panels integrated into the roads and buildings, water-reclamation and rain-capture systems, and heavy stack graphene batteries that could run the entire city for decades without a joule of power from an outside source. Pundits joked that his city could be carved from the Earth and sent into orbit without as much as a flicker in the lights for a hundred years.

He held up three fingers to summon the appropriate aide and heard the pitter-patter of feet behind him.

"Where are we on Project Blue?" he half whispered.

"*One* of the employees sent an update. There was some damage to the systems. He didn't elaborate but the timeline is still intact. The lamprey will disengage and return to Luna on schedule. There were...um...some fatalities when the systems malfunctioned. I've prepared a press statement and double-checked with legal. There's no chance of a wrongful-death suit thanks to the standard hold-harmless agreements all our void employees sign," said the aide, a young woman whose name Ibarra hadn't bothered to learn.

"No press release. All the miners were sequestered from outside contact until the end of their contract. Not a word to anyone, even their families, until then," Ibarra said.

"Mr. Ibarra, our previous focus groups on accidental employee deaths indicate we'd take a hit in public perception if we delay—"

Ibarra stopped dead in his tracks. He didn't move or say a word. A second passed and the aide took the hint and shuffled back to the entourage without a peep. Ibarra held up five fingers and continued down the hallway.

The next aide sauntered up from behind with hardly a sound. He stole a glance at her and grinned. The half-Asian, half-Anglo Ms. Martel had been with him longer than any other employee. Even though she was a few years older, she looked hardly a day over forty, thanks to the best augmetics and rejuvenation therapies his money could buy.

"How is our colony fleet doing?" he asked.

"All ships are in place and their slip coils are almost fully charged. The robot crews on Titan and Iapetus report the habitats are complete. Applications for the next wave of colonists increased 22 percent once we posted the photos," she said, her voice as low and silky as the day they'd met decades ago.

"And the *Lehi*?" he asked.

Martel cleared her throat.

Ibarra stopped and twisted the handle on his cane. A resonance field sprang from the handle, which would cancel out all sound from the conversation before it could travel two yards from the cane.

"I'm not getting any younger," he said.

"The *Lehi* is green across the board. The crew doesn't know what's in the hold and we've scrubbed all the details from every system that was involved with its construction. If word gets out what we've put in there...."

"It won't matter. It's illegal on Earth, not the moons of Saturn," he said.

"It might be too much for some governments. We could face nationalization of a significant amount of our assets."

Another aide ran up to the edge of the sound bubble holding an Ubi in front of his face. He waved at the pair and tried to yell to them, his words lost to the resonance field.

"Must be important," Martel said.

81

"Better be." Ibarra shut off the field.

"Sir, multiple sources report that the Chinese fleet is mobilizing. What do we do?" he asked. Ibarra struggled to remember who this aide was...someone Martel poached from the CIA. He'd gone two years without being fired, something of a record.

"Send me the projections." Ibarra turned and made his way back down the hallway. He swore this thing got longer every time he walked it. The elevator was a dozen yards away.

"But, sir, shouldn't we warn our fleet? So much capital invested in our ships and the Union Navy is at risk," his intelligence aide said, dogging his steps.

A transmitter in Ibarra's cane signaled the elevator door to open. Ibarra stepped in and turned to face the aide, who almost stepped into the elevator with him. Ibarra stabbed the cane into the aide's chest and shoved him with what little strength his old limbs could muster.

"No concern for the thousands of lives on

82

those ships? Empty out your desk. See Martel for your debriefing," Ibarra sneered. He lowered his cane and the doors shut. His final look at the flabbergasted aide, his jaw hanging slack, gave him a little laugh.

Ibarra waited for the biometric sensors in the elevator to read two thousand separate biometric markers on his person. Lasers scanned everything from his fingertips and iris patterns down to the cracks in his heels and the DNA he exhaled. Once the computer was satisfied with his identity, the graphene-reinforced steel plates beneath the elevator retracted to allow passage deep into the Earth. Only one other human being could get past the security screening, and she'd learn her destiny soon enough.

The elevator descended thirty-seven stories into the Earth before the doors opened with a ding to reveal a set of gleaming vault doors made of lead and lined with a silver fractal metal that he'd never bothered to name. Another bioscan and the vault doors swung inward.

The vault was a squat cylinder with a flat bottom and a rounded top. Lights embedded along the walls cast a uniform glow over bare concrete floors and walls. This was the first thing he'd built with his first billion, this vault and the officer tower above it.

In the middle of the room was a black plinth. Floating a foot above the plinth was the silver needle of light, the probe that called him decades ago.

"Hello, Marc. Things are progressing well," the probe said.

"*How* well? The Chinese are moving faster than we'd anticipated. Tipping off Union intelligence about that crooked captain may have saved our entire plan," Ibarra said. He shuffled forward and scooped up the probe, where it floated an inch above the palm of his hand as they spoke.

"The Chinese are a new variable. Success is now 28 percent, assuming the *Lehi* survives to phase two," the probe said, its light pulsing along with its words.

"And if the *Lehi* is hit?"

"Zero, unless a population can be evacuated from the system. And the chance of that being approved is slightly higher than zero. With intervention and elimination of the Chinese variable, the projections rise to 37 percent. Shall I intervene?"

Ibarra tossed the probe into the air where it floated of its own accord. He leaned against the plinth and sank to the ground. He tapped the tip of his cane against the soles of his shoes as he contemplated their next move.

"Have we done everything we could, old friend?"

"My initial projections of humanity's survival were much lower. We've used your species' fractured nature as an impetus to drive innovation, which should mask my intervention if the Xaros show an interest in your history. The slip-coil drive is as far as I could take you before the enemy would detect my overt assistance," the probe said.

"Heh, the slip coil. If only we had twice as many drives, twice as many ships in the fleet...."

"We could produce only so much stable quadrium for the drives within the constraints of manageable advancement. Anymore and the enemy would suspect outside assistance. Any outside—"

"Assistance and the probability of success is zero," Ibarra said in time with the probe.

"I've told you this for decades, and still you refuse to accept it. Your species is either exceptionally stubborn or lacks higher cognitive functions," the probe said as it floated toward Ibarra and stopped in front of his face. Its silver glow refracted off tears streaming down Ibarra's cheeks.

"Your eyes are secreting."

"This is it, Jimmy. Decades of manipulation, choosing which countries succeed and which fall into chaos, the wars...all those people we let die on Mars. All this work and I won't get to see the end of it." He wiped the tears off his face.

"You are...Moses. Judeo-Christian figure."

"The Jews knew Moses was in charge and

where he was taking them. He also didn't work with a frigging floating needle."

The probe's light went discordant for a moment, which it did the few times Ibarra had ever managed to annoy it.

"I am a sentient intelligence filled with the combined knowledge of countless civilizations sent across the void to help you hairless apes avoid extinction. I am *not* a needle. Also, given our first encounter, comparing you to Moses—and his burning bush—is apt."

Ibarra swatted at Jimmy with the tip of his cane. It passed through the probe as if nothing was there.

"What do we do about the Chinese? A low-grade engine malfunction or should a few of their torpedoes cook off in their tubes?" Ibarra asked.

The probe didn't answer.

"Jimmy?"

"There's a mass shadow approaching the heliopause. The Xaros. They're here."

Ibarra grabbed the plinth and pulled himself

to his feet. His heart quivered and his mouth went dry.

"How long until they can detect the fleet?"

The probe was silent, its light crackling as the entirety of its computing power came to bear.

"At least thirty-seven hours, best case. Twelve hours, worst case," it said.

"Activate the drives now. We can't afford to take any chances," Ibarra said as he shuffled toward the elevator.

"Done. The slip coils will fire in eight hours. What about the Chinese? I can sabotage a bulk of their fleet but I can't stop the wing of bombers in the Chinese Trojan horse. There's an escort carrier, the *Breitenfeld*, within their engagement envelope," the probe said.

"Don't do anything. The risk is too high that the enemy might find your fingerprints in their systems," Ibarra said. *How many thousands of men and women on the Breitenfeld have I just consigned to death?* Ibarra ran his thumb over the worn nub of his cane's handle, wrestling with the choice to let the carrier fend for itself when he could save it with a word.

"I suppose I must remind you who is on that ship, mustn't I?" the probe said with a chiding tone. "Stacey is on the *Breitenfeld*. You know how integral she is to our mission."

Ibarra went pale as the implications hit him.

"I thought she was on the *Tarawa*."

"No."

"But—"

"Still no. I can tip the odds in their favor without an unacceptable risk of compromise. Also, loss of the *Breitenfeld* has a significant impact on the next phase of the operation."

"Fine. Do it. Protect her at all costs," Ibarra said. The elevator door opened as he neared.

"Done. My estimation of the enemy's arrival was off by six point four three days. I must be slipping in my old age. Marc, a moment," the probe said, the needle of light morphing into a halo the size of Ibarra's head. "Will you imprint now? There's nothing more you can do."

Ibarra shook his head as the elevator doors began to close.

"I built this house of cards. I'll watch it fall down."

****

The *Breitenfeld's* mess hall was cramped with almost a hundred Marines and naval ratings packed together for their assigned meal time. Space was a premium in the space navy, and every cubic meter that could be cut from crew comfort—in favor of weapons, armor and machinery that powered the warship—was.

Standish placed his tray into a food processor and a covered plate wet with condensation and drink pouch rolled onto his tray. He sneered at the plate and picked it up, almost losing his lunch when a sailor jostled his tray.

"Hey! You mind?" Standish said to the sailor's back as he walked off without so much as a raised hand in apology.

Standish navigated the mess hall, dodging more people seemingly determined to ruin his meal. A low rumble of clicking silverware and grumbled conversations surrounded him. Each service man and woman on the *Breitenfeld* had a set window of time to get their meal and eat it, Automated cooks kept food ready, and the mess hall had patrons almost every hour of the day.

Standish squeezed between rows of seated diners and set his tray down next to the rest of his squad. He sat between Franklin and the bulk of a sailor, his thin frame gave him just enough wiggle room to get his arms over his meal.

"Makes you miss field rations, doesn't it? Just grab a plate and sit down under a tree and not know if the guy next to you skipped his last shower," Standish said.

The sailor to Standish's left gave him a sidelong look and shrugged his shoulders.

"Hot chow three times a day?" Vincenti asked. "Better than wondering how long you can last on whatever pogey bait you've got stuffed in your ruck." The Italian Marine twirled his fork in a plate of pasta and took a bite.

"Let's see what I got," Standish pulled the plastic top off his meal and sighed at the meal: a rib eye steak with roasted potatoes and asparagus.

"Man, this crap again," he said.

"What, you got the jackpot. I got damn rice and lentils again, I swear the ship's computer thinks I'm a vegan," Walsh said.

Standish pushed his plate at the medic and took the bowl of legumes and grains in trade.

"Thought you'd like steak," Torni said.

"I do," Standish said. "I love steak. Marinated steak, grilled steak, tri-tips, BBQ, all that. But 'steak' is the word. Not the reconstituted vegetable paste that the ship tries to pass off as steak. I want the real thing, made from cow."

"No one can tell the difference between the paste steaks and the real thing. The texture and taste are identical." Walsh cut off a hunk of steak and put in his mouth, content as he savored the bite.

"Yeah, but when I eat the ship's 'meat' I

know it's a lie. Call me a purist," Standish shoved lentils around his bowl, his appetite gone.

The double doors to the mess hall opened, and a pair of soldiers in green jumpsuits entered, their uniforms stood out in the sea of black and tan uniforms of the sailors and Marines. That one of the soldiers was in a wheel chair, pushed along by the other, brought the din of the mess hall down a few octaves as many did their best not to notice the strange arrival.

A soldier, a rail thin man with a mess of unruly black hair, pushed the wheel chair bound soldier up to a small table against the bulkhead. The soldier in the wheel chair, a woman with gentle features and skin the color of desert sand, looked over the mess hall.

"Holy...is that them?" Standish asked. "Is that the Iron Hearts? I didn't know they could leave the suits."

"That's two out of three, Bodel is the man, Kallen the woman," Vincenti said. Vincenti and Kallen locked eyes and traded a nod.

"And don't call it a suit, it's armor. They get a little mad when you call it a suit and they use those big metal hands…" Vincenti reached toward Standish with a pair of fingers and closed them with a squish sound.

"They wouldn't do that," Standish said.

"I've seen it happen," Vincenti said "to a Chinese soldier."

"No way," Standish crossed his arms over his chest.

"There we were—no kidding—deep in some East Timor jungle holed up in an abandoned hotel with the rest of the battalion," Vincenti said. "The Chinese had us pinned down for days, and we were down to a couple of bullets and foul language to defend ourselves. They brought up twenty—"

"It was five." Walsh said.

"*Maybe* five tanks, old ones from the Second Pacific War but with new active protection systems. We had nothing that could hurt them. Acera's on the IR screaming for help, and of course we've got no air support. Then he hears 'Stand by' on the net.

"You ever see an armor lance, all three suits, fight? Ten feet tall, moving with all the grace of a dancer, faster than you or I could. The armor, the Iron Hearts sitting over there, show up and tear the Chinese apart," Vincenti bite his lips for a second before continuing. "One of them, I think it was Bodel, he rip the turret off the Chinese tank. Grab the Chinese inside and—" Vincenti slammed his hand against the table, causing Standish to nearly jump out of his seat. "My *nonna*, she had chickens. One night a wolf gets in the coop…next morning the whole thing's covered in blood. It was like that when the Iron Hearts came to save us. I have bad dreams, right? Same as every combat vet. But the dreams that wake me up are the ones with *them* in it." Vincenti nodded his head at the two soldiers.

Bodel had returned with two plates of food, and was spoon feeding Kallen.

"Why doesn't she use an exo-suit to eat and walk around?" Standish asked. "And what happened to her? I didn't think you could be in the

95

military...like that."

"They have to synch with their armor, they use anything else that interacts with their nervous system and their synch isn't as strong," Walsh said. "Armor selection is tough, ninety-five percent wash out rate for volunteers. Kallen can synch with the armor, that got a lot of waivers signed."

"Where's the third?"

"Elias? Don't ask about him," Vincenti stood up and put a hand on Standish's shoulder "there are rumors." He policed up his tray and left.

"What kind of rumors?"

"You want to go over and ask them?" Walsh asked.

"No. Hell no," Standish said.

"Eat your reconstituted bean paste and just be happy they're on our side," Walsh said.

Standish watched the two armor soldiers as he ate. He looked down to open up his desert, when he glanced back at the Iron Hearts, Kallen was staring right at him.

She winked.

****

For all the expertise the Ibarra Corporation boasted in space flight, construction engineering and advanced robotics, they sure had a lot to learn about public affairs, Admiral Garrett decided. He'd been sitting with a long line of Colonial executives and dignitaries on a rickety stage for the last half hour, waiting for his chance to get away from the civilians.

The last batch of colonists had finally arrived on the *St. Augustine*, a six-mile-long passenger ship that rotated habitation modules around the ship's axis to produce gravity. Ibarra's people were getting the colonists "camera ready," reminding them of the approved talking points and reminding the family members of the amazing opportunity they had to take part in the Saturn colonization—what was a few weeks in cramped quarters compared to that?

The truly rich colonists were on the sleek

pleasure liners—private cabins, robot concierge, artificial gravity and no labor—that made trips to Mars and Venus. The wealthy would wait for their upscale homes to be built on the moons around Saturn, all part of the package.

As soon as the civilians exited their shuttle, they'd add to Garrett's growing list of problems. This ship held ten thousand Ibarra Corporation employees and their families, all of whom had unique and urgent problems that only Admiral Garrett could solve.

Garrett wasn't used to complaints when he toured ships. His time on naval vessels was spent conducting inspections, attending meetings, and making decisions. Not listening to a woman complain that she couldn't bring her ferrets with her on the trip to Saturn when the employee manual *clearly* allowed for pets under a certain wright.

He glanced at his Ubi for the hundredth time. Still no urgent call for him to leave the festivities. He had a press briefing on the *America* in an hour, but no way to get away before then.

An air lock opened, and two lines of people shuffled into the cargo bay and crowded around the stage as if they were at a concert and not in front of the fleet's admiral.

Garrett looked over the colonists. Most were men and women in the deep-blue Ibarra Corp work overalls, employees destined to assemble the space station, hydroponic farms and the rest of the infrastructure that would make human settlement possible. There were plenty of children in the crowd, many up on their fathers' shoulders so they could glimpse the luminaries responsible for their care during their exodus from Earth.

A little girl with unruly blond hair and green eyes waved a grubby hand at him. Garrett, his face a mask of stone, waved back.

The CEO of the colony mission blathered on and on about the corporate vision for what Marc Ibarra expected from them, all of which sounded like he'd cribbed his speech from motivational posters from the walls in Euskal Tower.

Garrett saw himself as a leader, one proven

by combat and trained to win wars. He wasn't meant to nursemaid a bunch of civilians from one end of the solar system to the other. He never understood why Ibarra had insisted he command this mission, but when the president of the Atlantic Union "strongly encourages" you to take an assignment, there wasn't much of a decision to make.

He leaned forward and looked hard at the civilians, their faces full of wonder and trepidation. He'd been in the navy for so long, sometimes he forgot about the people he'd sworn to defend.

****

Navigating the gnarl of asteroids between the *Breitenfeld* and Ceres was a routine matter—if Ensign Stacey Faben could use the navigation computers. Under analog conditions, she had to rely on the scopes mounted on the *Breitenfeld*'s hull and a bricked Ubi for calculations. By the turn of the century, school children carried more computing power in their cell phones than NASA used for initial moon landings. The Ubi at her fingertips was more than adequate for the task at hand, even if it wasn't linked to the rest of the ship's systems.

Simulations like this were as close to actual maneuvers as the ship's computers could make it; all her screens and feeds were indistinguishable from their real world inputs, which she could return to with the flip of a switch.

A stream of vector calculus equations crossed her visor and she solved a course plotting that gave the *Breitenfeld* a three-kilometer buffer between it and a pair of nickel-iron asteroids several times the size of the *Breitenfeld*. She switched through different angles by pressing tactile buttons on the side of her quad monitors. With tech like this, she wondered how the old American space shuttle pilots even managed to land in one piece.

"Conn, receive new course heading," she said. A press of a button on the Ubi screen and the heading went to the ensign at the ship's helm.

"New heading, aye," said the Conn.

Stacey kept her focus on the spinning rocks ahead of the *Breitenfeld*, waiting for the inevitable monkey wrench in the simulation. The *Breitenfeld*'s icon shifted on her screens, no feeling of engines firing or g-forces pressing against her like a real maneuver.

She did feel footsteps reverberate through her seat as someone approached. Glancing at a small mirror above her workstation, she saw Captain Valdar looking over her shoulder. Valdar had bounced from station to station as the analog drill continued, occasionally conferring with his bridge crew as their involvement in the simulation waned.

Here it comes, she thought.

An asteroid, a fractured mountain spewing fragments, spun into view from behind one of the larger asteroids in their path. Stacey didn't need to consult her Ubi to see the new asteroid would intersect with their course.

"Conn! Prep evasive maneuvers," she said. Lights in the bridge flashed red as the warning to strap into the nearest acceleration couch went out. Stacey touched the Ubi to input new calculations— but got no response.

The Ubi screen flashed yellow and read: MALCODE WARNING. Enemy defenders had broken the ship's firewalls and slagged the onboard computers. Now, the only computer she could rely on was the one between her ears.

The irregular asteroid, a long spike jutting off its central mass and spinning like a broken propeller, continued straight for the *Breitenfeld*.

"Astrogation, waiting for that new course," the Conn said.

Stacey bit her lip hard enough to draw blood and felt a solution come together.

"Gunnery, fire two rail shots at zero-eight-hundred mark one-three-thousand on my order. Conn set engine six deflection by twelve—No! Give me the Conn," Stacey said. The equation changed the longer she spoke and her solution would be useless by the time it left her lips.

She flipped a switch on the side of her chair

and two control sticks sprung from beneath panels on her workstation. She canted the *Breitenfeld* on its port side and redlined the engine burn, ignoring the shouts of protest from the engineering pod.

"Gunnery…fire!"

Two rail shots zipped away from the *Breitenfeld's* icon and impacted the approaching asteroid on the blade-like protrusion. The kinetic impact from the rail shots slowed the asteroid's oscillation and the blade passed behind the *Breitenfeld* with an uncomfortable five hundred yards to spare.

Stacey let out a cheer and raised her arms in triumph. Captain Valdar cleared his throat and her arms came right back down.

"End simulation, return computer assistance to all bridge functions," Captain Valdar said.

Stacey's work pod retracted the analog screens into the pod's torus and holo-screens snapped into being.

Earth reappeared on the porthole in front of Stacey as the simulation's faux-view on the synthetic diamond glass ended. She had a waning crescent view, most of it the night side of the planet, the glow of cities delineated the coastline. Thin strands of light marked out the lattice of hyperloop tubes connecting the major cities of Asia. Moscow to Beijing. Beijing to Tokyo and stretching into the dawn leading to San Francisco. Even with the animosity between the world's powers, people still loved to travel.

"Ensign," Captain Valdar said, "that was some impressive work just then."

Stacey rotated her pod to face her commanding officer.

"Thank you, sir. I try."

"You try, but you did the vector calculations of this ship, the asteroid variable and the mass deflection from the rail cannons all without the aid of a computer. If I hadn't watched you do it myself, I wouldn't believe such a thing was possible." Valdar stepped closer to her pod and opened the control panel on the outside of the torus.

A privacy filter went up around them,

blocking the rest of the bridge crew from hearing their conversation.

"I read your file. You broke atmosphere for the first time at ten years old, graduated from MIT at fifteen with two doctorates. What I don't understand is what you're doing in the navy. Someone with your…background would have other options available to them," Valdar said.

Stacey felt her face chill as the blood drained away. He knew. Of course he'd know. He was the captain of the ship and responsible for everything that happened on it. Knowing that a VIP like her was part of his crew would be in his purview.

"This is how I'll get deeper into space, sir. Closer to the science I studied in school," she said.

"You could have joined the colony fleet."

Stacey pursed her lips. "They're only going as far as Saturn. The Union fleet will set up outposts on Pluto, Eris, even Sedna. I'll join the company once my contract is up. I'm not saying a faster-than-light slip-coil drive might be ready by then," she glanced around quickly, "but I hear things."

"Very well, Lieutenant Faben, keep up the good work." Valdar ended the privacy screen and returned to his command chair.

"Faben" wasn't Stacey's true last name. It was Ibarra. Hiding behind a *nom de guerre* while serving in the navy was a necessity. Having the only heir to the Ibarra empire openly serving the Union Navy would put a giant target on any ship she crewed boarded, and the fame attached to her name would just make her job—and the job of those around her—that much more difficult.

The Ubi in her thigh pocket buzzed with a new message. She tapped the Ubi through her overalls and the message came up on the corner of her holo display. A time-locked e-mail from her grandfather. She squinted at the release time, which was blank.

He must have fat fingered the time code. I'll let him know later, she thought.

"Captain Valdar," said the officer in the engineering pod, "sir, we seem to have a malfunction in the slip-coil drive."

Stacey and the rest of the bridge crew pretended to stay focused on their workstations, but every ear was cocked to Valdar as he sat in his command chair. He pulled up the engineering feed and swiped through overlays.

"Malfunction how?"

"It's started the charge cycle. The Ibarra techs running the device don't know why it's doing that," the engineer said.

"EWO?" Valdar asked the electronic warfare officer, who was responsible for the integrity of the ship's computer systems and disrupting any enemy systems in turn.

"Nothing, sir. All firewalls and active protection measures are intact," the EWO replied.

"Commo, send an update to the flagship. Tell them we're working the issue," Valdar said.

"Right away, sir," said the platinum-blond officer in the communications pod. Stacey liked to tease the Norwegian officer that his head could be used as a beacon if the ship ever lost all power. "Sir, the rest of the fleet is reporting a similar malfunction. Every ship with a slip-coil drive."

"Sir," the engineer said, "the Ibarra techs say they might be able to do a hard shutdown but they'll need corporate approval for that. Worst case, the drive will fire in…forty-nine minutes."

"And what then?" Valdar asked.

"The course to Saturn is already laid into the slip coils, sir. We're locked out of our navigation systems," the Conn said.

Valdar glanced at Stacey, who gave a miniscule shrug of her shoulders in return.

"Well, this is damn peculiar," Valdar said.

****

Lawrence flapped his hands in the air, stepped up onto the tips of his toes and exhaled loudly.

"Three…two…one, I've got this," he said. He massaged his cheeks and snapped his fingers next to his ears. A passerby might assume Lawrence suffered from a host of nervous ticks. His pre-speech rituals were odd but they readied him for engaging with the media. Old Man Ibarra had told him his public-speaking skills were a key factor in his decision to make Lawrence the CEO of the Saturn Colonies, that and his command of an infantry company during the Jeju Island campaign.

Lawrence had always wondered why Ibarra insisted on staffing the colony with so many former military men, but asking Ibarra questions was a sure way to get fired.

The door to the briefing room opened and an aide waved Lawrence inside.

There was no press room on the *America*, so one of the many briefing rooms for the fighter squadrons served as a stand-in. Lawrence entered the room and gave the assembled journalists his plastic-surgery-perfect smile. Every seat was packed with reporters, personal recording drones hovering in the air above their respective owners like starving hummingbirds. Every major news network on Earth was here for this—humanity's first colony expedition since the Mars landings forty years ago.

"Hello everyone, I'm Theodore Lawrence, chief executive officer of Saturn Expeditions, a wholly owned subsidiary of the Ibarra Corporation. Thank you for making the long trip from Earth to this fleet anchorage. There's not a lot of scenery on that trip and if your Ubi battery dies, it feels a lot longer than fifteen hours." He flashed his gleaming white teeth with the award-winning smile and got a few decent laughs from the crowd.

"But the trip this colony is about to embark on is a bit different than a shuttle from Luna to Earth. It took the first colony ship nine months to reach Mars, and at the same speed this fleet would reach Saturn in almost three and a half years. You've all had a tour of the *Mayflower*–class colony ships and know how cramped they are. We wouldn't have had so many volunteers if we advertised those conditions in the brochure." Again with the smile, nowhere near as many laughs.

"But thanks to yet another breakthrough

from the scientists and engineers at the Ibarra labs, we have the slip-coil drive, a modified Alcubierre engine that can create just enough of a dip in space time to propel our ships at enormous speeds and cut the travel time to Saturn to a mere eight days. I'm sure you've all seen the—"

"Mr. Lawrence, why is the Ibarra Corporation only taking Ibarra employees on this mission? There are far more qualified and eager people to participate in this mission than whoever's willing to agree to your company's draconian personnel policies and restrictive background checks," the reporter from a South American net channel asked.

"The Ibarra Corporation is the single source of funding for this mission, and since no other sovereign nation seems interested in joining us on this historic moment we—"

"You have an Atlantic Union fleet escorting you! What does a colony need with a military escort that could wipe out the Martian colonies?" asked the only journalist from the Chinese Hegemony, Hu

Bing, seated a few rows from Lawrence and surrounded by news organizations from countries occupied by China. Lawrence had come prepared for a hostile audience.

"Our armed escort is fully funded by the Ibarra Corporation and isn't technically part of the Atlantic Union until it returns from Saturn. After the...security incident on Mars, we decided an abundance of caution was needed to secure our long-term investment," he said. Calling the Chinese seizure of the joint American-Japanese cities on Mars a "security incident" was being polite. It was entirely possible that all nine billion human beings on Earth would see this exchange and being testy wouldn't help with public perception.

"Your company has no right to Titan or any of the other moons. China established sovereignty on those worlds three decades ago with the *Daoda Yuan* missions," Bing said. The sycophant reporters around him nodded in support while most of the rest of room rolled their eyes or huffed their dismissal.

"I'd like to remind you of the Treaty of

Saigon, which the Chinese Hegemony is a party to, that allowed for unrestricted access to any place in the solar system where a physical presence had already been established. The Huygens probe from the now-defunct European Space Agency has been on Titan since 2005, and the rights associated with that probe were sold to the Ibarra Corporation long before the treaty. I fail to see your objection," Lawrence said.

Instead of going to the next challenge as Lawrence's public-relations strategists had anticipated, Bing snatched one of the floating camera droids and threw it at Lawrence with the speed and accuracy of a major-league baseball player. The droid hit Lawrence right in his perfect teeth. His hands flew to his mouth as pain lanced through his face. Hot blood flowed through his fingers and he stumbled against the back wall.

He heard rapid-fire, high-volume Chinese ringing through the briefing room as strong hands guided him away. Those same strong hands slammed him against the bulkhead and Lawrence found himself face-to-face with a very angry-looking Admiral Garrett. The admiral bunched his hand into Lawrence's bloodstained suit and lifted him an inch into the air.

"You care to explain why the slip-coil drives are powering up?" Garrett asked, his voice a low growl.

Lawrence gagged on blood running down his throat and felt a loose tooth with his tongue.

"Whaa?" His fattening lips provided a new obstacle to speaking.

"Every slip-coil drive in the fleet is cycling—your passenger and construction ships, every one of my warships. Why? We agreed to leave tomorrow and now you pull this kind of crap? What's your game?" Garrett asked.

Lawrence glanced down at the hands pinning him to the wall. They looked like they belonged to a farmhand and could do even more damage to his face if Garrett was so motivated.

"I don't know. The drive techs on the ships were supposed to wait until I gave the order—and I

115

haven't. Swear," Lawrence said, his bulbous lower lip making his words sound like baby babble.

"Shut it down. We aren't leaving until *Breitenfeld* joins the line."

Lawrence winced and poked at his split lip.

"I can't. No one can. They're the most sophisticated things we've ever developed, and a bit experimental. We've never tried to shut them down while they're engaged so we made sure it was impossible. The drives will form the slip bubble around every ship and take us straight to Saturn," Lawrence said. Garrett's shovel hands finally let him go.

"Experimental?"

Lawrence froze in place. He shouldn't have said that.

"Well, given the expense and rarity of the quadrium in the engines, we didn't do a full test. But the math works and Mr. Ibarra is never ever wrong about these sorts of things. If I didn't think it was safe, would I be on this ship?"

As a trained expert in negotiations, the

twitch to Garrett's lips and his balled fists gave Lawrence the hint that the admiral wasn't taking the news well.

"Sir!" An officer ran down the corridor, one of Garrett's senior staff members if Lawrence remembered right. "You're needed on the bridge, priority message from the Pentagon," the aide said.

"Get those reporters off my ship *now*," Garrett said. He turned away and stepped down a side corridor with the aide.

From the briefing room, Lawrence heard shouting in multiple languages as another personal drone crashed against the wall.

"Return to your seats or we will use non-lethal force to restore order!" boomed from the briefing room. One of the onboard Marines had activated his anti-riot broadcasts.

Lawrence tapped his fingertips against the blood seeping down his shirt and felt another loose tooth.

"This wasn't in my job description."

In the *Breitenfeld's* sick bay, Hale raised his right arm above his head, then swung it forward and backwards as if he was a windmill. He was sure he looked as silly as he felt. The medic on the other side of a glass panel tapped at a holo display invisible to Hale. Patient information was exclusive to the medical personnel until they deemed it necessary to share. Seeing just how bad one was hurt tended to impact a patient's resolve to hold on to life.

The sick bay's surgical robot had mended his broken bones and re-knit his torn skin and muscles in a few hours; the human doctor had stepped in only a few times to correct the robot's work. If his injuries had been worse, he could have been evacuated to the full surgical suites on the *America* or the *Constantine*, which were on par with the best facilities on Earth. Worse case, his arm could have been amputated and replaced with a bionic until a vat-grown replacement could catch up with him, a more extreme option that would only be considered in a time of war.

"Good thing we're exempt from the new skipper's analog drill. Manual surgery like that would've taken forever, not to mention recovery time," the medic said. "Bring your arm across your chest for me and pull it hard, please."

Hale complied as scratches of pain emanated from the pink scar tissue on his bicep.

"Little neurological sensitivity, but that'll fade in a few hours," the medic said. He closed his displays with a swipe of his hand and tossed a uniform jacket to Hale. "I'll mark you fit for duty. Come back if it falls off," the medic said.

Hale slid his stiff arm into the jacket and left the sick bay.

An alert display in the corridor marked the ship as still under an analog drill. This didn't mean much for Hale and his Marines; during a void engagement the Marine complement would join damage-control parties and repel boarders as needed. Trying to run a ship without the aid of the central computer core was a problem more for the bridge crew and the sailors.

"This new skipper is a ballbuster, no?" a woman said, a heavy French accent caressing her words. Black hair fell down her shoulders in loose waves and her dark eyes shown like obsidian in stark contrast to her alabaster skin. She put a vapor wand to her lips and took a deep breath. "Valdar flunked the entire bridge crew on the first drill. They almost passed the second," she said, vapor riding her breath like fog drifting over a bay.

Lieutenant Marie Durand looked Hale up and down and poked at his right arm. "Doesn't look so bad. You OK?"

"I've had worse. I'm better than those miners at any rate," he said. "As for a ball buster of a CO, he's not so bad, really—Valdar, I mean. Just has high standards for his people, even higher standards for himself."

"You know this how? Talk to a guy for two seconds and you know everything about him? Maybe you should have gone intelligence instead of

Marine Strike Corps."

"He's my godfather," Hale said. "He evacced my dad from Okinawa during the war, got him and the rest of the wounded off the island before the Chinese could overrun them. One of the civilians on the ship was my mom—that's how my parents met. He and dad were close before the battle and they stayed in touch after my dad was medically retired. My brother and I would visit Uncle Valdar every once in a while when we were growing up. He was there when I pinned on my butter bars."

"The captain is your godfather. I'm not sure if that means you can get away with anything or nothing."

"Let's keep that secret between us and not find out how much I can get away with. Wait…aren't you part of the drill?"

Durand rolled her eyes.

"Please, everything we do in the fighters is analog. The squadron finished the drill in thirty minutes. So I came to check on you," she said.

Durand glanced around, then leaned in and pecked Hale on the lips. "Your Marines won't stop bragging about you. Why don't we go to our spot and I do a bit more than brag?" Her hand brushed over his thigh.

"Marie...," Hale's voice cracked with nerves as he double-checked that no one else saw their public display of affection. They'd kept their relationship quiet for weeks, a minor miracle on a ship the size of the *Breitenfeld.* One wrong look in front of witnesses and the scuttlebutt would begin in earnest. "Marie. First, yes. Second—"

"Battle stations! Battle stations! All hands to battle stations! This is not a drill!" the speakers in the bulkheads blared. Red running lights snapped to life on the bulkheads.

Durand and Hale traded confused looks as they took their helmets from their carry pouches. A translucent net around Durand's locks pulled her hair into a bun to accommodate her helmet.

"Stay safe," Hale said. He squeezed her hand before stepping past her and taking off in a run.

"*Et toi*," Durand called out. *You too*.

****

Captain Valdar strapped himself into his command chair. Void combat meant rapid acceleration and deceleration, and despite all the advancements made by the Ibarra Corporation, the law of inertia still meant a messy end to anyone not strapped down for maneuvers. Someone tossed him a proper void helmet, larger and better armored than the one he carried in his suit.

The helmet fastened with a twist and he connected it to the airline coming from his command chair. His suit could provide air on its own for up to six hours, but running off the ship's air was vital for longer engagements.

"Scope, what've we got?" Valdar asked.

"Showing twelve Chinese Jiantou fighters and twenty Chui bombers on acceleration toward us," Stacey said. "They launched from a cargo ship in high anchor over the moon, same way they hit Mars during the war."

"Another Q ship, what a surprise," Valdar said without humor. "Give me a course projection."

He turned his chair around and directed it on the rail to the holo table.

An icon of the *Breitenfeld* hovered over the table; red triangles marking the Chinese ships appeared moments later. A cone sprang from the triangles, the edge barely touching the *Breitenfeld*. The colony fleet and its Atlantic Union escorts were dead center in the course projections.

"Sir, that's barely a wing of Chinese planes against our entire fleet. What do they think they're going to accomplish?" Commander Ericson asked. The two carriers in the fleet could have twice as many fighters in space before the Chinese were within engagement range; at first glance, the Chinese effort seemed futile.

"They're going for the colonists," Valdar said. "They damage the civilian ships and the whole mission gets scrubbed. Get me Admiral Garrett on the line."

"Do they really think they'll get through?" Ericson asked.

"They don't have to get through," Valdar said. "They just have to get close enough to launch their torpedoes. Those civilian ships are glass compared to us. Any damage and they aren't going anywhere."

"Sir, Admiral Garrett."

A hologram of the admiral's face came up on the control table.

"Valdar, I've got your tactical feed. You've authorization to launch and engage any hostiles. Get with the rest of the fleet as soon as you can. The rest of the Chinese fleet is mobilizing and the rest of the Union fleet is going to sit this one out," Garrett said, his words tinged with venom.

"What? Why?" Valdar asked. He picked up a light pen and drew intercept vectors for *Breitenfeld's* fighters.

"We aren't technically part of the Union while we're on this mission and China just declared war on the Ibarra Corporation, not the Union. Seems no one in Geneva is that anxious for another world war," Garrett said.

"More contacts!"

Red icons indicating unknown contacts flared at the edge of the table. Dozens more joined them and Valdar watched as "unknown" icons resolved into cruisers, carriers and destroyers.

"Looks like their entire fleet. Not ones for half measures, are they?" Valdar asked.

A course for the *Breitenfeld* came up, taking it directly into the Chinese line of advance. The course came from Admiral Garrett.

"Isaac, the fleet needs thirty minutes to engage the slip coils. Thirty minutes and the civilians will be safe. Can you give it to me?"

Valdar acknowledged Garrett's course and looked at the admiral's projection.

"You don't have to ask, sir. I was going to do it anyway," Valdar said.

"Fight your ship," Garrett said and cut the transmission.

Valdar opened a channel to the flight deck.

"Commander Albrecht, how soon can you launch the Eagles?"

"Ninety seconds until the first sortie," the air boss answered.

"Good hunting," Valdar cut the channel.

"Sir! Transmission from the Q ship," said the officer at the communication pod.

"Show me," Valdar said. He didn't bother standing up for this or removing his helmet. Showing that he was ready to fight might defuse the situation before it escalated into a shooting match.

The image of a Chinese officer, clad in the People's Liberation Army Space Navy's red and gold void suit, his head bare, came up on a holo display in front of Valdar. The Chinese officer sneered at him.

"Forces of the illegitimate Ibarra flotilla. You are in violation of the UN declaration on system settlement. Return to Luna anchorage immediately or we will seize your ships by force," he said in heavily accented English.

"*Cao ma de!*" Valdar said and cut the line. The bridge was stone silent as the crew stared at their captain in shock.

"Did I say that right?" Valdar asked.

"You actually told him to go…you know…his horse, but I'm sure he knew you meant his mother," Stacey said. "Mandarin is a tonal language. He might think you called his horse a—"

"Malcode warning!" the EWO announced. Pods shifted to haptic keyboards and flat display screens.

Valdar keyed his throat mic for a ship-wide announcement.

"*Breitenfeld*, this is your captain. The Chinese have heartburn over our mission and are on an attack vector to the colonial flotilla—unarmed ships full of innocent men, women and children. Any of you who've fought the Chinese before know they aren't afraid to target those who can't fight back. Let's kick the Chinese in the teeth so hard they think twice about ever following us to Saturn."

****

Durand ran up to her Eagle as Valdar's speech ended, the distinctive white skull and crossbones over a black field, the squadron markings of the 103rd squadron to the fore of her cockpit. A pair of smaller skulls were to the side of her cockpit, kill markings of the two Chinese fighters she shot down during an 'accidental' incursion into Australian airspace. The void fighter moved along the conveyor belt leading from the hangar to the twin catapults that would launch her and her wingman into the fight.

She leapt onto the ladder against the side of her fighter and vaulted into the cockpit. There were a dozen critical pre-flight checks to do before launch. By the book, she had time for no more than two. Her hands flew over the controls, activating the navigation and weapon systems.

Her crew chief, a stocky Scotsman named MacDougall, ran airlines into the back of her helmet and she felt cold, stale air puff into her helmet. He fastened her restraints as she brought up her custom holo displays.

"Knock 'em malky, lass," MacDougall said.

Durand, despite speaking English fluently, had no idea what MacDougall just said to her.

MacDougall saluted her and jumped down. He unhooked the ladder and the cockpit closed around her. The noise of the flight deck died away as the cockpit sealed.

Her F-99 Eagle, designed as a void fighter, looked more like a wide dagger blade. Wings, ailerons and rudders remained within the fighter until it broke into atmosphere. Twin variable engines and small thrusters around the hull gave her more maneuverability in space than she would ever have in atmospheric flight.

She tested the rotation on the twin gimbal-mounted gauss cannons under her fighter. Both cannons could rotate and shift on their mounts to provide 360 degrees of fire; a holo screen showed the gun camera feed and offered deflection-assisted aiming. She had five hundred rounds for each cannon, no more than thirty seconds of continuous fire.

She glanced to her right, where the rail lance barrel jutted from the hull. The lance was a miniature version of the rail cannon mounted on the *Breitenfeld*, designed to damage lumbering capital ships and ground targets.

Her mouth went dry as she brought the lance online. The weapon drew significant power out of her batteries and every shot came with a significant risk of knocking her fighter offline. Losing all power in the middle of a dogfight was a sure way to end up as a mark on the enemy's hull and Eagle pilots had modified an old sniper's mantra for the cannon, "One shot, you're killed."

Durand's fighter shifted to the ready deck, next in line for the catapult. Adrenaline coursed through her veins.

"Gall, you ready for this?" Ensign Jenkins, her wingman, said over their commlink.

Durand looked up at Jenkins in the Eagle directly across from her.

"I don't think it matters, Burro," Durand said, using Jenkins' call sign. "It's happening anyway."

Clamps fastened around her landing gear and shifted her fighter into the catapult, which would slingshot her from the hangar with enough velocity to hold her own in a dogfight.

"Eagle 3-7, prepare for launch," came the warning over her helmet IR.

Durand pushed herself deep into her acceleration couch and braced herself.

A hum filled her cockpit and a whine escaped her lips.

The catapult accelerated her at four times the force of Earth's gravity and the hangar sped past in a blur. The void enveloped her and her engines burst to life. The location of her flight came up on her cockpit display and she launched her Eagle into a steep climb.

Jenkins, who launched seconds behind her, joined the climb at her side.

"Gall, Burro, form up on me. You're on the

attack run," Commander Albrecht said over the squadron channel.

"Attack run? On what?" Durand asked. She nudged her Eagle higher, flying level with Albrecht and his wingman as they burned away from the *Breitenfeld*. More icons streaked from the *Breitenfeld* toward her, the last of the squadron's twelve fighters to join the formation.

"Red and green flights will interdict the Chinese as best they can. Blue flight will break from the scrum and make a gun run on that Q ship. That 'unarmed' merchant ship is heading toward the fleet at full speed. My best guess is it's got internal rail guns and will try to nail the civilian transports once it's inside the fleet's APS bubble," Albrecht said.

Each warship had an active protection system, a linked system of radar-guided missiles and gauss weapons designed to intercept incoming rail cannon rounds and knock incoming rounds off their intended angle of attack. Chinese rail guns fired projectiles too fast to be seen by the naked eye and the reaction time of the human beings manning the APS was limited. The chance of intercepting incoming rounds using radar and flack rounds was high, so long as there was time to detect the threat. As the Chinese got closer, the chance of an APS interception dropped.

"Why haven't the fleet's cruisers drilled that thing yet? No way some merchant ship could handle forty rail shots at once," Jenkins asked.

"Fleet—and *Breitenfeld*—are charging their slip-coil drives. Can't shunt the power to weapons, something about exploding, so we're all she's got." Albrecht said.

Red triangles popped onto Durand's display, enemy icons.

"Bogies inbound!" she shouted on the squadron channel, the announcement reverberating through the squadron.

"We've got…eighteen Jiantou fighters and six Jian bombers inbound," Jenkins said. Icons on Durand's display shifted to match the new designations. A line of ice ran down Durand's spine as fear broke through her adrenaline rush. The Jiantous were the best fighters in the Chinese arsenal and the Chinese wouldn't trust those planes to average pilots.

"Two to one. Not great odds but it's quality over quantity, right?" Jenkins asked.

"Suddenly quantity has a quality all its own, *n'est pas?*" Durand said. She felt the cold touch of sweat beneath her flight suit and tightened her grip on her control stick. The icons on her canopy grew larger; she could just make out the Chinese thrusters against the Milky Way's mélange of stars.

"Effective range in thirty seconds, synch target computers," Albrecht said.

Durand clicked a switch on her weapon control stick and the Eagles' onboard computers calculated firing solutions for each fighter. Each gauss gun would engage separate targets so long as their firewalls held up.

"Please hold," Durand said to herself. The EWO on the *Breitenfeld* would fight in the cyber realm and winning—or losing—that fight would end this fight in short order.

"Malcode warning," her onboard computer said. Amber warning icons flashed as the Chinese hacked into her ship's control systems. Her ship's firewalls would protect her for a few seconds, seconds she used to break the compromised systems away from the ship's controls with the push of a button.

"*Breitenfeld* EWO reports Chinese systems impacted. They're running new attack malware. Don't plan on getting our comps back anytime soon," Albrecht said.

Durand's gauss cannons returned to her control. She locked them in place. The only way she could aim them now was to point her fighter at her target. *Over a hundred and fifty years of air combat and I have to fight like I'm in the skies over Verdun*, she thought. She cut control to the gun stick and put both hands on the control stick in front of her; the trigger on the control stick would suffice.

The threat icons blinked away; the afterburners behind the Chinese fighters flickered

136

like torchlight.

"Even playing field again, except they brought twice as many to the game," Jenkins said.

The threat icons returned, their Identify Friend or Foe broadcasts marking them for Durand's truncated tracking computers. If she was close enough to read their IFF, they were close enough to read hers.

"Prepare for a pass. Blue flight, keep your burn going. No dogfighting if we can avoid it," Albrecht said.

Durand clicked her mic twice to acknowledge.

The Jiantou fighters, red and gold craft that looked like double-bladed arrowheads, formed a semicircle in front of the manta-like Chui bombers. The Chinese attack wave and the *Breitenfeld's* fighters adjusted course to fly straight toward each other. Durand lined up her crosshairs on a Jiantou and watched the range indicator, the distance still in red, her target still beyond the effective range of her gauss cannons.

Over the radio, she heard someone reciting the Lord's Prayer. The range on her target blinked amber—nearly there.

"Prepare to jink," Albrecht said, panting into his mic.

Durand caught a glint of sunlight off her target's canopy. The range icon went solid green.

"Jink!" Albrecht shouted.

Durand slammed a foot against her rudder thrusters and hard banked her Eagle on its side. Her hand squeezed the control stick hard enough that her knuckles popped.

The vibration from her cannon roared through her cockpit as it fired. Tracer rounds, treated to burn white hot as they shot through the cannon's barrels, zipped past her target. Red bolts streaked past her cockpit. She fought against a scream and smashed her fighter to the side with a thruster burst.

The Jiantou flew past her, her canopy darkening to block the blinding light from the passing engines. She glanced over her shoulder. The

Chinese fighter stuck to its course instead of turning to fight.

The HUD on her canopy showed three blue icons breaking through the swirling mass of Eagles and Jiantous; the rest of her flight had survived the first brush with the enemy, but red X's covered two of the squadron's icons. One flew from the dogfight on a steady course, propelled by whatever momentum it had before being damaged. The other X hung in space, the fighter destroyed.

"Get him off me!"

"Splash one bandit!"

Panicked transmissions begged Durand to turn around. Durand hated to leave her squadron behind and outgunned, but her mission demanded she keep her burn going for the Chinese Q ship. The ivory-white spaceship, a bisected cylinder decorated with an enormous white crane and hanzi characters, maintained its course to the colony fleet. At this range and with her gauss cannon, the ship was practically a barn door for her to hit.

"We have a read on that thing's ACM?" she

asked.

"Assume military grade. Don't waste a shot and risk going dark," Albrecht said.

"We've got company!" announced Sledge, Albrecht's wingman. Five Jiantous had broken from the dogfight and tore after Durand and her flight. Durand saw the Chinese fighters' afterburners flaring white-hot as they closed.

Durand pushed her engines to full military power, as fast as she could go without engaging her own afterburners. Her Eagle had enough power for the rail gun or the afterburners, not both. They had tens of seconds before the Jiantous were on them.

The Q ship was still beyond their effective range. Durand magnified the Q ship's image with a gesture. Two prongs of a rail gun jutted from the prow of the ship, already sizzling with electricity. Flak batteries had sprung up on the hull from compartments.

"Sir, it's got one big goddamn rail gun, not an internal battery like we thought. That thing's bigger than the guns on the *Charlemagne*," Durand said. If the effective range on the Q ship's gun was longer than the batteries on the *Charlemagne*...

"If it takes out the *Breitenfeld*, the rest of the fleet are sitting ducks. It'll pick off the colonists long before the rest of the fleet can engage it," Durand said to Albrecht and the rest of their flight. Modern void capital ships relied on their APS and maneuvers to avoid damage; a single hit from the Q ship's rail gun would rip a ship inside out.

"How long until it has a shot on the *Breitenfeld*?" Albrecht asked.

"Maybe another minute. I don't think we can hit that ship *and* deal with the ones on our ass before that happens," Durand said.

"Gall, Burro, do a tumble as soon as our pursuit is in range and continue the attack. Sledge, you and I will make an out-of-range rail shot to spoof the defenses and buy them time," Albrecht said.

Durand put a hand on the ventral/dorsal thrusters and felt her chest tighten. Tumble shots always made her queasy. The Jiantous bore down on them, nearly in range.

"Three...two...one...mark!"

Durand flipped her fighter over and kept her momentum toward the Q ship. The stars swirled around her and the target icons came around. She pulled the trigger on her gauss cannons and raked rounds across the Chinese fighters. One exploded, dirty red flames flaring from the machine before the vacuum snuffed the wreck into nothing but expanding detritus.

With no time to celebrate, Durand flipped her fighter back toward the Q ship and gunned her engines.

Sledge and Albrecht fired their rail guns and the magnetically accelerated slugs crossed half the distance to the Q ship before a swarm of rockets and flack intercepted the shots. The recoil from the shots robbed the two fighters of speed and they bellied over to face the remaining four Jiantous.

Durand glanced over her shoulder, no Jiantou on her six. Tracer rounds flared behind her like a swarm of fireflies in the night sky.

A burst of light erupted in front of her. Shrapnel from a flak round peppered her canopy, turning the right half into a mess of craters and leaving a crack like a bolt of lightning deep in the synthetic diamond canopy.

Durand sent her Eagle into a barrel roll and dove out of the line of fire. A peal of explosions filled her previous flight path. A dozen warning icons demanded her attention, which Durand ignored as she jinked her fighter and varied the speed of her attack to spoof the anti-aircraft batteries trying desperately to kill her.

"You all right?" Jenkins asked.

Ice crystals crept across the inside of her canopy, absolute zero's effect on ambient moisture. Durand flipped a panel of switches on her left side and her fighter sucked the atmosphere from her cockpit. A glance at her mostly green weapons panel gave her hope.

"Venting atmo…gun still works. Get ready to fire," Durand said. The Q ship loomed ahead, flak batteries flashing yellow from gauss fire.

"I'm hit! Hit—" the transmission from Sledge cut out.

The range reading on Durand's canopy flashed green.

"Fire!"

The recoil felt like her fighter had run into a brick wall. Her restraints kept her in her seat but her arms and head whipped forward. As her chin struck her chest, her helmet kept her from losing teeth but the hit felt like a boxer's uppercut.

She shook her head to refocus and saw the Q ship still ahead. Two new holes clean through its hull marked her and Jenkins' hits.

Jenkins' fighter soared ahead of Durand.

Durand yanked her control stick to the side and opened her throttle to regain speed.

Nothing. The Q ship veered across her canopy.

"Second shot charged!" Jenkins said.

Durand's cockpit was dead; emergency lights flickered around her. The only display still working was for the battery and it read:

CHARGING. Her rail shot had overloaded her systems. She was a sitting duck.

"Firing!" Jenkins shouted. Durand saw her ship slow as the rail gun strong-armed her forward momentum. A flak round burst just below Jenkins' fighter and it lurched higher like it had been kicked.

Three more flak shells burst around Jenkins. The Eagle disintegrated in a flash of flame, reducing her and her ship to ash and twisted metal.

Durand reached out, her hand striking the canopy. Jenkins was gone, just like that.

Durand sat back, ready for her turn in the fire. Her hand went to a crucifix beneath her flight suit, no time to say a proper prayer. But there was still time to be of use in this battle. She squinted at the Q ship, trying to find where Jenkins's last shot had hit.

"*Breitenfeld*, any station on this net, the Q ship is damaged, venting atmosphere." Lightning arced between the long prongs of the rail gun. The burst from the gauss cannons had ceased and the Q ship rotated slowly away from Durand, bringing the top of the ship into view. A black maw on the rear of the ship arced electricity from the within, like a thunderstorm in the night.

"The battery stacks are hit!" The exit wound from Jenkins's last shot might be enough to kill the Q ship. "I say again, the ship's battery stacks are—"

White lightning leapt from the battery stacks and arced back against the hull. The Q ship shimmered as raw power flowed through it. The white hull blackened as it burned. The spine of the ship cracked and the lightning ceased, leaving an afterglow on Durand's eyes. Durand watched the Q ship float on, like a dead animal on a lake's surface.

"Gall, Burro, you read me?" Albrecht said.

Lights returned to the cockpit and a slight nudge against her chest told Durand the engines were functioning again.

"This is Gall. I went into reboot after my first shot but I'm coming back online. Burro is…down," she said.

"Can you make it back to the *Breitenfeld* or do I have to squeeze you into my cockpit? No time for a pickup," Albrecht said.

Navigation beacons returned to her HUD and the Eagle's maneuverability returned slowly.

"I can make it back. It'll be slow and if we run into any more—wait. Where are the Chinese?" None of the threat icons were on her HUD.

"EWO cracked their attack programs and their firewalls. We got aim assist back and finished them off. I got one without help but the last three almost got me," Albrecht said.

Durand flew toward Albrecht's blue icon. A yellow border on the icon told of significant damage to the ship.

"I'm coming up on you," she said. Albrecht's port engine was a ragged mess. Gauss bullets had badly drilled the rear third of the fighter. That it could still put out any thrust was a miracle.

"I don't know what's holding you together. Don't sneeze," she said.

"You don't look too hot yourself. Get back to the ship—hurry," he said. She could see him beneath what remained of his canopy as she sped by. Gauss rounds had perforated the canopy and knocked a third of it into the void.

"I'm not going to leave you out here," she said, slowing to match his speed.

"There isn't another bogey for a million kilometers in any direction and my landing will be uglier than a soup sandwich. Get on the deck before I wreck it on my way in."

"This is Captain Valdar." The new captain cut off Durand's attempt to argue. "Search and rescue has the last of our pilots. The slip coils are malfunctioning. Return to the ship with all possible speed or you're going to float out here until the Union decides to send a ship, or until the Chinese do."

"Acknowledge, *Breitenfeld*, we're limping but we'll make it home," Albrecht said. Valdar's icon dropped off her HUD. "You heard the man— get moving."

Durand grumbled and gingerly increased power to her engines. She questioned the wisdom of rushing to a ship with malfunctioning engines but she decided to take her chances with Ibarra engineering over a Chinese prison.

She flew past an Eagle wing, spinning lazily in the vacuum, the serial number of the fighter half-missing and blackened.

"How many did we lose?" she asked.

"Five," Albrecht's voice cracked as he spoke. "No damage to the *Breit* or the fleet and we swept the sky. Damn fine job."

Jenkins's final moments replayed in Durand's mind and she felt like anything but a "damn fine job" had just transpired.

She shook her head and focused on the *Breitenfeld*, the aft hangar gate open to receive her. With the malcode threat gone, she queued up the auto landing sequence. Sparks shot from the panel and a malfunction icon came up on her HUD.

"You think?" She keyed her throat mic, "Deck, I'm coming in on manual…have fire and rescue there just in case."

A panel descended from the ceiling and lights of the optical landing system, called a meatball by tradition, flashed to guide her in safely. She lowered her speed and focused on the meatball, making minute adjustments to her course.

The lights ahead of her wavered, like a sheen of water vapor passing in between her and the ship. She blinked hard. *Must be the adrenaline wearing off,* she thought. The *Breitenfeld* wavered again and she swore she could see the star field beyond the ship.

"Anyone else see this?" she said.

"Focus!" Albrecht ordered.

Durand followed the meatball's landing path and lowered her landing gear. Gravity returned as she crossed the hangar's threshold. Her Eagle wobbled against the new force and her rear wheels struck the deck.

What should have happened next was her forward gear hitting the deck and the vectored thrusters around her ship bringing her to a quick stop.

Instead, her forward strut cracked in half the instant it made contact and her plane's nose struck the deck. Durand's Eagle ripped across the flight deck, spewing sparks and whirling into a lazy spin as it almost cut a furrow against the graphene composite steel.

Durand almost ejected, then remembered the unyielding bulkhead just above the flight deck. She caught sight of the forward edge of the flight deck as her fighter spun, the precipice becoming another item on a very long list of things that were about to kill her.

If she overshot the runway, the *Breitenfeld* would smash her like a bug against a windshield.

Friction against the deck slowed her Eagle and Durand braced herself against the back of her seat to eject if she went over the edge. Maybe she'd be blasted out into space instead of against the hull.

A few yards from the edge, her forward motion came to a sudden halt.

Durand, not waiting to test her luck, unbuckled herself and pulled the emergency release on the canopy. She heaved the canopy aside and leapt from the cockpit. Earth-normal gravity brought her to the deck and she fell with all the grace and dignity of a toddler's first failed attempt to walk across a living room.

"Move! Get clear, lassy," came MacDougall's voice over the IR.

She scrambled back to her feet and ran toward a waiting team of crewmen and medics behind safety bumpers on the left side of the runway. She looked over her shoulder and saw MacDougall in a lifter exo-suit standing behind her Eagle. The suit's clamps had grappled onto the tail section—and stopped her from going over the edge.

"Albrecht is coming in. He's in worse shape than I am," she said. She pointed toward the rear of the runway. Albrecht's Eagle loomed in the darkness.

"No thank ye at all. I'll remember that the next time you're about to go ass over teakettle—"

Shouts broke over the IR. A scrum of sailors, masters at arms by their shoulder brassards, shoved and wrestled with three Chinese pilots whose red flight suits were tight enough to give them all away as women and which shone like rubies against the white-armored sailors.

One of the Chinese snatched a pistol from a sailor's holster and fumbled with it.

Durand drew her gauss pistol and aimed.

A white flash erupted from her weapon and her target doubled over, clutching a thigh. The pistol fell to the ground and was kicked away in the confusion. The other two Chinese converged on their wounded comrade, pointing at Durand and putting themselves between her and the third pilot.

Clumps of blood warbled into the airless hangar, the wounded pilot's cries trapped within her helmet.

Durand felt an atavistic need to hurt the Chinese pilots again for Jenkins' death and for the rest of her fellow pilots that she'd never see again.

"Get out the way so I can shoot her again!" Durand yelled. That the Chinese couldn't hear her IR didn't matter to her.

The masters at arms peeled two of the Chinese pilots away and slapped restraining wires around their wrists, arms and knees. The two bound pilots struggled with all the dexterity of an inchworm as the men at arms carried them away.

A sailor stepped between the wounded pilot and Durand.

"Ma'am, I need you to holster that weapon," he said.

Durand lowered the pistol to her waist, watching as two men at arms held the wounded pilot down and sprayed quick foam into the entry and exit wounds on her thigh. Restraining wires went around her wrists and arms but the fight had gone out of her.

The Chinese pilot, who would have been pretty had her face not been a rictus of hatred, shouted at Durand as she was carried off.

"Ingrates. We pick them up out of their dead bomber just like international law demands, and this is how they repay us," a sailor said.

Durand shook her head and set her pistol to safe. She looked back to the end of the hangar to check on Albrecht's approach...and did a double take.

Long red lines faded into being just beyond the edge of the runway and a keening hum assaulted Durand's senses. The lines thickened, green forks of lightning arcing between the lines, and the space between them filled with an ivory light that grew in intensity.

Durand wrapped her hands and arms around her head to save herself from the onslaught, but the assault continued until all she could feel was white light stabbing into her eyes and a buzz that eradicated the memory of any other sound she ever had.

I'm dying, she thought. *All that and this is how I die.*

She felt a slight pop in her ears…and it was over.

Durand peeked between her fingers and saw the world as it should have been: a flight deck in the midst of recovering its fighter craft from a battle.

Crewmen gawked around them, everyone looking as shocked as she felt.

MacDougall was still at the rear of what remained of her fighter. The mechanic looked around him liked he'd just heard the whisper of a long-lost loved one.

Durand's priorities came back in a rush.

"Albrecht! Get that ship clear! He's coming in," she said.

She looked back to the far edge of the runway and saw nothing but empty space where she'd seen her squadron commander only seconds ago.

Albrecht was gone.

****

Captain Valdar, still strapped in his command chair, sat very still. The blinding light and overwhelming noise had ended only moments ago. Every display in the bridge blinked with error messages.

"What the hell was that?" he asked. He hit the control stick on his chair, but there was no response. He cursed and unsnapped his restraints.

"EWO, were we hacked?" Valdar asked. He struggled from his chair—the white noise had done something to his inner ear and holding his balance was difficult, like after three too many cocktails.

The EWO shook her head and tossed her hands in the air.

"All our higher systems were air-gapped and unpowered. There was nothing *to* hack," the EWO said.

Valdar turned around too quickly and had to steady himself on his chair.

"Comms, send a status report to the fleet. Tell them…something," Valdar said. "Your guess is as good as mine right now."

"Everything's down, sir. I can get on the hull and use an old signal lamp if needed," the communications lieutenant said. Her holo displays wavered, then snapped into focus. "Oh, there we go. One moment, sir."

Functionality returned to the rest of the bridge pods, but several of the holo screens wobbled from some sort of error.

"Engineering, how're we on life support, battery power?" Valdar asked.

"Batteries are at 95 percent and taking power from the fusion plant, hull solar panels fully functional. The slip-coil drive is…well…that's funny," the engineer tapped at his console.

"Sir, fleet command wants to know if we experienced an anomaly. Seems it hit every ship," the communications lieutenant reported.

A gasp from Stacey silenced the bridge.

"No! No, this can't be right," Stacey said.

"What is it, ensign?" Valdar asked.

"Sir, I—sorry, there must be an error in my scope. The Earth is…wrong, somehow," she said.

"Show me. Everyone," Valdar punched a key on the briefing table.

A hologram of Earth appeared in front of Valdar; the half of the planet their scopes could see was half-lit by the sun. He stared at the sunlit side, unable to find what had startled his astrogator.

"What? What's wrong?"

"The dark side, sir" she said.

Valdar looked closer; there was nothing but an abyss of darkness beyond the thin line of twilight. Valdar shook his head in confusion, then his jaw went slack.

It was dark, black as death on the Earth's night surface. There were no outlines of mega-cities hugging the coasts or the meridians of hyper-loop trains that connected the globe.

The bridge was eerily silent as the Earth rotated into the night, the darkness uniform as the abyss.

"Comms, what're we reading from Earth?" Valdar asked, his voice low.

Valdar heard the clack of fingers against a keyboard and the buzz of error messages.

"Nothing, sir. No location beacons, no Internet, not even radio…nothing from the rest of the solar system. All I'm getting is tight beam IR from the rest of the fleet," the Comms officer said.

"Faben, use the scopes to look at…Copenhagen. See what's there. Whatever hit us might have been an EMP," Valdar said. Stacey took to her assignment with a nod; the telescopes on the *Breitenfeld* were strong enough to make out license plate numbers on Earth at this distance. An electromagnetic pulse could wipe out unshielded power systems. The effect was used extensively during the Second Pacific War and both the Chinese and Atlantic Union kept the weapons in their arsenals. Valdar believed it was a distinct possibility that the colony mission to Saturn had triggered World War IV.

"Comms, do a wideband broadcast. Ask if anyone can hear us," Valdar said.

The Comms pod buzzed with an error message.

"I'm locked out, sir. All I have is IR tight beam, and I can only access the fleet—not the relays on Luna or Berlin."

"Um, sir?" Stacey said. "You'll want to see this." Her hands were shaking as they hovered over her keyboard.

"Show me. Show everyone."

Video of the ship's telescope feed of Copenhagen came up on the bridge's forward holo. Valdar recognized the Kastellet, the historic five-pointed fort surrounded by a moat, next to the city's bay. The wooded park in the center of the fort was as Valdar remembered it. The last time he'd been to the Kastellet, the skyline of one of Europe's great economic hubs was as memorable as the views across the Baltic Sea. But on the projection, all the buildings, skyscrapers and the harbor around the Kastellet were gone.

Grass and new-growth forest filled the area where civilization should have been.

"Zoom out. Find something. Stockholm, Berlin," Valdar said, his mouth dry.

The telescope feed flashed from city to city. There was nothing but meadows where there had once been buildings. She cycled the feed through Paris, Rome, Vienna—all the same.

"There! I saw something," someone said.

Stacey focused the scope on a four-lane highway, which cut off in the middle of a grass field, as if whoever built it had hit an invisible wall. She ran the scope along the highway where tufts of grass peeked through cracks in the road and overgrown weeds along the shoulder looked as if no one had touched the road in years. A still-intact road branched to the north.

"Which way?" she asked.

"To the north is Melk, Austria, my hometown. Please," the lieutenant in the gunnery pod said.

The feed moved north and the gunnery lieutenant let out a prayer as buildings came into view. Part of the town was gone, erased just like every other place they'd seen. The façade from an apartment complex was missing, the interior exposed like a half-complete autopsy.

"Zoom in on that building," Valdar said.

The feed morphed. The exposed building looked as if it had been sliced by a laser scalpel; pipes and fiber-optic cables hung from the split walls like collapsed arteries. The exposed room had a kitchen table—a third of it missing—lying across the floor, broken plates sprinkled around it.

A shadow flit across the feed.

"What was that? Find it," Valdar said.

The feed remained steady despite Stacey's stabs against the keyboard and mumbled curses. Her Ubi emitted a series of double beeps warning of an incoming message. She slapped at it to turn it off but it kept beeping.

The forward projector and every screen on the bridge cut to black as Stacey's Ubi went silent. A half second later, a tired old man appeared on the screen, his eyes full of sorrow and his shoulders slouched.

Marc Ibarra.

"This message is for my fleet. What I have to say is hard to accept, but you must listen." Ibarra looked up at the camera. "As of now, you are all that is left. Every human being on Earth, the moon, Mars, everywhere…is dead."

Valdar squeezed his hands into fists. *No, this can't be right. Not my family*, he thought.

"Soon after you left, a swarm—an alien

163

armada, arrived. It scoured the solar system clean of any and all human life, any sign that we ever existed. There was no way to stop it. What I did to you was our only hope of survival.

"The slip-coil drives are stasis generators. They brought each ship out of the time-space continuum for thirty years. If they functioned properly, the swarm never detected your presence at anchorage, scoured the solar system, and moved on to the next star system. If they did detect you, then they are waiting and all hope is lost."

Valdar looked at the gunnery officer, who shook his head. Nothing on the scope.

"The swarm will leave a residual force to erase everything we've built. They are few in number but you must not underestimate them. Even with the full might of the fleet, I'm not sure you can beat what remains.

"To survive, you must remain radio silent for as long as possible, tight beam communications only. They aren't looking for you but they'll attack the moment they detect you. Then, you must get my granddaughter to my headquarters in Phoenix immediately. She is the key to the next battle. She must survive.

"Stacey," the bridge crew snapped around to look at her as Ibarra continued speaking, "all the answers I can give you and the fleet are waiting."

Ibarra took a deep breath and wiped a tear from his eye. "Go. Go now. For what little it's worth, I'm sorry. There was no other way."

The screens blinked back to normal.

Stacey sat back against her pod chair, her face a mess of confusion and fear.

"Sir, priority message from Admiral Garrett," said the Comms officer. Valdar tapped the pad on the back of his left hand to take the call. Valdar's visor opened a video window only he could see. Garrett looked older than the last time they'd spoken.

"Admiral," Valdar said, "we just received a message from Marc Ibarra—"

"We got it too. Every single screen in the fleet had it. Everything Ibarra said checks out.

Astrogation looked at the orbital position of the planets and they're right where they should be if the year is 2089, but Ceres, the dwarf planet in the asteroid belt, is somehow missing," Garrett said.

"It pisses me off to take orders from Ibarra, but this is—I don't know what this is. Not yet. You get Ibarra's grandkid to Phoenix with your Marine complement and get out of there without a peep. The *Breitenfeld* and the rest of the fleet will stay put. The heat flare from our engines is pretty damn noticeable.

"Now, if you'll excuse me, I have to figure out what to do with half a million civilians who're trying to lose their minds. Godspeed," Garrett said and cut the call.

"Lieutenant Faben," Valdar said. Stacey looked up from her Ubi, her face pale. "Do you have any orbital assault training?" She shook her head.

"Urban warfare?" A shake.

"Do you know how to use a gauss rifle?" Another shake.

"Report to Major Acera on the flight deck. Get moving. See what they can teach you on the way down," he said. He keyed a ship-wide announcement from his wrist pad.

"*Breitenfeld*, this is Valdar. I don't know any more, or any less, than you do. We have a mission, orbital insertion on Phoenix and an immediate extraction of whatever Ibarra wants us to find there. Focus on that. That mission is all we are and all we have. We will piece the whole story together later.

"Make ready for orbital assault. Valdar, out."

CHAPTER 4

Lieutenant Hale rechecked the power charge on his gauss rifle for the umpteenth time and glanced at Ensign "Faben," who was strapped in next to him. The name plate his visor put out over her was tied to the bio-tags she wore around her neck, not the truth.

"Ten minutes out," Major Acera announced to the Marine company over the IR net. Hale and his team shared a drop ship with their sister strike squad; the rest of Acera's Marines and a platoon of mechanized armor were split between five other drop ships.

"Faben, is there anything else you can tell

us?" Acera asked.

Stacey didn't respond. Hale nudged her with his elbow. Her head popped up from the Ubi screen she was reading.

"What? Right, sorry. I've got a note from Grandpa on my Ubi. It says I'm supposed to go to his private elevator in the Euskal Tower and take it into the basement. He said the sensors are gene-coded to me only. If the power's out, there's a battery-stack access point next to the door," she said.

"Like he planned this whole thing," Vincenti said. Franklin, seated next to him, struck Vincenti with his elbow.

"I see the schematic for the battery stack, sir. We can run it off our spares," Hale said.

"We'll set down five kilometers south of the target building. Maintain radio silence unless detected, IR only," Acera said.

Stacey, clad in her shipboard skin suit and work overalls, looked like a child next to Hale in his assault armor, the graphene composite plates could take a direct gauss shot but made him feel like he was wearing a barrel around his chest. The extra battery and ammo packs mag-locked to his lower back and thighs crowded Stacey against the bulkhead but she hadn't complained.

He glanced at the anti-armor grenades mag-locked to his upper chest. The grenades would fire off a depleted uranium slug or a molten lance against an armored target by way of a shaped-charge explosion within the grenade. If he used the EFP setting, the grenade would blast well short of the target to fire off the explosively formed slug. Hale never cared to learn the physics behind the device; he just needed to know how it worked. The anti-armor grenade's blast was little threat to Hale in his armor, but Stacey wasn't so well protected.

It took eight hours to properly fit someone into void rated combat armor—time the mission couldn't give her.

Stacey had a small-caliber gauss pistol on her chest harness, which was adequate against unarmored targets and little else.

"Did Ibarra say anything about what's down there? Aliens, right, but what kind?" Standish asked.

"He didn't say," she said with a shrug.

"Why the hell not? If it's twenty feet tall and has tentacles for a face, we'd fight that differently than we would... brain thing riding around a mech suit, right?" Standish said.

"Ibarra Corp developed our gauss rifles and just about every other piece of gear we have. If he did plan this, then maybe we can hurt whatever's waiting for us," Franklin said, patting the rotary cannon at his side. "And we have the Iron Soldiers with us."

The mechanized armor platoon that fell under Acera's command was part of the Union Army; referring to them as Marines was a mistake and an invitation to a fistfight.

"Plenty of Ibarra tech on Earth when we left. Didn't seem to do them any good," Standish muttered. No one argued with him.

"Sir," Cortaro spoke to Hale over a private

channel, "my family lives near the drop site. Scope shows my house still there. You think…we can maybe…?"

"Not just yet," Hale said. "My parents aren't that far away either. I want to go as much as you do, but it'll have to wait until this is over."

Cortaro nodded. "Hoo-ah, sir. You're right. I shouldn't even have asked. Don't tell no one, OK?"

"I bet they're OK. Just get through this fight," Hale said. Cortaro had a wife and five children in the Phoenix suburbs. All his Marines had family on Earth; all were just as worried as Cortaro. Even if Ibarra was wrong and there were survivors from the alien invasion, thirty years had passed. What was left of the world they knew?

"Stand by for atmosphere," chimed the drop ship's computer.

Wisps of fire streaked past the windows as the drop ship dove to the Earth. The first bit of turbulence felt like the ship dropped a meter. Marines cursed and braced themselves against their seats.

"Put your head against the seat and get ready for G's" Hale said to Stacey. The ship shook like a rat in a terrier's jaw. Combat drops were designed for speed, not comfort.

"'Get ready for G's,' he says. 'Go on the orbital assault. It'll be fun,' they said," Stacey murmured.

"We can all hear you," Hale said. The drop ship banked from side to side and Hale's head bounced against the restraints.

A red light flashed in the ceiling.

"Breaking maneuvers in three…two…," the computer said with an inappropriate level of calm.

Hale squeezed his core muscles and thighs. The drop ship pulled from its dive and Hale felt the press of five times his weight against his body. He strained to keep blood in his brain until the maneuver ended, the unnatural press leaving him like the dimming of a blinding light.

"We've got a winner," Walsh said.

Stacey sat slumped against her restraints; the maneuver had caused her to black out.

"Her readings are OK. Wake her up," Walsh said.

Hale reached over and pressed a button on the top of her helmet. A second later, her body shook as a mild electric shock went down her spine and a whiff of ammonia filled her helmet.

Stacey jerked away and tried to rub her offended sinuses.

"Ugh, this is why I went space navy," she said.

"Thirty seconds to insertion. Assume drop line positions," the computer said.

Hale disengaged his restraints and sprang to his feet. He pulled Stacey from her seat and guided her to Torni, who attached a D-clip on a line running from her armor to Stacey's chest harness.

"What do I do?" Stacey asked.

"Hold on tight," Torni said as she wrapped an arm around Stacey's waist and grabbed the line running from the ceiling to a panel beneath her feet.

Hale went to his drop panel and locked his feet into the restraints. Clamps locked around his feet and he removed his rifle from its chest mount. The ship shook as it lost speed. An amber light pulsed on the bulkhead.

"Marines, our mission is stealth and reconnaissance. Don't fire unless our lives depend on it," Hale said.

The amber light pulsed faster and turned green. Hale mag-locked his hand to the cable and nodded his head to pray. *God, please don't let me screw this up.*

The panel beneath Hale's feet broke from the drop ship and plummeted, taking Hale with it.

Blast from the drop ship's engines knocked him from side to side as the cable lowered him to the ground, his augmented grip keeping him from taking the much quicker gravity-assisted way down. He scanned the terrain around the drop point—overgrown weeds and covered play parks for children.

The sky was overcast, a gray sheen so dull he couldn't find the sun. Five other Marines descended alongside him, more from the other drop ships. A pair of Eagles, wings and rudders extended for atmospheric flight, hovered over the drop ships by turbo fan engines built into the wings.

The panel smacked into the ground and the clamps on his feet disengaged. Hale jumped away and ran for a block building sitting astride an unkempt soccer field. He slid against the wall, kicking up a plume of dust and pebbles. Walsh and Standish stopped on either side of him, rifles scanning for targets.

"This is Red 1, boots dry," Hale said on the company IR net. On Earth, ambient moisture would absorb the IR transmissions, limiting the effective range to a hundred yards. Major Acera, huddled against a jungle gym set with the first sergeant and a pair of Marines shepherding a mortar tube, gave him a thumbs up.

Torni and Stacey ran over to join Hale, Stacey's labored breathing drowning out the local IR net. The rest of Hale's Marines descended from their drop ship.

"I know this place," Stacey said. "I had my

eighth birthday party right over there." She pointed
to a covered pavilion.

Hale was about to give her a quick lesson in
radio discipline when he noticed something in the
dirt, a glint of metal. Grabbing it with his fingertips,
he lifted it slowly as sand grains fell away from a
dull steel rod connected to a lump. The whole thing
came loose with a jerk and Hale held it in front of
him.

The metal rod was attached to a ball joint;
another metal rod dangled from the joint.

"Walsh, is this what it looks like?" Hale
asked the medic.

Walsh snatched the joint and held it up to
his visor.

"It's a prosthetic leg, newer model too....
Hold on, this kind of prosthetic is supposed to be
covered in replacement tissue when installed.
Where's the rest of him?" Walsh asked. He glanced
around the corner and froze.

"Sir, this is weird," Walsh said.

Hale leaned over Walsh to see what held

Walsh's attention. The medic pointed at a hole in the concrete the diameter of a clenched fist. The hole extended through one wall and through another; Hale could see gray sky through the hole.

"Some sort of laser, fired from the sky, maybe," Hale said.

"Lasers leave scorch marks. That left a perfect cross-section of the wall when it went through it," Walsh said.

Cortaro and the rest of Hale's Marines went prone next to the perforated block house, their active camouflage morphing to match the sandy ground.

"Armor drop, prepare to move out once they're on the ground," Acera said over the net. The IR net had limited range from person to person, but the IR would rebroadcast received messages, creating a web that could extend for miles.

Two of the drop ships lowered their ramps and tilted nearly parallel to the Earth. Two huge humanoid shapes, their legs tight together and arms crossed over their chests like pharaohs in their crypts, slid from the drop ships.

The mechanized armor suits unlimbered in midair and hit the ground so hard Hale felt tremors. The armor that landed closest to Hale knelt for a moment, then stood to its full ten feet. Pale beige armor plates swirled as the active camouflage adjusted to the terrain.

The M-37 mechanized armor suits were one of the great innovations to come out of the Second Pacific War between the Chinese and America and its allies, where crewed tanks proved too vulnerable to urban terrain and relentless electromagnetic attack. Neither the Chinese nor Atlantic Union belligerents could hack the human nervous system so an engineer at MIT figured out a way to integrate a mechanized suit of armor with a human brain.

The first deployment of a half-dozen mechanized armor at the Battle of Brisbane routed the Chinese invaders and accelerated their development. All six of the original Black Knights died in subsequent battles, their armor recovered and put on permanent display at the armor training center at Fort Knox. Hale remembered running past each suit during pilot selection, the battle damage that felled each suit never repaired, still as raw as the day it died.

The nearest suit took a dark metal Gatling cannon off the mag-lock on its leg and connected a belt of gauss bolts to the cannon's magazine. Twin spikes of launch rails were visible, sticking up from the suit's back, as it strode over and bent at the waist to bring the sensor box that made up its head level with Stacey.

"I'm to keep you safe," came over the IR net, the voice tinny and mechanical. The pilots couldn't speak while suited up, their entire nervous system given over to controlling the armor. A separate system kept the pilots alive while they were curled up inside the armored wombs within the suits.

Stacey backed away from the suit and bumped into Torni.

"First Lieutenant Elias, at your service," the suit said and tapped a quick salute against its head.

"Armor, go tracked. Low profile needed," Acera said over the net.

Elias' leg panels snapped open, revealing treads. The treads extended with a mechanical whine and the legs hinged at the hips to bring the tracks into contact with the ground.

"Stay behind me, crunchies," Elias said and rolled to the north.

"I swear those guys give me the creeps," Standish said.

Hale shared the route to the Euskal Tower with his section and fell into his position as his Marines formed a wedge behind Elias. Hale grabbed a bewildered Stacey by the back of her chest harness and put her two steps behind him.

"Stay with us and keep your head down if things go sideways, OK?" he said.

She nodded.

Hale glanced over his shoulder as the drop ships and their fighter escort broke away and flew south. They'd hole up in a canyon until they were needed for extraction.

As their engines died away, an unnerving silence surrounded the Marines. They marched past a suburb that had been home to tens of thousands of people, but nothing moved around them except for the wind whispering through mesquite trees, doves whinnying through the air, and the *flap, flap, flap* of a ragged American flag on a pole outside a grade school.

"Oh wow," Standish said, pointing to a distant mountain range where a mile-long spaceship lay broken against the peaks and valleys. The ship had survived reentry scorched and mostly intact. Sections of the hull had been ripped away, exposing the internal beams and hinting at what remained within.

"It's the *Midway*. I can see her hull numbers," Cortaro said. The Atlantic Union's flagship was the best assignment for a sailor's career and every position, from cook to captain, was a hard-won contest. Now it lay in the sun, rotting like a giant animal.

"Focus. Keep moving," Hale said.

Hale looked into a car parked on the roadside, blanketed in years of blown pollen and dust, a fist-sized hole in the roof and a dusty Ubi on the passenger seat the only clues as to what happened to the driver.

A tumbleweed meandered down the road, thumping lazily along.

Hale tightened his grip on his gauss rifle. Euskal Tower loomed ahead of them, wavering as dust blew through the sky.

A gust of wind sent a line of dirt snaking down the road and a radiation warning icon pinged on his visor.

"Walsh, how bad is it?" Hale asked.

"Trace alpha and beta particles, minimal gamma rays. Nothing to worry about, but definitely more than what's normally in the atmosphere," Walsh said. The medic tapped at his forearm computer.

"What caused it?" Hale asked.

"There hasn't been a nuke power plant for decades, but modeling fits with atmospheric nuclear weapons decades ago," Walsh said.

"At least there was a fight," Franklin said, hefting his gauss cannon against his hip. The micro grav emitters around the barrel glowed as they kept the barrel level to the ground.

"Eyes open, mouth shut," Cortaro said.

The march continued through the empty city. Packs of wild dogs barked and howled in the distance, none daring to come close to the Marines as they passed.

A sign, rattling against its frame, welcomed them to the Ibarra Corporation headquarters. A twenty-foot wall surrounded the enclave and prominent warnings against drone trespassing ran along the wall. Hale's diagram showed an entrance to the compound, but their map must have been extremely dated.

"Let me get a look," Standish said. He grabbed a vine attached to the wall and started climbing.

"No, wait!" Stacey called out. Standish froze, his hand almost over the top of the wall.

"Grandpa put almost every electronic countermeasure he could invent into that wall. Anything with an electrical impulse goes over it— all hell will break loose. All the entrances will be blocked."

Standish dropped to the ground and dusted himself off.

"You think it's still active after all this time?" Hale asked.

"The batteries are supposed to last for fifty years and the top of the walls have ingrained solar panels to keep them running even longer," she said.

"Then how do we get in?" Cortaro asked.

Stacey looked up and down the wall, then took off her right glove. She pressed her palm against the wall, and a second later a red arrow pointed to the left along with "32m."

"I put a couple backdoors in the program so I could sneak out as a teenager," she said.

Thirty-two meters away, Stacey put her hand against the wall again and a section sank into the ground, just enough for an adult to get through on their hands and knees.

On the other side of the wall, Hale saw a wrecked building and lumps of concrete on the ground.

"Something happened over there," he knelt down to cross through.

"Hale, hold up," Major Acera said over the IR net. Hale pointed to Standish and then to the entrance.

"Sure, if anyone's going to get their face eaten by an alien, it should be me," Standish said as he scurried through the entrance.

Acera jogged up and looked into the hole in the wall.

"Can you make it bigger?" he asked Stacey.

"No, sir, this was all I ever needed to get in and out. Never thought I'd have to bring a walking tank with me," she said, pointing to Elias.

"I'm not a tank. I am armor," Elias said, lifting a leg off the ground with flexibility impossible to any human, and got to his feet. The treads returned to the housings in his suit's calves and thighs. "If you need us, just start shooting," he said.

Acera touched his forearm computer. "Second platoon, secure this exit and provide security for the mortar tube. First and third platoons are with me to the objective. Let's go."

Marines followed their commander through the tunnel.

"Ibarra never mentioned any of this to you? No 'aliens are coming—here's my super-secret plan to save us'?" Hale asked Stacey.

"Never. He was so security conscious about everything, real paranoid. He got hacked in the '20s and never trusted a networked device again. Weird that the inventor of the modern world was pretty much a Luddite, right?" she said.

Hale looked south where blue-black storm clouds crept through the sky toward them.

"Monsoon season," she said.

"We're up," Hale said as he followed the last Marine through—and found a war zone on the other side. Building walls had crumpled during some long-ago onslaught. Broken windows and lumps of concrete knocked from walls by gauss fire littered the ground. The rear of the wall surrounding the compound had hastily erected firing stoops built against the wall, much of it crumpled to the ground.

"Last stand?" Cortaro asked Hale as their Marines crept into a wrecked building; their training demanded they seek cover whenever possible.

"I hope not," Hale said.

"Oh no," Stacey said from behind them. "That's my house!" She ran past Hale before he could stop her, flitted around the rubble and ran into a once-elegant townhouse, Hale on her heels.

"Stop! Damn you," Hale reached out, his fingertips scraping against her back.

She pushed past a door swinging on its hinges and came to a sudden stop once she made it down the hallway beyond the door.

Hale brought his gauss rifle to his shoulder and set his weapon to FIRE. He stepped in front of her and saw what brought her to a halt.

Half the house was missing, seemingly

erased from existence, the floor tiles, refrigerator and part of a bed, perfectly sliced away. Hanging in the emptiness was a cube, cobalt blue around the edges, the faces faded to the color of a sky filled with gossamer clouds. Golden flakes floated within it.

"What is that?" Stacey asked, her voice filled with awe.

The cube rotated in place, randomly changing directions as if buffeted by a phantom breeze. An ice-blue light flared above them. Hale grabbed Stacey by the waist, swung her back into what remained of her home and snapped his weapon up toward the light.

Another cube, barely the size of baseball, floated toward the larger cube. Its light drew sharp shadows across the floor, mimicking a day's worth of the sun's passage in a few seconds. A tight beam of white light connected the two cubes and the smaller cube passed into the larger one, which pulsed and grew several inches bigger.

"It's beautiful," she whispered.

"Hale, get back here. We've got contact," Acera said over the IR net.

Hale grabbed Stacey by the carry handle on the back of her harness and gave her a tug as he backed out of the room. She stutter-stepped backwards, her eyes locked on the cube.

Hale found his Marines, with the exception of Sergeant Cortaro, bunched up on the corner of a mostly intact home, where gauss rounds had stitched up the walls and knocked gouts of plaster and concrete away. Vincenti pointed to Hale and then to the door.

"Attach a line to her if she tries to run off again," Hale said to Torni, finally letting go of Stacey as he stepped into the house.

Cortaro was at the top of a flight of stairs on his hands and knees. Windows ran along the upper hallway above Cortaro's head. A low buzzing sound pulsed through the house and windows rattled in their frames.

Hale crouched and climbed up the stairs, careful not to flag his location by sticking his rifle barrel into view of whatever was making that noise beyond the windows.

"Sir, this is *loco*," Cortaro said. "Come see."

Cortaro led Hale into an adolescent's bedroom, dolls and plush toys from girlhood shoved to the fringes of the room in favor of shift-posters of pop stars and a burgeoning collection of clothing.

Another of the perfect holes ran from the wall to the bedframe. Something glinted underneath the bed. Hale pulled an Ubi out from under the bed and saw a light-red dust covered the screen. He handed it to Cortaro.

"They're built to last. Maybe we can charge it," Hale said.

"Look through that hole. You'll see it," his team sergeant said.

A buzz went through the wall like an electric current as Hale brought his eye to the hole.

"Three stories up, your two o'clock."

Hale found it hovering midair, a black and gray oblong shape next to the sliced remnants of an air conditioner. It was a little more than a meter long and held its position perfectly, like it was bolted into place. Hale toggled his magnification lenses to zoom in. It looked like a drone, like those sent into Europa's oceans years ago. Four segmented stalks moved around the air conditioner, red light arcing between the stalk tips and their focus. The air conditioner disintegrated where the red light touched it, small blue motes sublimating from the metal and floating around the drone.

Four different stalks converged into a point behind the drone and blue light identical to the cube he and Stacey had seen emanated from the convergence. The blue motes fell into the convergence like it was a black hole.

Hale magnified further. The drone's surface was gray and black bands and mottled patterns like Damascus steel wavered across the surface, never still. A stalk moved from the convergence to the air conditioner, sliding effortlessly across the drone's surface.

The drone lacked any other features. It was just the stalks connected to the ellipsoid body with the swirling patterns.

The buzzing intensified, in time with a pulse of red light from the drone.

"Hale, take your team and the principal to the tower. We'll keep an eye on that thing. Call out if you see another," Acera said.

"Roger, moving."

Hale and Cortaro crept out of the house. The lieutenant pulled his Marines together into a huddle.

"Whatever that thing is, it looks armored. Switch to high-powered shots but make them count. We're a long way from a resupply," Hale said.

"Faben—Ibarra, whatever—stay close and stay quiet," he said to Stacey, who nodded quickly.

"Follow me." Hale turned and switched his rifle to high power. A warning icon popped on his visor, alerting him to the power drain he placed on the system. The batteries on their gauss rifles would run dry after ten shots. They carried spare batteries, but not enough for a prolonged fight.

A threat icon on his visor's mini-map, fed to him by the Marines watching the drone, remained steady. They moved another two hundred meters toward the looming tower, and the threat icon faded away.

"We're out of IR range. Stay sharp," Cortaro said.

They came up to a wide intersection, the road twisted and broken. Hunks of solar-panel glass that made up the road had melted, like a flash-frozen lava flow.

Walsh used a mirror to look around the corner, then sprinted across the roadway. He was halfway across when he did a double take at something in the debris. He got to the other side and pointed to what he'd seen.

"Sir, there's an armor suit in the road," Walsh said over the IR.

"I'll look it over. Leapfrog me," Hale said. He sprinted across the road and vaulted over a lump of panel glass into a depression. An armored hand and forearm stuck up from the dirt, bent into a claw. Hale swept dirt away and found the shoulder and unit patch. He recognized the worn insignia instantly, the *fleur-de-lis* over an eight-pointed shield and the words *Toujours Pret*—Always Ready. The armor belonged to the 2nd Dragoons, a unit that had served the United States of America and the Atlantic Union for over two centuries.

He ran his hands under the shoulder joint and found a button, right where it should be. A panel popped open on the shoulder, a blank screen underneath it. If the suit had power, the screen would have lit with the pilot's vital signs. Hale grabbed a wire from his helmet and was about to connect it into the screen's port when he told himself, *No, this isn't my mission.* There was no way the pilot could still be alive. Even with the coma protocols, the womb could keep the pilot alive for only a few days at best. Hale hoped the pilot died quickly and not screaming inside the suit. A shiver passed through Hale and he crossed the road.

"Anything?" Walsh asked as his hand went to a laser cutter locked to his thigh. The cutter could open the suit's armor like a tin can if needed, but it would take time.

"No power, not worth the risk to have a loose EM broadcast either," Hale said.

Standish, the point man, held up a fist and the team froze in place.

"Contact, one drone, two hundred meters," Standish said.

The drone descended from an upper level of the Euskal Tower, its stalks bent in half and sunk into the body. It floated to a few feet above the road and zipped around the corner, out of sight from the Marines.

"There any other way into that tower?" Hale asked Stacey.

"I'm fresh out of secret passages," she said.

"It didn't notice us from this distance. Maybe we can sneak past it," Cortaro said.

"If not…," Franklin said, patting his Gustav.

The Marines continued past the remnants of a bank, the vault door perforated with holes. They came to a wide boulevard running past the Euskal Tower, a hundred meters bereft of cover and concealment. The double doors to the tower hung from their hinges.

Hale peeked around the corner, searching for the drone.

A buzz rattled the walls of the bank.

Standish and Franklin jumped away from the building like it was on fire, scanning the sky with their weapons.

"Christ, that's close," Standish said.

"Go, now!" Hale said and then tore across the road, dodging stopped cars and leaping over a rail guard. His lungs burned as his sprint brought him to the tower's entrance. He leaned back and slid into the tower, his Marines right behind him. Torni had thrown Stacey over her shoulder and carried her across the road.

There was no sign of the drone, nothing but labored breathing over the IR.

The foyer was overgrown with now-dead potted plants that had burst from their pots and pressed into the ceiling like smoke from a nascent fire. Fish tanks, their water brown from algae, filtered the sun's light into an ugly brown miasma through the hallway leading to a glass and gold elevator.

"That's your elevator, right?" Hale asked Stacey.

"Not exactly." She kept her head low and ran down the hallway, stopping to the side of a gilded elevator, and ripped vines from the wall. A panel hinged open, a receptacle the size of a soda can waited to be filled.

"Franklin, a spare," Hale said. Franklin unclipped a battery from his belt and tossed it to Stacey. She placed the battery and shut the panel. A soft whirr came from behind the wall.

"Cortaro, I'll go down with her. Secure this spot," Hale said.

"For how long, sir?" Cortaro asked.

Hale looked at Stacey, who shrugged.

"No problem, sir, we'll just stay here. With the aliens," Standish said.

The wall next to the main elevator opened. Vines cracked and fell away as the doors to the auxiliary lift rolled aside.

Stacey took a hesitant step into the elevator and Hale followed her a second later.

"Now," Hale said "how do we—"

The doors slammed shut lightning fast. Hale's breathing quickened as he realized just how enclosed—and tiny—this space was. He reached out to touch the walls, which were solid. There was no emergency exit, no way out of here. He concentrated on the lights along the ceiling, the sound of his breathing. He wasn't in the womb; this wasn't the test. His panic died down but it stayed over his shoulder, waiting for him to lower his guard.

"Remove headgear for biometric identification. Lethal countermeasures are authorized by subsection twelve dash nine comment three by your employment contract. You have twelve seconds to comply," a monotone voice said from a speaker in the ceiling.

Stacey twisted off her helmet and tossed it to Hale. She used her teeth to strip off a glove and placed her hand on a pad that extended from the wall.

"Say your name for voice print identification," came from the speaker.

"Stacey Fabe—Ibarra! Stacey Ibarra!" She winced as Hale's count to twelve elapsed.

A bell dinged.

"Welcome, Stacey Ibarra. One moment please."

They heard the plates beneath the elevator shifting aside and felt the elevator descend.

Hale, who barely fit in the elevator, shifted in his armor.

Stacey ran a hand through sweat-soaked hair and pinched the bridge of her nose.

"I hate this," she said. "I was *it* growing up. I had five aunts but I was the only grandchild. I think I was five when I realized that I was going to inherit the biggest business in history. No pressure, right? 'Hey Stacey, sure hope you're good to manage millions of employees and trillions of dollars in assets soon as Gramps kicks the bucket. Whole world's counting on you.'

"Now, I'm supposed to be the lynchpin for all of humanity. I just wanted to be an astrophysicist. Me and a bunch of telescopes, grant money and a house full of cats if I never got married."

Stacey sniffed, fighting tears.

"I wanted to be an armor pilot, but that didn't work out," Hale said.

"What happened?"

Hale's teeth clenched as prickles of fear ran down his spine, his nascent claustrophobia coming to the forefront of his emotions.

"I failed the last isolation test. And—could we not talk about that? In here? Right now?"

"Sorry. So, you and Durand, eh?" Hale's growing unease vanished. How the heck did she know about him and the fighter pilot?

The elevator came to a halt and the doors opened with a ding.

Hale pushed past Stacey and leveled his rifle at the plinth in the middle of the room. Lying next to the plinth was a desiccated body, an ornate cane clutched in its hand.

"Grandpa?" Stacey stepped around Hale and walked up to the body, her hands at her mouth. She knelt beside the body, its skin shriveled and eye sockets empty. Wisps of white hair wavered in a slight breeze.

"Is this what he wanted us to find?" Hale asked.

A column of white light burst from the plinth. Stacey fell back on her haunches with a squeak. Hale jumped in front of her, holding a hand in front of his face to block the light.

"Stacey, I'm so glad to see you," came a voice from the light, a voice familiar to Hale, but with a deep resonance—Ibarra.

"What are you?" she asked. The light dimmed, fluctuating as if the light source was just under water.

"I am an approximation of Marc Ibarra. His memories and personality were imprinted onto my matrix. More of him will be apparent as my higher functions come online," said the light.

"I'm first Lieutenant Ken Hale of the Atlantic Union Marine Corps. You want to explain just what the hell's going on out there?"

The light shrank to the size of a needle and sparkled.

"You aren't using unshielded electronics. Good. Have the Xaros detected you? Where is Ceres?"

"The what?" Hale asked.

"The big ugly footballs that wiped out humanity, you dolt—the Xaros! Do they know you're here?" The light quaked with anger.

"No, no, I don't think so," Stacey said. "We couldn't *find* Ceres when we looked for it."

"I know where it's going. This is working better than my projections. Stacey, pick me up," the light said.

Stacey backed away, a grimace on her face.

"Stacey Prudence Ibarra, I did not raise you to be chicken. The fate of the world really does depend on us leaving as quickly as possible. It's not like I'm asking you to repopulate the Earth with this knuckle-dragger," the light said.

"Knuckle-dragger?" Hale said with indignation.

"Wait, you *are* my grandfather," Stacey said. She stepped over Ibarra's desiccated corpse and reached out to the sliver of light that contained his mind. Her hand opened and clenched a few inches from the light, like it was a burning ember.

"For Pete's sake," the Ibarra light said. The light snapped into Stacey's hand and she yelped in surprise.

She held her hand by the wrist and tried to shake the light loose, but it had embedded in her palm.

"Stop sniveling. I know that didn't hurt. You wouldn't believe where I had to carry this thing for the first decade. Now let's get out of here," Ibarra said.

Stacey rubbed her palm against the side of her thigh and looked at Hale with desperation.

Hale grabbed her by the wrist and pulled her toward the elevator.

"Where are we supposed to take you?" Hale asked.

"My fleet, and hurry. There's more at stake than just the survival of what little remains of humanity," Ibarra said.

****

Cortaro pressed his back against the wall as the buzzing sound continued. The probe had meandered back to the tower since Hale and Stacey took the elevator and was dismantling an office several floors above them.

The sergeant looked over the Marines, each pressed against the walls out of sight from the probe, their faces hard against the stress of being so close to an enemy they didn't know how to fight. Standish, the Marine Cortaro thought would crack under the pressure first, nodded his head back and forth slightly, a song on his lips that he didn't sing over the IR net.

Cortaro shifted slightly to peek at the battery

powering the elevator—still above three quarters charge but draining fast.

As he leaned over, the Ubi Hale recovered from the girl's room caught a direct ray of sunlight in Cortaro's mesh pouch. The solar power lining of the screen converted the energy into battery power and brought the Ubi to life.

The Ubi vibrated in the pouch and, in a high-pitched voice, said, "Please return me to direct sunlight." Marines snapped their head around to the sudden noise.

The buzzing of the probe ceased.

Cortaro ripped the battery from the Ubi and held very still.

A hum filled the air and set Cortaro's teeth on edge. A shadow passed across the hallway as the probe floated along the outer wall. The shadow's stalks writhed as the humming grew louder.

Cortaro shifted back away from where he'd been sitting, praying that he'd killed the Ubi before that thing knew exactly where his Marines were hiding. Seconds ticked by like hours and the humming faded. Cortaro let out a sigh of relief—just before an amber beam shot through the wall and struck the gilded elevator with a hiss. Cortaro saw the burning point of one of the probe's stalk tips twist toward him in the new smoking hole in the wall. Cortaro rolled away as a second beam cut through where his head had been.

"Contact!" Vincenti yelled. He sprung to his feet and fired his gauss rifle at the drone. On high power, the bolt left his barrel at three times the speed of sound and blew out half the windows in the hallway with the sudden sonic boom.

The bolt hit the drone with the clang of a metal girder snapping in half and knocked it spinning into the wall. Stalks shot out of the drone and embedded into the tower, whipping it against the wall so hard that it embedded itself in the marble facade. The drone swung loose from the crater, like a condemned man hanging by his noose. A deep divot in the swirling gray and black surface marked where Vincenti's round had impacted.

The rest of the Marines were on their feet,

weapons trained on the drone.

"I think I got it," Vincenti said.

Franklin's Gustav hummed as a full-power shot readied in the weapon's chamber.

"Let me double-tap it," Franklin said.

"No," Cortaro said. "If you miss, you'll take out half a floor and everyone from here to Phoenix will see it."

One of the drone's stalks fell from the wall and twitched in the air.

"What's it doing?" Vincenti said, his voice reedy with fear. "Should I—"

A crimson blast from a stalk struck Vincenti in the chest and he crumpled to the ground. The drone sprang into the air, stalks swirling around it.

The team unloaded on the drone without orders. Hits from high-velocity slugs sent the drone tumbling in the air. A shot from Torni sheered two stalks from the drone. The dismembered limbs floated in the air like falling leaves, then disintegrated like they were burning from the inside out.

Two new stalks grew from the drone within seconds and their points joined together. A yellow beam scythed through the air, missing Torni's head by a handbreadth as it slashed through the foyer. Glass and masonry blasted loose where the beam struck. The ornate elevator erupted outward as the beam passed across it. Shards of glass careened off Cortaro's armor as he lined up a shot on the drone.

Cortaro put two rounds into the drone and a crack burst across its surface. The crack expanded, showing the drone's innards: a chrome and gold crystal lattice that sparked with energy.

Franklin's Gustav boomed and the drone burst into a million pieces. The remnants floated in the air, golden spurts of energy arcing between the spinning fragments of the drone's inner workings. The pieces burned away within seconds; the destruction left behind was the only remnant of the drone.

Cortaro ran to Vincenti, the Marine's team icon reading an error.

"Walsh, get over here!" Cortaro said. The

medic didn't answer as Cortaro rolled Vincenti onto his back.

Vincenti had a perfect hole in his armor and the interior of his visor swirled with a deep-red smoke. Cortaro put his fingers under Vincenti's jaw to unlatch the helmet and pulled it free.

A gout of red smoke wafted from the helmet. Cortaro looked down where Vincenti's head should have been but nothing was there. More red smoke drifted up from where the blast struck Vincenti and from the hole in the neck armor.

Cortaro dropped Vincenti's helmet and got back to his feet.

"Walsh?" Cortaro asked. He turned around and saw Torni and Standish standing beside where Walsh lay on his back—in pieces. The drone's yellow beam had sliced through Walsh's chest, cauterizing the flesh with a black glaze of seared blood. Cortaro was thankful he couldn't smell anything with his helmet on.

"Franklin?"

"I'm fine. I think I see another one coming

right for us," Franklin said. "Make that three." He hefted his Gustav and braced himself for the recoil.

The sound of straining metal groaned from what remained of the elevator. The false doors to the private lift partly opened and closed, accompanied by a warning buzzer.

"Lieutenant Hale, going to need you to hurry the hell up," Cortaro said into the IR net, unsure his words could reach him. He took cover against what remained of the wall. Franklin's Gustav fired with the clang of a church bell and Cortaro aimed at the approaching drones.

****

The elevator carrying Hale and Stacey jerked to a halt. The lights switched to amber and pulsed.

"That's not good," Hale said, tapping at the control panel.

"What happened?" Stacey asked the sliver of light in her palm.

"I don't know. The shielding is too strong for me to reach out," Ibarra said.

The building rocked and the elevator lights went solid red.

"Those are the emergency brakes. We are definitely stuck now," Ibarra said. Thuds reverberated through the elevator and a tremor made the floor tick-tick-tick against Hale's boots.

"That's a firefight." Hale pawed at the ceiling panels, which refused to budge. He switched his gauss rifle to low power and pressed the muzzle against the ceiling. "When all else fails, we can shoot our way out."

"Don't! I designed this to withstand gauss fire. One shot and you'll turn our ride into a blender," Ibarra said.

"If you designed this, then how did you intend to get out in case of an emergency?" Stacey asked.

"I didn't," Ibarra said.

"Some genius you are," Hale said.

The elevator rumbled, then went into free

fall. Stacey screamed and braced herself against the sides. The elevator slammed to a halt and sent her and Hale to the ground in a jumble of limbs. The elevator heaved upwards, paused, and then moved up again.

"What the hell is going on?" Hale asked.

"Ah, OK. We'll be fine in a minute," Ibarra said. Their ascent continued in pulses.

Stacey pulled her sidearm from its holster and powered it up. The lights in the elevator cut out. The only illumination came from the glow from Stacey's palm and the lights on their weapons.

The elevator fell on its side, taking its passengers down with it. It tumbled to one side, then slammed against the ground with a metallic slap. Metal groaned and light burst through rents in the elevator door. The tips of gray tendrils bent the metal with ease.

The doors ripped away and Stacey fired her pistol. A gauss round bounced off the head of Elias' armor. The suit, its grayscale armor blending with the clouds above it, shook its head from side to side.

"You're welcome," Elias said. The suit's huge arm reached into the elevator and scooped Stacey out.

Hale stood up and looked around. The elevator lay in what remained of the Euskal Tower's VIP entrance. Most of the roof was blasted away, the carpet scorched and smoking.

Hale's visor struggled to update as information flooded it.

"Sir? You get what we came for?" Cortaro asked. "Major Acera wants us to leave like yesterday."

"We've got it. What happened? Where are Walsh and Vincenti? Why aren't they on my screens?"

"They're down, sir. Those things...they're murder," Cortaro said.

Hale looked at the remains of his two Marines lying side by side outside the wrecked entrance. Two men gone and he hadn't been there when it happened. Guilt hit him in the stomach like a fist and he climbed out of the elevator. He got two steps toward Walsh and Vincenti before Cortaro put a hand to his chest.

"I have their tags. We have to go before more show up. Mission, sir. Remember the mission," Cortaro said.

Hale clenched his jaw and forced himself to look away.

The sound of gauss fire reverberated through the city. Red and yellow flashes burst from the perimeter wall near their exit.

"We destroyed the drone that Acera was watching soon as you made contact. More must have shown up," Elias said. "The major sent me over as soon as that fight was over. He figured you might need me."

"There are fifteen Xaros drones approaching this location from the northeast. I suggest we leave now," Ibarra said.

Elias' head snapped down to look at the glowing light in Stacey's palm.

"What the hell is that?" Elias asked.

"It's the mind of my dead grandfather

215

imprinted on some sort of alien intelligence," Stacey said.

"Sure. Why not. Not like this day can get any weirder," Elias said.

A horn honked from behind Hale. A white truck with a double cab pulled up beside them, Standish behind the wheel. He reached through the open driver's window and slapped at his door.

"Mount up! Told you I could hotwire this thing to run off my suit battery," he said.

"Stacey, get in the backseat," Hale said. "Torni and Cortaro on her sides. Franklin, get in the back with me. Elias, can you keep up with the truck?" Hale pulled himself into the back of the truck, which rode low on its axles from the weight of five armored Marines.

"Three Xaros inbound, six hundred meters and closing," Ibarra said.

"Go. I'll take care of this and catch up," Elias said.

Hale nodded to the hulking suit of armor and knocked twice on the top of the truck, which

216

lurched forward, slammed to a halt, and spun its wheels in place before jerking forward.

"You can hotwire but not drive, eh, Standish?" Torni asked.

"Ha ha, you'd rather walk?" Standish asked. Their truck turned down the four-lane road heading south to their exit. Red and yellow lights mixed with the pale white flashes of heavy gauss fire.

"Where did you learn to steal cars?" Franklin asked.

"*Steal* is such an ugly word. This is a military re-appropriation," Standish said, weaving their truck between dead cars.

Booms from Elias' cannon reverberated between the buildings.

"Sir, if I fire my Gustav, it'll probably flip this truck right over," Franklin said to Hale.

"I know. You're still the best shot out of all of us. Give me your grenades." Hale handed his gauss rifle to the heavy gunner and got three anti-armor grenades in return.

A black oblong shape swooped out from

behind an office building and bore down on the truck. Stalks grew from the drone's body, their tips burning like embers.

"Incoming!" Hale yelled. He twisted the fuse on the anti-armor grenade to "EFP" and hurled the grenade at the approaching drone. The grenade tumbled end over end, the radar and IR sensors in the warhead scanning for an appropriate target. The grenade locked on to the drone and exploded. The explosives behind the tungsten plate morphed the metal into an oversized bullet and shot the projectile at the drone at a velocity of nearly a mile per second.

The projectile struck the drone and slammed it into the road. The drone tumbled end over end, smashing into an antique sports car and embedding in the wreckage.

"That got it," Hale said.

"No, sir," Franklin said, "it ain't dead just yet." Franklin put a gauss round into the wrecked nest where the drone lay, shoving the mass to the side.

The drone burst from the wreck, its stalks tearing the old car into bits as it extracted itself. It floated a meter above the road and raced after the Marines.

A gauss round hit the drone dead center and managed to slow it down. Hale threw another grenade but the projectile missed the drone and blew a crater in the road. The drone slalomed toward them, fouling Franklin's next shot and evading a third grenade.

"Damn things learn fast," Franklin said.

All but two stalks retracted into the drone and it sped forward so fast Hale saw it as a blur. Hale pulled a grenade off his belt and set it to "Shaped Charge."

The drone reared up just behind the truck, its stalks raised like a tarantula about to strike. Franklin fired and the round impacted with a spark, sending the drone back a meter. The drone's stalks slammed down, barely missing the truck before it impaled itself into the road.

Hale tossed the grenade at the stationary

drone and turned his head aside.

The grenade exploded, sending a molten lance of tungsten at the drone. The lance punctured the drone's carapace and shattered everything within.

The drone disintegrated without a sound.

"Hot damn, sir! That was awesome!" Standish yelled and almost tossed his lieutenant over the side by swerving too sharply around a school bus.

"Red 1, this is Gall. Can you read me?" Durand's voice broke over Hale's IR net.

"This is Red 1. We have the package. Can you get to us?" Hale said.

"I'm assuming you're the white truck heading south. Stand by," she said.

The sound of breaking glass and cracking masonry demanded Hale's attention. A drone burst through a building and pounced at the truck. Standish jerked the truck into a fishtail and spun around the drone.

A stalk split the air over Hale's head and

slashed through the tailgate like it was made of paper. The truck slammed into the concrete divider and ground to a halt.

Three stalk tips converged, a yellow light brighter than the sun burning between the points.

Franklin got off a hip shot that hit the rear of the drone. It veered to the side but the stalks held their aim.

Standish got the truck moving just as the drone fired. Brilliant light, brighter than a million candles, flashed in front of Hale and annihilated the road. Hale tried to blink away the afterglow and fumbled with a grenade.

Standish hit a pothole and the grenade flew out of Hale's grasp and bounced down to the road.

Hale's strained eyes caught another shape speeding up from behind the drone and Hale's heart sank at the idea of fighting a second drone.

He blinked hard and saw Elias, his legs in their tracked position, slam into the drone and wrestle it to the ground.

The suit ripped stalks from the drone and

hammered blows against the carapace, the suit's armored fists sounding like blows against an anvil. Elias picked up the drone and slammed it against the road. The drone skipped away like a stone across a lake.

Elias' treads morphed back into his legs and he took his Gustav heavy rifle from his back.

The drone stopped its skip midair and launched itself back at Elias like a bullet. A stalk speared out and drove straight through Elias' head. The suit twitched then fell to its knees.

The drone grew more stalks and readied another blast.

"Uh, sir?" Franklin said.

Elias' suit twisted around at the waist and blew the drone apart with a single shot. Elias stood and ran after the truck, a gout of sparks pouring from its ruined head assembly.

"His real head is in the armor's chest," Hale said.

A drop ship roared overhead and kept pace with the truck.

"Hale, there are more bogeys inbound. I can't put down to get you," Durand said over the IR.

Hale looked over the cab to see how much road they had left. His idea just might work.

"Gall, lower your ramp and fly as close to the front of the truck as you can. Standish, hold your speed. We're going to do an alley-oop with the principal," Hale said.

"I'm sorry—you're going to what me?" Stacey asked.

Hale punched through the cab's rear glass, which shattered into uniform cubes, and pulled Stacey out by her harness. As Hale grabbed her by the shoulder and belt, Franklin mimicked the hold.

The drop ship came down ahead of them, flying almost ten feet above with its rear hatch open.

"What…what…what are you doing?" Stacey demanded, struggling against the Marine's grasp.

"Gall, get ready to cut speed in

three…two…," Hale said.

"Can we talk about—" Stacey's plea turned into a shriek as Hale and Franklin hurled her straight up, their augmented strength hefting her level with the open drop ship.

The drop ship slammed its reverse thrusters and Stacey's forward momentum carried her over the drop ship's lowered hatch and into the hold. She rolled across the deck and crashed against a bulkhead. The rear hatch sealed shut and Durand hit the thrusters.

The crew chief ran over and touched Stacey on the shoulder.

"You OK?"

"Ensign Faben/Ibarra is uninjured. Please return us to the fleet at once," Ibarra said, the light on Stacey's hand pulsating with its words.

"Holy shit!" the crew chief squealed and backpedaled away from Stacey.

"What's going on back there?" Durand said over the intercom.

"I don't know where to start. Can we please

leave?" Stacey asked. She sat up and looked at the light glowing in her palm. The light held steady and she clenched her hand into a fist.

****

The truck pulled up to a mess of rubble. Buildings smoked and popped as small fires burned inside them. Hale and Franklin leapt from the truck before it came to a complete stop, their weapons up and ready. The crawlspace used to gain entrance had been blown into a breach big enough for two Marines to walk through at a time.

Major Acera was supposed to meet Hale here, but the only Marines waiting for them lay in the rubble, limbs bent at cruel angles. Each bore the perfect holes of the Xaros weapons. Hale picked up the left arm of one of the Marines; the ID tags that should have been under the Marine's forearm Ubi were gone.

Hale hated to see Marines left on the battlefield but nothing could be done for them now.

He keyed in coordinates for each body; the information would pass on to the graves registration teams to collect the bodies later.

"Ident chips are gone. They were leaving on their own terms, not running," Hale said.

Elias rolled up and got back on his feet.

"I'm not picking up anything on my IR," he said. Each suit came with an IR net booster. If Acera or any Marine tied to his net were in line of sight, Elias would have connected to him. Grabbing his sensor "head," Elias tried to crunch it back together. A misshapen lump held firm for a second, then fell over again.

"What now, sir? Those two drones took off after the drop ship but more will come," Cortaro said.

"Move to the landing zone. They won't leave until we get there," Hale said.

"Assuming they know we're alive," Standish said.

"Less talk, more moving," Elias said. The suit stumbled over a lump of concrete and a blurb of static shot from its speakers.

"You OK in there?" Standish asked.

"My primary cameras are shot, some damage to my gyroscopes affecting balance," Elias said.

"Can't you get out of there and walk?"

A flap snapped down on the suit's upper torso and it leaned toward Standish. A slit in the armor came level with Standish's eyes as a sliver of pale white skin, so translucent that pulsating veins were visible, twisted behind the slit and a pair of pale blue eyes stared at Standish.

"Death before dismount, crunchy. Let's get moving," Elias said.

Hale picked his way through the breach and looked toward the distant landing zone. Smoke rose from a dozen different places between his Marines and their escape.

"Double time," Hale said and started running, which was easier in their armor than running unarmored. The suits lengthened strides and optimized the swing of the arms to keep a kinesthetic rhythm. They ran almost a kilometer, passing newly collapsed homes and burning vehicles, before they heard the sharp whine of gauss weapons fire.

Hale ran toward the sound of battle, his Marines behind him.

A gauss round snapped past Hale and blew through a garage door. Marines' locations popped onto Hale's visor as the IR net established itself.

"This is Red 1. Five Marines and one armor coming in!" Hale shouted into the IR net.

"Hale? Did you get her out?" Acera asked, the sound of gauss blasts and the swoosh of Xaros beams crowding out his words.

"She's away and with the precious cargo," Hale answered.

"Bring the armor up. We need his rail shot," Acera said. An enemy icon blinked onto Hale's mini-map.

Hale waved to Elias to follow him, the suit too damaged to receive updates from Acera.

"Sir, a rail shot in atmosphere?" Hale said.

An explosion blew through the three-story city hall. Hale not only saw the explosion, he heard it up close and personal as it overwhelmed the IR net.

Someone screamed in pain on the net, then cut out in a hiss of static.

"Yes in atmosphere! I'm bringing it to you!" Acera said.

Hale whirled around and pointed at Elias. "Ready your rail shot!"

Elias skidded to a halt and raised a foot off the ground. A spike shot from his heel and imbedded in the ground. He jammed the spike deep into the ground and repeated the anchoring with his other foot.

The paired rails on his back lifted up and hinged down on his shoulder. Electricity crackled between the rails and Hale's visor roiled with static.

"Ready," Elias said.

A lone Marine ran across the road ahead of them. He twisted around and fired off a high-powered shot from his hip. The round blew a crumbling wall to dust, which billowed like a growing cloud.

A high-pitched whine rose in Hale's ears and a dark mass appeared in the dust cloud.

"Shoot it! Shoot it!" Acera shouted.

"Shoot what? I don't see—"

A giant stomped out of the dust, twice the height and width of Elias' armor. It was hunched over, a wolf-like head lower than its shoulders. Black armor swirling with gray fractals gleamed with a chrome reflection. The giant's arms ended in glowing points of light at the apex of dozens of stalks protruding from its forearms.

One of the trunk-like arms pointed at Acera and a spear of light erupted from its cannon. The light blew through two rows of houses, sending roofs spinning into the air like startled birds. The giant came to a stop, then slowly turned its attention toward Elias. The lights in the center of the hand cannons grew brighter.

"Hold on to something," Elias said. Electric arcs sizzled up and down his rails and Hale fell to the ground, his arms wrapped around his head.

The rail gun fired with the force of a thunderclap as it accelerated a cobalt-jacketed tungsten slug the size of Hale's forearm from zero to 25,000 miles an hour, fast enough to send the slug into orbit, straight at the Xaros monstrosity. The slug ignited the oxygen in the air as it flew to its target, a laser-straight contrail of fire in its wake.

The slug passed through the Xaros giant and blew it apart. Hunks of the giant tumbled away from Hale and Elias, caught up in the hurricane force winds that followed the slug's passage. The Xaros disintegrated within seconds of its destruction.

Hale looked up and saw flaming trees up and down the road, burning like torches. The tinkle and crash of breaking glass from across the neighborhood surrounded Hale, the overpressure from the rail gun's blast damaging far beyond what lay in its line of fire.

"Major Acera?" Hale asked. The major's location pinged from the center of a wrecked house across the street.

Hale ran across the street, adding a waypoint for what remained of his team to converge where the major should have been. The house was a field of blackened rubble, scorched remnants of a family home jumbled with wood and concrete. Acera's marker bobbed from place to place within the rubble.

"Sir? Where are you?" Hale said through his helmet's loudspeakers. He grabbed a chunk of masonry and threw it aside. Acera's location icon switched to amber and blinked—he was wounded. Hale kicked aside a ruined doll and ran deeper into the rubble field. Acera's icon flitted from place to place as the metal in the rubble, heat from the rail shot, and the burning remnants of the home all conspired to block Acera's beacon.

"Come on...where are you?" Hale said.

"Sir! I'm picking him up," Cortaro said from the edge of the wreckage. The team sergeant's reading came up on Hale's visor. The two icons wavered around a cracked wall canted over a support beam.

"I've got him too," Standish said. A third icon floated around the canted wall. Hale stumbled over the debris toward where the readings triangulated.

He found Acera under the wall, the lower half of the major's body pinned beneath it.

"Hale, take this." Acera tossed a tube to Hale, a pyrotechnic that could send up a cluster of burning lights. "Use it to bring in the evac and get out of here," Acera said, his voice straining against the pain of his shattered legs.

"No, we're not leaving you," Hale said. He mag-locked the star cluster to his thigh and pushed at the wall holding Acera to the ground. It was a solid mountain. Hale's Marines joined the rescue effort, jamming their gauss rifles into the voids between the wall and the ground, trying to pry Acera loose.

"Five drones combined to make that walker. Blew both our fighters and a drop ship out of the air before the last two got away. Get that intelligence back to the fleet and leave me, Marines! That's an order!" Acera said.

Hale's team grouped together at one edge of the wall and tried lifting it in a combined effort. The wall shifted, then sank even deeper.

"Get out of here! Now!" Acera said again.

Hale tapped at the side of his helmet and shrugged his shoulders.

"Lift again," Hale said, "on three...two...." The wall elevated with a groan. Elias stood at the other end of the wall, holding the wall aloft with a single hand.

Standish and Cortaro dragged Acera clear of the wall, his lower leg armor cracked and caked in blood.

Hale held the star cluster in front of him and slapped it on the bottom. Three gold lights popped from the cylinder like a military-grade Roman candle from his childhood. Icons of approaching Marines crept onto his visor, what little remained of their landing force.

The whine of approaching drop ships grew louder.

Hale looked back to the Euskal Tower, the lower floors engulfed in flames. A line of destruction traced his path back to where he'd left two of his marines on the battlefield. Honor demanded he recover them, but this battle was beyond what the Corps expected of him. This was about survival.

CHAPTER 5

Hale triggered his helmet's release and slid it off his head. The air in the drop ship smelled of ozone and blood, but it was cool and being able to scratch his face was a welcome relief. The drop ships had just left Earth atmosphere. It would be hours before they made it back to the *Breitenfeld*.

He looked at his Marines, each coming down from combat highs in their own way: Standish wolfed down a pouch of spaghetti and meatballs. Franklin slept against his restraints. Cortaro's attention focused on an Ubi, not the one he normally played games on as his adrenaline waned. Torni, who kept her blond hair slightly longer than

236

the male Marines' high and tight, ran an alcohol pad over her exposed skin.

Habit made Hale look for Vincenti and Walsh, but they were gone.

Looking down at his filthy armor, Hale saw his was just as stained with soot, blood and pulverized concrete as the rest of the Marines in the drop ship. Remnants from another squad of Marines sat across from him. Elias and another armor soldier took up most of the deck between the two rows of seats. The armor was in travel configuration, arms and legs tight together and strapped to the deck.

Hale keyed a channel to Elias.

"You OK in there?" Hale asked, keeping his voice low.

"I've had worse," Elias said.

"When was the last time you were out?"

Seconds ticked by as Hale waited for Elias' answer.

"You can't stay in there forever, Elias, especially not after the system damage you've taken. Did you get any over feed when you got hit?"

Hale asked. Armor pilots often reported feeling pain when their suits took damage, which the suit designers claimed was impossible. Pilots, not wanting to risk admitting to neurologic issues and thus losing their suits, referred to the phantom pain as "over feed."

"Some, but it's gone," Elias answered. "I'll come out when this is over. Can't risk losing resonance with my armor."

"You're going to get wither if you're in there for much longer. You know the risks."

Elias's armor rocked slightly.

"You see that? I'm fine. Just because you got through phase three of selection doesn't mean you earned your plugs. Now piss off," Elias killed the channel.

The Ubi on Hale's forearm vibrated, a call from Captain Valdar. Hale put his helmet back on as Valdar's holo image appeared to Hale. "Yes, sir," Hale said.

"Status report," Valdar said.

"Nineteen confirmed dead, twelve missing

in action, five wounded. The enemy is some sort of drone that Ibarra calls the Xaros. Ibarra, Marc Ibarra is somehow—" Valdar raised a hand.

"We've spoken with *it*. Admiral Garrett sent the drop ship with both Ibarras on to the *America*." Valdar shifted his head from side to side, examining Hale. "You look like hell, Kenny. Ibarra said you saved their bacon down there."

"I lost Marines, sir. I should have done more. I should have done better."

"This is war, son. You can do everything perfect and still lose good men and women. You're the Marine commander until Acera is out of his medically induced coma and back in the fight. Understand?"

Hale nodded. His first command beyond his team wouldn't be that large.

"Admiral Garrett has the fleet—" Warning lights flared behind Valdar. He stepped away from the camera and returned a moment later, his face pale.

"Hale, you've got incoming on fast

approach from Luna." Valdar looked aside. "At least fifty contacts. The destroyers *Tucson* and *Salzburg* are screening between the moon and *Breitenfeld*. Get within their anti-aircraft range and they'll cover you the rest of the way home. I can't get fighters to you before the drones catch up, but we'll try."

"Suit up! We've got incoming!" Hale shouted. Marines scrambled to put their helmets back on and reseal their suits for void operations.

"Wish us luck," Hale said to Valdar.

"*Breitenfeld*, out."

Hale stood up and helped a wounded Marine, his abdominal armor scorched and cracked, from his chair.

"Pilot, I've got one Marine without suit integrity. Once I get him in a pod, go zero atmosphere and lower the rear hatch," Hale said through the IR net. Hale half dragged, half pushed the protesting Marine into a life pod the size of a coffin and sealed the pod shut. The Marine banged against the pod's door feebly, demanding he be allowed to come out and fight.

Cortaro pulled his Marines to their feet and pushed them toward their assignments. "Standish, top gun. Torni, bottom. Franklin, get your Gustav on a pintle."

Standish and Torni climbed into the turret pods. Standish flashed a double thumb and pinky "hakka" sign as his pod swung into the lower gun.

Whirling red lights gave Hale two seconds' warning before the atmosphere in the drop ship was sucked into holding tanks. His armor shifted and popped as it adjusted to void conditions.

The rear hatch descended without a sound, the Earth and the moon hanging in the space beyond, pristine and calm as ever.

Cortaro took careful mag-locked steps out onto the hatch. One wrong step or a sudden maneuver would send him into the void, and it was a long way down. Cortaro lifted a metal hinge from the hatch and set it upright. Franklin locked his Gustav onto the rod and dialed in left, right, up and down limits for his weapon—firing a weapon into the ship carrying you was discouraged.

Cortaro ran a lifeline from Franklin's armor to the deck and did the same for Hale, who knelt beside Franklin's weapon position and mag-locked his knee and shin to the hatch.

Hale checked his rifle's batteries. He had enough charge left for four shots on high power.

Yellow light swept over the hatch as the drop ship's afterburners flared. The acceleration tugged Hale to the abyss but his mag locks held him in place. An ammo canister flew past him and tumbled into nothingness.

The glow from the afterburners subsided.

"That's all the burn we've got left. We're about to have company," Durand said over the IR.

Stars wavered as the Xaros drones cut between them and Hale. Moments later, Hale could pick out the gray-black dots of the drones moving against the backdrop of space. Target icons popped onto his visor.

"Standish, Torni, this is no time to save ammo," Hale said.

The turret gunners answered with bursts from their twin gauss cannons. Yellow tracers streaked across the void and into the mass of drones. The turrets on the drop ship carrying the Acera and the remainder of their company joined the fusillade.

The drones jinked away from the gauss rounds, shunting from side to side with more g-forces than any human pilot could tolerate. Target icons winked out as the converging gauss fire found targets—no satisfying bursts of fire or sympathetic detonations from whatever powered the drones. They evaporated from existence with each solid hit.

"Damn things are quick!" Standish shouted.

Franklin's pintle-mounted cannon peeled off a trio of rounds. Hale's visor darkened in response to the blasts a mere meter from his head.

The drones were close enough that Hale could see their stalks, tips glowing with foul intent.

"Targets are four hundred and fifty—"

A red star came to life against the darkness and a crimson beam burst forth. Light the color of hell's mouth filled the drop ship and a flash blinded Hale. He blinked hard, the afterglow of the passing Xaros blast still burning against his retinas.

"Report!" Hale shouted.

"I got it! Everyone OK in there?" Torni asked.

Voices crowded the IR net and Hale's vision returned. The beam had cut through the deck between him and Franklin. A red-hot metal trough cut from the edge of the hatch and descended into Standish's turret.

"Standish? Answer me," Hale said. The Marine's team icon held firm but there was no answer.

Another burst from Franklin's cannon brought Hale's attention back to the battle. He aimed his rifle at a drone building up a blast and fired a high-powered shot. The recoil rocked him against his magnetic hold on the deck. He reacquired his target and watched it spin against the backdrop of space. A second round cracked it in half and it dissipated.

Two Xaros blasts cut past Hale's drop ship.

"*Hit! We're hit!*" yelled the other drop ship pilot.

The Xaros pursuit slowed and the cloud of enemy icons contracted. The drones swarmed together, a murmuration crackling with electricity.

A burning yellow needle of light penetrated the mass of drones and burst. Yellow slivers flew out of the new explosion and terminated where they impacted with a drone, wayward bolts accelerating beyond the swarm.

"*This is Commander Rikon of the* Tucson. *We'll keep up the anti-aircraft fire. You get your ass back to* Breitenfeld," came over the IR net.

The drop ship sped past the *Tucson*, a destroyer. The fleet's destroyers were nimble ships designed to destroy hostile fighters and torpedoes. The "hedgehog" shells fired by its turrets managed to have some effect on the swarm. As the *Tucson* sent another shell into the swarm, threat icons blinked away, but the contraction of drones continued.

The other drop ship dropped behind Hale, one of its engines a burning ruin. Explosive bolts cut the engine off and the engine flew away, severing the limb to save the body.

"Tucson, *we can't make it to the* Breitenfeld. *We'll need a tug from you.*" The other drop ship slowed and drifted toward the destroyer.

"What the hell?" Franklin said.

The target icons on the drones now read as an error and all the icons massed into a single point. Hale looked through his rifle's scope and zoomed in. The individual drones were gone. They'd fused into a single entity that looked like a hollowed-out log, long stalks whipping through space around it.

A red ember grew within the center of the Xaros construct.

"*Tucson*, you need to—" Hale never had a chance to finish his warning.

A laser pulse tore through the *Tucson* like it wasn't even there, cutting it in half. The *Tucson* languished for a moment, then both halves exploded. Debris pelted Hale's armor hard enough to sting. Instinct brought his hand up in front of his face so he didn't see the lump of twisted metal that struck his forearm.

A jagged bolt of pain tore up his arm, joined by an acid bite of freezing cold. A hunk of metal was stuck in his arm. White geysers of air tinged with the red of his evaporating blood spat from where his suit's integrity was compromised. His visor flashed a red and black PRESSURE warning.

Hale pawed at his belt, struggling to find the canister he needed to save his life. Breathing became harder as his air became thinner with each passing moment.

His injured arm jerked away from him. Cortaro yanked the shrapnel from Hale's arm, the final two inches covered in blood that crystalized in the void instantly. Blobs of blood spurt from the wound. Cortaro put a nozzle against the suit's breach and sprayed a milky white foam into it, finally separating Hale from space. Cortaro squeezed the canister and a separate nozzle popped out of the other end.

The team sergeant stabbed the air canister into a plug on Hale's chest and a wave of pressure flooded Hale's suit. He gasped a full breath of air and struggled to get back to his knees.

The Xaros ship rotated and brought its cannon to bear on Hale's drop ship.

"Gall. Do something," Hale said.

A hedgehog shell exploded on top of the alien ship, the spikes ricocheting off its hull.

"This is the Salzburg. *No effect from our cannons. Switching to torpedoes,"* came over the IR.

The Xaros ship froze and shifted toward the *Salzburg.* The remaining destroyer ejected three torpedoes from its external launchers. The torpedoes hung in space for a moment, then their engines flared to life. But instead of rocketing toward the Xaros ship, they looped around and made straight for the *Salzburg.*

The drop ship's top turret fired, smashing one of the torpedoes to pieces. The *Salzburg*'s point defense crew, caught flat-footed by the sudden attack from their own weapons, struggled to engage the second and third torpedoes.

Durand banked their drop ship hard and put the *Salzburg* between them and the torpedoes.

Cannon fire blossomed along the *Salzburg* as it tried to defend itself. The cannons cut off and a blast of light and flame erupted from destroyer's hull. A torpedo had found its way home.

The airless void extinguished the flames, leaving a burning light racing toward the drop ship. The third torpedo bore down on the drop ship like a wolf chasing down a rabbit.

"*Shoot it!*" Durand said over and over again.

Every weapon left to Hale and his team cut loose on the torpedo, which danced around their shots with preternatural grace. Hale switched his rifle to low power and fired from the hip. He fought against the recoil that pulled his shots higher with each blast. Hale yelled as the torpedo came so close he could almost read the words stenciled on it.

The rear of the torpedo kicked up and it exploded in a flash of red and yellow.

Hale ejected the spent battery on his rifle and slammed a fresh charge.

The Xaros ship was still there, a baleful eye of red energy growing within it.

"Sir, it was an honor," Franklin said.

Hale swallowed hard and got to his feet. No way would he die on his knees.

The red lightning leapt from the center of the Xaros cannon and caressed its inner hull.

The Xaros ship crumpled, struck by a hammer blow that could have cracked a planet's shell. A gray flash of light struck the ship, sending it pin wheeling through space. A third strike split the ship like a log beneath a woodsman's axe. Embers spread across its surface and it disintegrated into nothing.

"*Drop ship One-Zero, this is* Breitenfeld. *You can thank our rail gun crews later. Make a manual landing. We can't risk any automation, not after seeing those torpedoes compromised,*" Captain Valdar said.

"The scope is clear, *grace a Dieu*. Buckle up

for landing," Durand said.

****

Hale jumped off the drop ship ramp and stumbled against the deck, his one good arm ill positioned to stop his fall. A crewman helped Hale to his feet and pointed to the turret beneath the drop ship. Sparks flew from the ring mount as engineers tried to cut Standish free. The Xaros laser had fused the turret's mechanics into a lump of slag and there hadn't been a word from him since the hit.

"We've almost got it open," the crewman said.

Hale pushed his way into the scrum around the turret. The graphene-doped glass of the turret was cracked and cloudy with damage, no way to see inside.

"Has he said anything? How is he?" Hale asked.

The turret broke free and fell to the deck with a metallic snap. Standish rolled out of the turret and lay limp as a rag doll.

Hale ran to his Marine, hesitant to touch him.

"Standish?"

Standish's armor shook with a sudden palsy, then the Marine sat up.

"Wow! That sucked. Suit went into low-energy survival mode and left me twisted like a pretzel for…." Standish stood and tried to scratch between his shoulder blades, then pointed at Hale's injured arm. "Damn, sir. Again?"

Standish looked around the flight deck. Crewmen rushed to extract the two armor suits and ready Eagles for their next sortie. Their banged-up Mule was the only drop ship on deck.

"Where's Major Acera and the rest of the company?" Standish asked.

"They didn't make it. Their ship went up with the *Tucson*," Cortaro said.

Standish's shoulders slumped and he nodded slowly. His dejection spread to what remained of Hale's team. Acera had been Hale's mentor and everything Hale thought a Marine should be. Now he was gone. Along with Walsh. And Vincenti. And every single person he'd left on Earth when he joined this fleet. But this wasn't the time for sorrow. Hale felt the weight of his rank on his shoulders and knew what he had to do.

"Sergeant Cortaro." Hale slapped his good fist against his chest armor with a clang. The sound jolted those around him. "Gather up every able-bodied Marine and get them to the armory. Do a post-combat inspection of every suit and weapon and get ready to launch again. Cycle platoons through for rest and food then get me a roster of who's left. We'll reorganize the company once I've got my arm taken care of," Hale said. A mission to focus on would better serve the Marines than idle time that would only let their collective losses overwhelm them.

The foam on his forearm had collapsed in the atmosphere of the flight deck and blood seeped from the wound.

"I'll take him to sick bay," Durand said. She

jogged his good elbow toward sick bay and took him away from his Marines without further discussion. Sergeant Cortaro gave him a quick salute.

"You alright?" he asked Durand.

"No, I'm pretty shit right now, and so are you. Don't say another word. If you fall on your face, I'm not sure I can drag you the rest of the way in that armor," she said.

Hale's arm throbbed, bolts of pain sending spasms through his bicep as they walked. For all the pain in his arm, it was nothing next to the emptiness of sorrow spreading through his chest.

CHAPTER 6

Admiral Garrett paced behind the chair at the head of a long table. His wardroom could host almost two dozen guests for formal dinners or staff meetings. For extreme circumstances such as this, it could accommodate many more with some technological trickery.

"Done yet?" Garrett asked the petty officer working on the holo emitter in the center of the desk.

"Almost, sir. The IR repeaters on each ship have to compensate for lag every time it—"

"Soon?"

"Two minutes," the petty officer mumbled.

Garrett turned to the other two people in the room, Stacey Ibarra and Theo Lawrence. Stacey stood against the bulkhead with her head down, like a scolded child. Lawrence shifted his weight from foot to foot and tugged at his collar.

"We are going to stay here until every single question is answered, and if I catch a whiff of bullshit from either of you, I will rip your face off in front of a live studio audience," Garrett said. "Get me?"

Lawrence brought his hands up in surrender and nodded quickly.

Stacey brought her head up, her lip quivering.

"Sir, I don't really know much," she said.

"Not you, ensign. That thing you're carrying," Garrett said.

Stacey turned her palm up and a pale blue light shown from her hand.

Marc Ibarra's face coalesced in the light and looked at Garrett with contempt.

"You could rip my face off now if that will

make you feel better," Ibarra said.

Garrett swiped through Ibarra's projection with no effect. Garrett grumbled and turned back to the conference table.

The holo emitter in the middle of the table clicked on and translucent projections of captains from across the fleet filled the seats. The projections changed to a captain whenever he spoke and side conversations rumbled through the room.

"All right," Garrett said, and the conversations died away. The captains turned their attention to Garrett, who sat down and motioned to Stacey to approach.

"Captains of the Saturn Colonial Mission, we have some answers. Finally. I'll turn this over to the one responsible for all of this."

Stacey held her palm toward the table and light swirled in the air in front of Garrett. A perfect 3-D image of Marc Ibarra made of blue and white light came into being.

"I am not Marc Ibarra. I am an artificial intelligence formatted with his memories and personality to aid in communication. The Marc Ibarra you know is dead. He chose to die with your species rather than join this fleet.

"I represent an alien confederation fighting against the Xaros, the drones that wiped out Earth and threaten all intelligent life in this galaxy. If we're lucky, in the next few days we can save what remains of your people and strike a blow in this war."

Military captains remained stoic as the civilian ship masters shouted accusations and questions at Ibarra who raised his hands in an appeal for quiet.

"What happened to Earth? Where is everyone?" asked a civilian captain, the questioner replaced as another echoed the question.

Ibarra's image flickered.

****

Cortaro ran a cable from the Ubi he'd picked up to a wall-mounted screen and Marines and

258

sailors clustered around it. The screen, and every other PA screen on the ship, matched the Ubi's display. Rumors had swirled through the ship about what was on the Ubi and Captain Valdar ordered its contents shared on the ship-wide address system without delay or filtering through the ship's leadership.

Cortaro swiped through the media files and found the last video entry. He'd already seen it a dozen times, each time harder than the last. He hit play.

A haggard face of a man with a red and white beard and a thinning hairline came up. A feeble light showed his face, the collar of his stained uniform, and little else. The collar held a commander's rank pins.

"This is Commander Phil Albrecht of the NAU *Breitenfeld*." Murmurs spread across the crowd watching the video. Albrecht looked years older than when he'd been on the ship, little more than twelve hours ago from the ship's perspective. "Or I was. No one knows what happened to the

Breitenfeld, or the rest of the fleet, after the malfunction. Now I'm the ranking officer of what's left of the military in and around Euskal Tower.

"We don't have much time. The next assault will—" Albrecht pressed a hand against his face and took a deep breath. "Sorry. The *Breitenfeld* and the rest of the fleet vanished right after the Chinese attack. The Ibarra Corporation thinks there was some sort malfunction in the slip-coil drive that sent the fleet into deep space instead of Saturn. Marc Ibarra is MIA and no one has any idea where he is. Must have snuck onto the fleet is my guess.

"The *Midway* picked me up outside lunar orbit and we were gearing up for a punitive strike against the Chinese when we detected the droids." Albrecht's gaze unfocused. He mouthed words several times before they finally came out. "At first, we thought it was some sort of meteor shower. There were so many contacts. The drones, robots— whatever! The swarm passed over Mars and wiped out everything.

"We got some video feed back before the

computers were compromised. Saw just enough to know the swarm was alien and our fight with the Chinese got put on hold. There were billions of drones. Do you understand? Hundreds of billions of drones. They didn't try to talk to us, didn't give us any kind of chance, nothing.

"We combined fleets with the Chinese and whatever the Russians had around Luna and tried to fight. I led a flight off the *Midway*...." Albrecht wiped a tear away from his face. "We hurt them, a few of them, with high-powered gauss and rail gun shots. Nukes, anything with an onboard system was useless. We were doing well, then the Chinese fired up their targeting computers. The drones compromised their systems in seconds, turned the Chinese guns against themselves, and wiped them out in minutes.

"The line held, but not for much longer. The drones were just toying with us, seeing what we were capable of. Then they joined together into a ship twice the size of the *Midway* and blew the fleet away. I saw drones bore into ships, heard the screams of the crew as the drones slaughtered them.

"The *Midway* took a bad hit and drifted into Earth's gravity well. I gathered up survivors and retreated. The spaceport near Phoenix was still functioning so we made planet fall there. Most of the planet was shut down. The drones ripped through the firewalls controlling the utility systems and cut the power to everything.   .

"We thought we could fight them on the ground," he said, shaking his head. "They formed into orbital platforms and hit anything that moved with disintegration beams. The armored corps at Ft. Hood never got out of the motor pool. Everything was just gone within hours. I managed to get into Euskal Tower with a few units of armor and sailors.

"We hunkered down, tried to raise resistance cells on the Internet until that went down. We went to radio but every time someone broadcasted they'd go dark within minutes. The drones would triangulate their radio towers and wipe them out. The old fiber-optic lines stayed up but…

"The drones sent swarms into the cities,

killed every man, woman and child. There was no place to hide. The disintegration beams cut through everything. There were some in deep bunkers, but the drones bored through the ground and wiped them out too. The deep-sea colony didn't last long, same with the cavern cities on Luna.

"It took thirty-six hours to wipe out humanity. Billions dead. No demands for surrender, no communication from the drones.

"For some reason, the drones weren't very interested in us down here. Only a handful of drones came to Euskal. We fought off the first wave, thanks to the armor suits. The second wave knocked us down to three suits and a dozen men and women with rifles. They're massing over the mountains now, thousands of them."

Red flashes of light lit the room behind Albrecht. Marines and sailors stirred from sleep and ran from the room.

"I don't have much time left. I'll broadcast this message on every wavelength I can. Maybe it'll catch up to the *Breitenfeld*."

A red beam sliced through the room leaving a burning line on the camera's pixels.

"*Gott mit uns!*" Albrecht shouted and cut the video.

Cortaro set the video back to the beginning. The room was silent, but for the sound of someone weeping in a distant corner.

****

Ibarra's projection leaned over the table.

"When the last human was dead, the Xaros left a small detachment to erase all trace of our · existence and the majority of their force dispersed to other stars."

"You knew! You knew, you son of a bitch, and you didn't tell us!" Admiral Garrett roared.

"Yes, I knew." Ibarra's image shifted into a single line of light running perpendicular to the table. "I arrived almost sixty years ago, and even if I'd taken total control of your civilization, it would not have mattered. In the fifteen thousand years we've fought against the Xaros, only two civilizations have withstood the initial contact with them. The first didn't survive the second attack. The second civilization survives only because it went into hiding. I am a herald of the surviving civilization. Both civilizations had thousands more years to develop before contact. I devised a scheme to give you a shot at surviving."

The light shifted to show a schematic of the slip-coil drive.

"Not an engine at all, but a stasis device. It sent each ship into a pocket universe where time essentially stands still. You disappeared before the Xaros could detect you and sidestepped time just long enough for the plan to work. The Xaros fleet, moving at nearly the speed of light, is too far away to turn around." The display shifted back to Ibarra.

"If you had these stasis devices, why is the fleet so small? Ten billion people and you only cared to save six hundred thousand?" one of the civilian captains asked.

"The slip drives ran off quadrium. I mined

265

out every last gram this solar system had to offer to make this fleet as large as it could be." Ibarra's image crossed his arms. "You can second-guess me all you like but none of your questions or good ideas mean a damn thing right now. I had sixty years to come up with a plan and I had the help of an AI more advanced than anything we could conceive. The choice was to save some of us and win this fight—or extinction.

"If humanity is still around to vilify me in a hundred years, then I've succeeded."

"What do they want? The Xaros?" Lawrence said, stepping away from the corner.

"They eliminate all intelligent life they can find. For so long we've wondered why the stars were so silent—no broadcasts from alien civilizations anywhere on the electromagnetic spectrum. The Xaros will send single drones to every single star to find intelligent life and suitable planets, but when they detect intelligent life through their transmissions, they come in force. We've been broadcasting a giant 'Kick Me' sign since the

1920s."

"The first species to come in contact with the Xaros gave them their name, which in that extinct language translates equally to death, annihilation and cruelty. The Xaros have never communicated with any species they've encountered."

Ibarra shifted into a model of the Milky Way where an arrow pointed to Earth's place in the galaxy. Stars at the western edge of the galaxy switched to red and a crimson tide rolled across the galaxy, covering almost three quarters of the stars, until it reached Earth.

"We're certain they originated from beyond our galaxy because elements of their makeup aren't found anywhere in the Milky Way. We don't know who sent them but there is more to their purpose than nihilism. They will erase all trace of living civilizations—we see that happening right now— but will preserve the remains of extinct races. And no, we don't know why."

"You keep saying 'we,'" Admiral Garrett

said. "Who do you represent and why shouldn't we toss you out of an airlock and go it our own way?"

Ibarra morphed into a silvery tear of light. It gave off a gentle glow that reminded Garrett of childhood Christmas trees.

"There is an alliance of intelligences against the Xaros, who, for all their technological prowess, are limited by the laws of physics. They can travel at a little more than 90 percent of the speed of light between the stars and that gives us our only salvation: time. We've had the time to organize and coordinate, to integrate species who could help in the fight. The alliance detected you sooner than the Xaros did and sent me to do what I could.

"So far, the Xaros know nothing of the alliance and we must keep it that way until we have the means to defeat them. As far as the alliance is concerned, humanity's extinction is better than my capture or detection by the Xaros."

Angry muttering filled the conference room. Holo projections jumped from captain to captain as accusations flew.

"You should have let us all die!"

"We won't be your pawns!"

"You expect us to trust you!"

Garrett jabbed a button on the table and the ship captains went mute.

The tear of light morphed back into Ibarra.

"Yes, we're expendable," Ibarra said. "In the end, any part can be sacrificed to save the whole. That is the morality of survival." Ibarra's image rotated around to look at Garrett. "The question is, will we do what we must to survive?"

"Wait just a damn minute," Lawrence said. "This isn't his decision. I'm the CEO of this fleet and our charter is very clear that I'm the one who—"

"Theodore, the next decision is strictly military and you're not in any position to second-guess it," Ibarra said.

"You. Are. A. Hologram! Marc Ibarra is dead and I'm the ranking officer in this company now. There's no need to risk the personnel and material expenditure following the plan of a bunch of whatever-you-are holed up on the fringe of the galaxy when we're dealing with annihilation," Lawrence said. Nods and silent cheers came from some—all of them civilian—captains.

Ibarra rolled his eyes. "This is why I didn't put any politicians in the fleet."

Stacey cleared her throat.

"If I may," she said. "Article five, subsection nine, paragraph twelve of the fleet charter puts Admiral Garrett in charge of the fleet until it reaches Saturn. We're still in transit, technically."

Lawrence raised a finger and opened his mouth to protest, caught himself, then furiously tapped at his forearm computer.

Garrett unmuted the captains and gestured to the table.

"Please. Continue."

"There's no 'please continue,'" one of the civilian captains said. "We aren't going to just let you—"

Garrett pushed a button and the captain

270

vanished. Another click kicked all the civilian captains off the line. Naval officers filled in the vacant seats.

"Thank you," Ibarra said. His image shifted into a rocky satellite pockmarked by asteroid strikes, small patches of ice glinting from its surface. It could have been any of hundreds of such bland planets and planetoids from Mercury to the outer Oort cloud. What set it apart for Garrett were the eight concentric rings around the orb and the glittering material between each ring.

"What are we looking at?" Garrett asked.

"Ceres, a dwarf planet that was, until recently, a resident of the asteroid belt. The Xaros are moving it into Earth orbit at the L1 Lagrange point between Earth and the sun. The rings nullify the planetoid's mass and provide propulsion. Fascinating, isn't it? They're rearranging the solar system," Ibarra said.

"Get to the point, professor."

The image zoomed in to what looked like a crown of thorns hundreds of kilometers in diameter, the gray-black metal of the crown swirling with the same patterns as the Xaros drones. Four dark cables ran from the crown to the surface of Ceres. The crown wasn't a complete circle. The last few degrees of the circle didn't connect, like the bare branches of two trees reaching for each other.

"This is a wormhole generator, a gate from one place in the galaxy to another. More importantly, it is an *incomplete* wormhole generator. Once the solar system was subdued, the majority of the Xaros droids reassembled themselves into the array around Ceres and this gate. The Xaros have a factory and are using the four space elevators on Ceres to shuttle material up to the gate. They are within days of completion," Ibarra said.

"Our exit from time-out, stasis—whatever— and this gate isn't a coincidence," Garrett said.

"No, admiral, it isn't. This is an opportunity that the alliance has been waiting for. We need you to capture the gate before it's complete." The image zoomed in further to a confluence of thorns where a dome almost as large as the *America* was seated.

"If it's heading for Earth, why don't we clear out the drones and wait for it to come to us?" Garrett asked.

"Two reasons. First, the drones on Ceres and Earth will replicate and double their numbers within the next seventy hours. We can barely beat them now. It would be impossible to beat them once they've replicated. Second, once the gate is complete, it will tie into the rest of the gates the Xaros have across the galaxy and the number of reinforcements that will pour through the open gate can be expressed only in scientific notation.

"You get me into the control room and I will take control of the gate," Ibarra said.

"Why do droids need a control room? They seem just fine in space," Stacey asked.

"That, my dear, is an excellent question."

Garrett stood up and put his hands on his hips. He paced around the table, captains watching him as he walked behind them. Officers who'd served with him since the Second Pacific War recognized when their commander was deep in thought.

"How many drones are we facing? Hundreds?" Garrett asked.

"Total single units: close to ten thousand," Ibarra answered.

"Impossible. The combination of a few dozen of those things almost took out *Breitenfeld*," Garrett said.

"You are correct. Good thing I took out an insurance policy before you left," Ibarra said.

His image shifted to a plot from the fleet leading to Ceres. An icon appeared over an asteroid idling along the fleet's route.

"I'll open an IR beam and—"

"Hello?" a hoarse voice came through the speakers. "This is Sven Thorsson of the Ibarra Mining Corp. I'm on asteroid IM-3637. There was some sort of malfunction with our power plant and…my limpet station is gone. I had no communications ability until a few seconds ago. Can anyone hear me?"

"Hello, Sven, this is Chairman Ibarra. Is the cargo secure?"

"Sir! Yes, everything is here. Where are you? What the hell is going on?" Thorsson asked.

"Just hold on, Sven. We'll send someone over to pick you up shortly. Ibarra out." He cut the channel as Thorsson's panicked voice tried to ask more questions.

Ibarra rubbed his holographic hands together.

"You're going to like this."

CHAPTER 7

Lieutenant Hale sat at a small desk in his bunk room. It was definitely *his* now; the other two lieutenants he shared the berthing with had died on the mission to recover Ibarra from his tower. The dead Marines' bunks had rumpled sheets and a few loose personal items—mini-Ubis for music, hard-copy photos and an antique Ka-Bar knife—still on them, as if the Marines would be back any moment to clean up before Major Acera saw the mess.

Hale's Ubi lay on the desk, projecting a screen and keyboard for him to work from. He stared at the blank screen and couldn't find any words. He'd sat down to write condolence letters to

Walsh and Vincenti's families. That was his duty, to explain how they died to those they loved so there might be some closure, some comfort in knowing that the officer who ordered them into battle cared about their well-being and didn't send them to their deaths without care or concern.

The words wouldn't come to Hale. There was no one to write them to.

The double beep of an incoming call snapped him from his reverie. Hale looked at the caller's name for a second, then accepted the call.

The screen changed to show his brother, Jared, his fraternal twin, who looked as bad as Hale felt. Jared served in a Marine infantry company, not as specialized as Hale's strike team but equipped with heavier weapons and more Marines than Hale's company.

"Ken! Thank God. I haven't been able to get through to your ship for hours. The IR lines are jam-packed and...are you OK?"

Hale held up his left arm, a pucker of synth-skin over the shrapnel wound.

"Nothing they can't fix," Hale said. "How're things on the *Charlemagne*? You good?"

"We just offloaded a civilian from an asteroid mine and a lot of weird ammo. You know anything about that?"

Hale shrugged. "I was there but I don't know what I saw."

Jared and Hale locked eyes. They'd shared a womb and hardly gone more than a day without speaking to each other since they'd learned to talk. Jared didn't need to ask how Hale felt. He could see it on his face.

"I've looked at the scopes of Earth. Mom and Dad's house is still standing. Most of the town is still there. You think there's any chance they're hiding out somewhere?" Jared asked.

Hale shook his head. "Everyone's gone."

Silence passed between them.

"Not everyone," Jared said. "I've still got you. You've still got me. We've got our Marines and we've got our mission, whatever the brass decide it is. Right?"

Hale smiled. Leave it to his brother to know what he needed to hear. "Right."

"What was it Grandpa used to say about fighting in Iraq?" Ken asked.

"'Leaving a job half-done is worse than not doing it at all.' We'll fight this out, kick those things in the ass so hard they'll run back to whatever hell pit they came from."

"Shit, those things have teeth?"

"No, they have these stalks that…are you screwing with me?"

"A little," Ken smiled. Jared looked off screen and nodded to someone. "I've got to go. Stay safe and save some aliens for me, *capciche?*"

"*Capache.*"

They tapped their knuckles toward each other and the call ended.

****

Cortaro opened a hatch and stuck his head into the compartment. The room was empty but for the three armor suits standing against the bulkheads in their coffin-like alcoves. Sailors and marines had nicknamed the compartment holding the armor contingent "the cemetery," and unless technicians were there to prep the suits for combat, it was just as quiet as its namesake's reputation.

He shut the hatch behind him and climbed the stairs leading to a catwalk that ringed the interior of the cemetery, giving easy access to the sensor platforms on top of the suits. Cortaro looked over the scorch marks across the chest of one of the suits, a pristine helmet attached to the suit's neck coupling.

"Never. Never on my best day would I climb into one of those things," he muttered.

He tapped at his cargo pocket. The Ubi he'd picked up from Ibarra's city was still there, just like the last dozen times he'd felt for it. Cortaro sat on the catwalk, his back to the suit, and dangled his feet over the side.

Sitting with his feet playing in the wind always made him feel better. As a child, he'd climbed through the old wrecks of the Minneapolis tenements ruined in the Intifada. He'd climb through ventilation shafts to get to the highest vantage point and stare at the long fall. That he'd joined the Marine Strike Teams known for orbital free-fall jumps came as a surprise to no one in his family.

Most of the *Breitenfeld* was a claustrophobic mess, but the cemetery gave him some breathing room.

He pulled the Ubi from his pocket and brought it to life. The Ubis held petabytes worth of data on their internals, and a near-perfect copy of anything on the web that the user had ever browsed or downloaded. Getting Torni to crack it wasn't difficult, not with her military-grade intrusion tools.

The dead girl that owned the Ubi had been a military brat and she'd had a keen interest in the fleet's disappearance. Several of her friends had fathers, mothers and relatives in the fleet. Pawing through the private moments of the dead bothered him, but if there was something he could find….

There, a memorial website set up by one of the fleet's many family support groups. Cortaro scrolled through the names of service men and women, most with a death date listed as the day the fleet blinked out of existence. Some were blank; most had postings attached to the name.

His heart skipped a beat when he found Jose Cortaro, his name, which had fifteen posts, more than any other he'd seen. He tapped the screen with a trembling finger.

The first post was his military biography: awards, deployments dates to and from the Australian DMZ and the Bali Incursion. It ended with MIA, Missing in Action.

"I'm not. I'm not missing. I'm right here, damn it."

There was a video of him coming home from the Bali Incursion taken by a cousin who was in on his plan. His wife and kids sat around a holo-screen watching a Spanish tele-novella when the doorbell rang.

"Pizza!" little Immanuel said and ran to the

door. Cortaro remembered hearing that clarion voice through the door and wiped away a tear.

The video showed Immanuel open the door and stare at his father, dumbstruck.

"Immanuel, hurry up and get the pizza. We're getting cold," his wife said.

"It's not pizza, Mama. It's Papa," Immanuel said.

His kids and wife tripped over each other to get to the door and the video turned to chaos as Cortaro was swamped with hugs and squeals of joy.

There were more pictures of him with his children: Josephina, Rodrigo, Pilar, Juan and Immanuel. Birthdays, quinceaneras, ball games. His wife, Consuela, holding on to him. She'd put on a lot of baby weight and never lost it, which he always insisted he liked.

Tears fell on the Ubi screen. He wiped them away and swiped the last entry open.

A video of Immanuel played, dated to a few weeks after the fleet vanished.

"Papa…Mama and everyone says you're not

coming back. They say your ship had an accident. But you told me you'd always come back, no matter what. So, maybe you can find this wherever your ship is. Come back soon, Papa. I miss you."

Cortaro broke down in sobs. He wished he'd been there when the drones came for them and he begged God to let him go back and hold his family for their final moments.

His crying ended when a huge metal hand touched his shoulder. Cortaro jerked away from the touch like it was a live wire, sending the Ubi flying into the air. The armor reached under the catwalk and caught the Ubi before it hit the ground.

Cortaro, on the verge of hyperventilating, crab-walked away from the armor.

"*Cono la madre, Mia!*"

"Didn't mean to startle you," Elias said.

"*Hijo de madre puta de metal!*"

The armor's head cocked to the side.

"What the hell, Elias? What're you doing in here?" Cortaro demanded. He swiped the Ubi out of the suit's fingers as Elias handed it back to him.

The soft whine of the suit's servos accompanied the suit's movements as it settled back into its coffin.

"I sleep in the suit. There's some synch loss every time we take off our armor, takes a while to get back to peak efficiency when we get back in," Elias said.

"God damn, is there anyone else in here?"

The suit next to Elias waved a hand. Cortaro rolled his eyes and made a prayer to the Virgin Mary in contrition.

"You'd be surprised how many people come in here to hook up," Elias said with a chuckle.

Cortaro recomposed himself. He was a Marine gunnery sergeant; he did not show weakness.

"Elias, you…you didn't see me like that. OK?"

"Your secret's safe," Elias said.

Cortaro nodded and turned away, making for the hatch.

"Cortaro."

He turned around. Elias' suit had a single finger over where the suit's lips would be, if it had them. Cortaro returned the gesture and left.

****

Stacey sat on a bunk, the only bunk in the small berthing. Normally, the room would belong to a field-grade officer in charge of a significant portion of the *America*'s crew and capabilities. The alien device in her palm made her something of a VIP, even more than her true surname ever did. With her knees tucked into her chin, she kept her hand with the alien inside of it under a pillow.

"Stacey, this is silly," Ibarra said, his words muffled by the pillow.

"No, this is just weird."

"I know it's a lot to take in, but we need to discuss the next step and what it means for you," Ibarra said. She took her hand out and his face materialized in front of her.

"Tell me," she said, "tell me how you did it.

You knew the Xaros could control computers, so you—"

"Arranged for the world's militaries to not trust computers, yes. It wasn't an accident that the Chinese acquired the computing power to crack the American and allied militaries' codes right before the Second Pacific War. Wasn't an accident that the electronic kill screens went up around borders to fry any drones and guided missiles that passed through them. There had to be a reason why humans flew their own planes and pulled their own triggers. If my involvement was too obvious, the Xaros would have suspected something and they would have waited here for the fleet to return until the sun burned out."

"Do you know how many people died in that war? Why didn't you give the capability to the good guys, let them beat the piss out of the Chinese like they deserved? What they did to Darwin made the Japanese in Nanking look like…Mormon missionaries in comparison!" She jabbed a finger into Ibarra's face.

"A single power would have stagnated. There wouldn't have been an effort to keep up a strong military against a peer with similar strengths—no need to build an escort fleet to take a colony to Saturn."

"You were behind everything, weren't you?"

"There was a resurgence of boy bands in the 2030s. I had nothing to do with that."

Stacey fought against a laugh and made an undistinguished snort.

"We need to talk about the next phase and your role in it," Ibarra said. "I always told you how special you were. That wasn't a grandfather's doting. It is true. You've been...engineered to do something wondrous—incredible—for humanity."

Stacey stayed quiet, her lips quivering.

"*Engineered* how?" she said, her voice hard.

"Once I had the capability, I changed the DNA that I would pass on to my children, and that DNA would change again with the next generation so that you could play a pivotal role in what has to happen next."

Stacey got off her cot and looked in the small mirror by the hatch. Her bright violet eyes had always been a source of curiosity for her family; such a contrast against her straw-colored hair led most to believe she wore colored contact lenses.

"What am I, alien?"

"Partly synthetic."

She pressed a fingernail against her cheek; the pain felt as real as anything. She took her hand away as a slow, horrifying realization came to her.

"Mom. She was one of six sisters. All my aunts, they never had babies. They tried and tried, but they all miscarried. Every single time. I was Mom's third pregnancy…The synthetic DNA wouldn't take, would it? Their bodies felt something wrong, something imperfect, and rejected the embryos."

"Stacy. Listen to me."

Stacey slammed an elbow into the mirror and pulled a hunk of mirror from the cracks, cutting her fingertips on the jagged edges.

"Do you know what that did to your daughters? Your *daughters*!" She brought the tip of the improvised knife against the palm of her hand where the probe resided. "My aunts looked at me with so much envy, so much sorrow, because I was what they could never have and you did it to them! Why?"

"To save us. All of us. It destroyed me to see them in so much pain, but it was the only way."

Stacey pressed the tip into her palm, drawing blood.

"Get out of me, you monster! I don't know what you think you're going to do to me but I won't be part of it." She grimaced as she ran the knife across her palm.

The sliver of light dimmed and faded to nothing. A chill ran up her arm, across her shoulder and thrummed against the base of her skull.

She dropped the hunk of broken mirror to the floor involuntarily. The pain burning across her palm ceased and she watched wide-eyed as the cut mended itself.

"Sweetheart, listen to me." Ibarra's words came to her as her own thoughts.

Stacey sobbed and tried to move, but her limbs wouldn't respond.

"Just get out of me."

"I can't. The Xaros would detect me outside your body and that is a variable we can't afford."

"You're going to stick me in that star gate, aren't you? Jam wires into my skull and force me to control the gate. Trap me in a tube and never let me move again. I'll be worse than the armor pilots," she said. She choked her tears back and concentrated on moving a single finger, railing against being locked into her own body.

"I told you it would be wondrous. And you might agree if you give me a chance to explain," Ibarra said.

****

The *Breitenfeld's* brig was a repurposed cargo hold, a bare room filled with a few cots and a chemical toilet bolted to the deck. The bars running from floor to ceiling were meant to keep cargo separated and were too far apart to be an adequate cell. Electrified slats mag-locked to the bars made the cell front look more like an irregular picket fence than a brig.

Torni stood guard over the three prisoners. As one of the few female Marines, she was of a limited pool that could watch over Chinese pilots stewing in the brig. Her shift had another two hours to go, and none of the prisoners seemed interested in causing trouble or doing anything to alleviate their shared boredom.

The round handle on the door twisted and Torni straightened up. Captain Valdar stepped into the brig, Durand a step behind him.

Valdar strode to the cell and the three prisoners rose to their feet. The tallest balled her fists and sneered at the captain. Another mumbled something undeniably rude and touched the synth-skin patch on her leg when she saw Durand.

Valdar tapped his forearm-mounted Ubi and

lifted his arm toward the captives.

"Do you speak English?" he asked. His Ubi translated his words into Mandarin and Cantonese.

The tallest walked up to the bars, staying outside arm's distance to avoid a painful shock.

"We all speak your mutt language," she said, her voice heavily accented. "I am Sub-Lieutenant Choi San Ma, People's Liberation Army Space Navy. We've given you our names and serial numbers as required per the Geneva Conventions for prisoners of war. We have nothing else to say." Valdar's Ubi translated Ma's words back into Mandarin before he could shut it off.

"Have you told them?" Valdar asked Torni.

"No sir, they weren't interested in speaking to anyone until you showed up," Torni said.

"I am the captain of the *Breitenfeld* and you aren't prisoners of war." He tapped his Ubi and the electrified slats fell to the deck. The bars pulled apart like an opening maw and retracted into their deck housings.

Torni shifted into a combat stance, ready to

react if the Chinese charged. The three pilots stood stock-still, poker faces intact.

"Lieutenant Durand has a proposal for you that has my full support. Either you make yourself useful or you keep quiet," he said. He gave Durand a pat on the shoulder as he left.

Durand stepped into the cell and looked the pilots over. Each was whipcord thin and identical strict haircuts framed their faces so equally Durand could almost believe they were sisters. The one she'd shot on the flight deck stared daggers at her.

"You're not prisoners of war because there are no countries to fight. You need to watch this," Durand brought up the videos from the Ubi Cortaro found on Earth and let the Chinese pilots watch. When it was over, the shortest pointed a finger at Durand.

"Lies! This is all a trick by your government to brainwash us into helping you," she said.

"I will take you to our scopes. You can look at the Earth for yourself. It's all gone," Durand said.

Choi sat on her bunk, forearms resting

against her knees. "If this is true, what do you want?" she asked.

Durand bit her lip before speaking. Twenty-four hours ago, she would have laughed herself blue if someone told her she was about to have this exact conversation.

"The fleet is preparing for an attack on the Xaros space station around Ceres. It's an all-out assault, no reserves, no holding back. We need every fighter we can muster in the void and you three…could pilot one of our bombers."

The pilot she'd shot barked a laugh. "What makes you think we could even fly one of your crates?"

"I've seen your cockpits. They're nearly identical to ours since China stole the designs," Durand said.

"Copied," Choi corrected.

"Semantics aside, we've got time to get you familiar with our Condors before the assault. You can join us or stay in this box. I don't know what we'll do with you once it's all over, assuming any of us survive," Durand said.

The shortest, and the youngest by Durand's guess, spoke to the other pilots in Chinese. An angry discussion followed, one Durand's Ubi couldn't translate from Mandarin or Cantonese.

"You want to help me out here?" Durand asked. The foreign conversation continued unabated. Durand turned to Torni and raised her hands in confusion.

Torni shrugged, "They aren't speaking Swedish."

"Village dialect," Choi said. "We will fly with you," the words came out of her mouth like they were laced with razors, "but only after we've looked through your scopes to Earth."

"Fair enough. You all have names?"

"I'm Mei Ma," said the pilot Durand had shot.

"Zhi Ma," said the shortest.

"You're all named Ma? You related?"' Durand asked.

Choi rolled her eyes.

"There are one point eight billion Chinese in the world and only a hundred surnames. The chance that three would have the same name is pretty high, wouldn't you agree?" Choi said.

"We're cousins!" Zhi piped up.

Mei jammed an elbow into her cousin's side.

"Fine. Whatever. I'm your squadron commander and you can call me 'Ma'am.' Let's go," Durand said.

CHAPTER 8

Hale pressed the battery release on his gauss rifle and knocked the battery off the top of it. He clicked the fresh battery in his hand into the slot and felt a thrum of energy shoot through the weapon. His empty hand slapped against an ammo drum on his belt and rammed it into the ammo well on the underside of his weapon. Recharging and reloading the rifle took less than two seconds.

Cortaro called out the time and Hale removed his blindfold.

"Not bad, sir," Cortaro said.

Elias, legs folded into travel mode, let loose a grunt—which Hale knew was high praise. The two Marines wore their combat armor, helmets resting on the waist-high ledge separating them from the VR firing range. A foot beyond the ledge, the ship looked like a purgatorial mass of gray, the default projection before the shooters loaded up firing scenarios from a simple known-distance range on the green fields of Ft. Benning to the orange skies and methane lakes of Titan.

"How much longer are we going to wait for this guy?" Cortaro asked. He sat on the pallet of ammo cases that had been delivered to the *Breitenfeld* a few hours ago, along with strict instructions not to open the cases until they'd received instruction from a specialist…who was supposed to have joined them fifteen minutes ago.

"This is a waste of time. Does the Ibarra Corp really think we can't figure out how to use bullets?" Elias added.

"Captain Valdar said hurry up and get down here. We did and now we wait. Some things in the Marine Corps won't ever change, even after the apocalypse," Hale said.

The VR room snapped from gray to void black. A tall Nordic man's projection, wavering around the edges, came into being.

"Ah, Lieutenant Hale. I didn't think I'd see you again, but this week's been full of surprises, hasn't it?" Thorsson said. "Sorry I was late, some training issues on the *Tarawa*."

"You're taking away our training time. · What are you going to tell us about bullets beyond 'put them in the bad guys until they stop moving'?" Cortaro asked.

"Don't call them bullets. They are works of art. Please, open the case," Thorsson said. The locks on the cases switched from red to green with a click.

Cortaro opened a case and pulled out a belt of silver-gray bullets, their surfaces riven with fractals.

"You're holding specially treated quadrium-jacketed tungsten rounds, similar to your normal gauss bolts but these do amazing things when accelerated to high speed," Thorsson said.

300

Hale brought the belt to his face for closer inspection; the bullets smelled of ozone and burning hair.

"What's quadrium?" Hale asked.

"An isotope of hydrogen that is a pain in the ass to manufacture and the most expensive substance in the solar system. Each round costs the Ibarra Corp almost four million dollars. Not that money means anything anymore. Now—the fun part!" Thorsson reached down and picked up a gauss rifle within his VR environment. He turned around and a floating Xaros drone materialized ten meters away from him.

Thorsson fired at the drone and lightning erupted around his target. The lighting arced back against the drone and it fell to the ground, smoking.

"I never get tired of that!" Thorsson said.

"Did you kill it?" Hale asked.

"No, as you see, the drone hasn't disintegrated. The quadrium disrupts the drones, stuns them. Then…." A mech suit's arm materialized next to Thorsson, a double-barreled gun mounted on its forearm. Two rounds fired from the gun, each shot so close it almost melded into a single sound.

The drone jerked and cracked open, the pyrite in the shell spilling out. The drone blinked out of existence.

"Where do I get one of those?" Elias asked, pointing to the gun that finished off the drone.

"The schematics are already with your ship's 3-D printing shop and should be ready soon. The first shot cracks the shell. The second cracks the nut inside. Now, the Q-rounds require a great deal of power to activate. You'll have to hot shot your gauss rifles," Thorsson said.

"*One* shot per battery? Not a lot of room for error," Hale said.

"You see that case of Q-rounds? That is *it*, jarhead. We divvied them up across the fleet but there will be no resupply. Don't miss. I'll leave a VR simulation of Xaros drones and proxy Q-rounds so you can practice." Thorsson checked his watch and sighed. "More ships, more Marines." His projection blinked away.

Cortaro lifted another belt of rounds from a case and twisted them like a wind chime.

Thorsson snapped back into reality.

"Oh, and they're a little radioactive. Don't handle them for too long if you have exposed skin or are outside your void suits." Thorsson vanished again.

Cortaro gently but quickly replaced the belt.

"We've got something now," Elias said.

"Still isn't much. What will kill these things? The anti-armor grenades can crack them but getting them to connect is iffy. High-velocity gauss rounds will do it but that takes several hits and they move damn fast. The rail guns will do the trick but the rate of fire is too low to take out the small ones…," Hale said, his mind trying to dissect the tactical problem.

"It takes…two and a half tons of force to crack the shells, maybe a bit less," Elias said. "Maybe there's a way to save a few Q-rounds." Elias raised an arm and the mechanical hand retracted into the forearm. A spike slid out and replaced the hand, nearly the length of Hale's arm.

"This is for enemy armor." The spike retracted into the housing, then shot forward like a piston's cylinder, stopping with a clang that rang Hale's ears with tinnitus. "If high-powered gauss rounds will crack them, this will do the trick too."

"You want to stab them to death?" Hale asked. "This is a void fight in the twenty-first century, not the Battle of Agincourt."

"Albrecht said the drones boarded ships, said he heard them slaughtering the crew. You want to fire those Q-rounds or high-powered gauss shots inside the ship?" Elias said.

Hale crossed his arms and leaned against the VR shelf. He was in charge of shipboard defense now and he felt shame for not seeing this problem before Elias did.

"Sir, why don't we get our Marines over here? See what we can figure out together," Cortaro said.

"Right, good idea. Elias, bring up the rest of

304

the armor."

"They're already on their way."

****

Fourteen Marines. Three suits of armor. That was all Hale had left to command. The Marines knelt and stood in groups of four arrayed across the VR shooting range. Franklin fired a single Q-round into the starry void simulation. The range rifle, designed to simulate the recoil, slammed into Franklin's shoulder like he was firing an elephant gun. Standish and Cortaro put high-powered gauss rounds into the drone crippled by Franklin's hit and their target disintegrated.

Franklin exchanged his spent rifle for a fully charged weapon with Torni, who swapped out the battery almost as fast as Franklin could engage another target.

Back when warships plied the seas by sail, American Marines would send their best shots into the crow's nest on top of the masts to pick off enemy officers during close-in fights. *How little things have changed,* Hale thought.

The second and third group of Marines repeated the firing drill.

"We can kill fifteen drones a minute like this," Cortaro said.

"Let's hope the drones are polite enough to come at us a few at a time," Hale said.

"Sir? I was thinking," Standish said. He stood up from his firing line and watched as Elias swung his spike into a holographic drone.

"Now we're in trouble," Torni said.

"You ever work on a cattle ranch? Because when it was time to slaughter a cow, we had to kill them in a way that was humane and not so messy— stay with me," he added quickly when he saw Cortaro frown. "We used pneumatic bolts attached to an air tank, called a captive bolt gun. Whack! Right on the cattle's forehead and they're out for good," Standish said.

"Cut to the chase before I think you're just goldbricking," Cortaro said.

"We can't use the armor's spikes all over the ship. They won't fit. But we could make a bolt gun like that, small enough to carry but with enough force to get the job done. Stun the drones with the Q-rounds and finish them off with the bolts," Standish said.

Hale thought for a moment.

"I hate to say it, but he might have a good idea," Hale said. "Get a design together in the machine shop and load up the plans to the fleet net. The 3-D printers shouldn't have a problem replicating whatever you come up with."

A peal of thunder burst from the trio of suits at the end of the line.

Elias stood at full height, both arms extending into the VR field. His right arm bore the holographic double-barreled gun Thorsson had shown them; his left arm had a miniature version of the rail gun he carried on his back mounted on it, also a hologram.

An ammo canister fed Q-rounds into the rail gun, which sent the Q-rounds sizzling through the air and into drones up to five hundred meters downrange. Elias' right arm engaged drones bearing down on the firing line.

"Are you dual targeting?" Hale asked.

A drone swept in and vanished into the edge of the VR field.

"Yes," Elias said, "works best when I'm not distracted."

Another suit, both arms carrying the double-barreled gauss guns, fired. Each gun fired on separate targets, winnowing the approaching swarm with marked efficiency. The suit's rate of fire stopped suddenly and the suit stepped back from the line. Its metal hands clamped against its head sensors as if it had a sudden migraine.

"He's redlined, isn't he?" Hale demanded. The link between pilot and armor put a tremendous strain on the pilot's nervous system and there were limits to what the human brain could handle. Hale's selection training at Ft. Knox had shown more than one vid of armor pilots reduced to vegetables from overloading their nervous systems by pushing their suits beyond the bounds of their design.

"He'll be fine," Elias said. "Leave our methods to us. It doesn't concern you."

"The hell it doesn't. I need you all in this fight and you're no good to anyone if you burn yourself out before the battle even starts," Hale said.

Elias growled and bent at the waist, lowering his suit's head level with Hale's. Hale didn't flinch as he locked eyes with the suit's lenses.

"We are armor." Elias slammed a fist against his chest with the clang of a tolling bell. "We are the Iron Hearts. We are the anvil that will break our foe."

"And we fight as one," Hale said, finishing the creed. "I may not have my plugs, Elias, but we *will* fight as one. Don't burn yourself out."

"This is *Ragnarok*, Hale. Armageddon. We can leave nothing on the table. No sacrifice is too great," Elias said.

"Only if we lose, and I don't plan on packing it in just yet. We will need armor after this battle."

The three suits remained silent but their arms and heads moved and gestured in conversation. Elias brought a fist up parallel to his shoulder; the old hand signal for "stop."

"We won't redline in training. No restraint in battle," Elias said.

Hale, who had enough experience to know when he couldn't push an argument any further—and that Elias could easily squish his head like a grape—nodded in agreement.

CHAPTER 9

Valdar moved the scope down the Virginia coastline. Past Mobjack Bay where he'd taught his boys to sail. Past the York River and onto the now bare isthmus where Newport News used to be. His mind traced where Interstate 664 had crossed the James River and he zoomed in on the lakeshore where his home should have been.

The house was gone, replaced by scrub forest reclaiming the neighborhood. Another decade of growth and there would be no sign that humanity had ever lived there.

"Sir?" Ericson said. "They're about to start."

Valdar sent the scope's view over the

Atlantic and stood up. He straightened his uniform and walked over to the tactical table where Hale, Durand and his senior officers waited for him.

Valdar took his place catty-corner to the end of the table; he wasn't the focus of this briefing.

The holo display in the center of the table lit up and a mass of light swirled above it, coalescing into Ceres, slowly rotating within its artificial rings. The crown of thorns over its north pole hung motionless.

Admiral Garrett's hologram appeared at the end of the table.

"All right, let's get this started," Garrett said.

The image of Ceres shrank and the fleet's icons appeared at the far edge of the projection.

"We're eight hours from the target, the Xaros gate designated Objective Crucible," Garrett said. "The Xaros have been busy since we broke clear of our moorings. Crucible is better defended now than when we first saw it. See for yourself."

The holo changed to the Crucible. Four

carrier-sized ships, resembling the much bigger brother of the Xaros gun that destroyed the *Tucson*, surrounded the alien star gate.

"I'll let our resident expert explain this," Garrett said. His image switched to Stacey, her face impassive.

"The Xaros drones extracting omnium from within Ceres combined into these defense platforms in the last half hour. Joining is a significant drain on their pyrite cores, so we won't likely see them morph into something larger or more maneuverable," Stacey said. Her voice was steady but seemed to originate from somewhere far deep within her.

"Fixed defenses, this fight will be an assault, not a meeting engagement like we'd thought," Garrett said.

"Why aren't they coming for us? They know our rail batteries could hit a stationary target from here," asked the captain of the *Falklands*, a Sikh man wearing the traditional turban, speaking with a heavy English accent.

"Because of this." Garrett tapped at his table and a swarm of drones, thousands strong, filled the projection. "This is every single drone from Earth and Luna. Once the last drone caught up with the swarm, it started accelerating. Massing against a foe seems to be their preferred tactic." The projection shifted; the mass of drones were gaining on the fleet. A convergence point lay ahead of the fleet, well short of Ceres.

The *Breitenfeld's* officers traded worried glances. The pursuit swarm looked like more than the fleet could handle.

"We prepared for this," Stacey said. The asteroid home to Thorsson and his hidden factory popped onto the projection, just ahead of the swarm. "The asteroid is lined with graphene-doped quadrium, which has a number of unique properties your science will appreciate once your knowledge of quantum mechanics advances for another thousand years. Namely, the Xaros sensors can't penetrate it, which is why they didn't detect the cache within this asteroid or my—excuse me, the

314

probe's—little hiding place beneath Euskal Tower.

"When you bombard quadrium with just the right kind of graviton particle, you get an incredibly strong gravity well in a localized space—a localized space that the swarm will completely enter in just a few seconds," she said.

The plot of the swarm bent toward the asteroid and swirled into it like ships sucked into a whirlpool. Debris spat away from the rock and it vanished from the plot, along with the entire swarm.

"The drones are tough, but even they will be ripped apart by a quantum singularity. A nice trick if I do say so myself," Stacey said.

"She acting funny to you?" Durand whispered to Hale, who nodded.

"Why didn't we use that weapon against the Crucible?" Valdar asked Garrett.

"We need the Crucible intact," Stacey answered. "Once we can use it, we'll either escape from this solar system or bring in reinforcements to defend it. Even if we win this day, the Xaros have already sent out a speed-of-light distress signal. The nearest Xaros drone is six light years away at Barnard's star. The drone in that system will replicate and bring another swarm equal to the one that wiped out Earth."

"Are we going to get any good news today?" Hale asked under his breath.

"The rate of fire from the orbitals is…a challenge," Garrett said.

A sped-up simulation of the fleet approaching the Crucible ran; the four orbitals destroyed the fleet within a half hour. Variations of the simulation ended the same way.

Valdar tugged at his mustache as he watched the fleet's demise over and over again. His eyes widened with an idea and he co-opted the display to run his own simulation.

"Sir, this is Captain Valdar of the *Breitenfeld*. I think we're looking at this problem the wrong way."

Garrett looked right at Valdar.

"I'm open to suggestions," the admiral said.

****

Torni shifted her knee against the hull of the civilian luxury liner and locked her knee armor to the metal plating. She pressed the arc welder against the launch rails she and Standish had been working on for the last thirty minutes.

Standish, welding on the opposite side of Torni, glanced up at the dark gray orb of Ceres, so close it was the same size as a penny held at arm's length. The glint of drop ship engines burning away from the cluster of luxury liners looked like a line of orderly comets.

"I heard some of the civilians were mad, mad, *mad* about losing their comfy bunks," Standish said. He brought his forearm up to wipe his brow and pressed it against his helmet uselessly. "Heard the Marines on the *Tarawa* had to crack a few skulls to get a couple civvies out."

"Entitled bunch of progs. Figured they'd all want off as soon as they knew what we were going to do with their ships. Good thing there aren't any courts to issue injunctions," Torni said in between zaps from her welder.

"Did we bring any lawyers?" Standish asked.

They both paused their work and shrugged in unison.

"Makes you wonder, don't it?" Standish asked.

"Wonder how you can talk so damn much?"

"No, wonder why Ibarra decided to make us his fleet. Guy had sixty years, right? Sixty years to screw around with politics and economies. He invented the first real graphene battery—made a fortune—and had some super alien computer to help him out. So why didn't he get the Chinese in on his plan? They were a hell of a lot more organized. Not a lot of dissent in their politics, kind of deal. I swear we couldn't get five guys and gals on the *Breit* to agree on pizza toppings."

Torni stood up and leaned back to work out a nasty kink. The fleet surrounded them in serene silence. Fighter and bomber flights weaved through the hundred ships that contained the last of humanity, from the stubby destroyers to the lance-like bulk of the carrier *Charlemagne*.

"You're American, right?" she asked.

"Canadian, eh?"

"When he was a boy, my grandfather lived in Stockholm. He and his family were there when the Muslims declared the city theirs. They were poor, and didn't have the money to pay the non-believer tax and wouldn't convert to Islam, so the Muslims enslaved them all. They murdered my great-grandfather. My great-grandmother didn't last much longer.

"He was in rags, starving, when the crusade came. He told me stories about the American soldiers, how they looked like knights in their body armor and the red Templar cross on their shoulder. They killed the Islamists, sent the rest of them back to their sand dunes in the Middle East. They saved him, fed him and showed him what strength really is. And they were all volunteers, every last one of them.

"No one had to order an American to save the oppressed. It's part of their nature to see others live free, even at the sacrifice of their own lives. Once the Germans finally followed the Americans' lead, and the rest of Europe got its act together, we had the Atlantic Union. Separate nations and peoples who would fight for each other. The Chinese didn't go to war to save Mongolia when the Russians conquered it."

"Huh," Standish said. "I never thought about it that way. Save those who'll sacrifice for the whole."

"Oye!" Crewman MacDougal shouted through the IR. He took great loping strides toward them over the hull. "Why're you and that Jessie slacking?"

"Shut ye geggie before I snip yer baws off," Torni said, flashing a "V" with her fingers at MacDougal.

"Give 'em to the jobby jabber, why don't you? Get that done and move to the next rack before the torps get here. We ain't got til morn."

MacDougal bounded past them, sending another invective to the next work crew.

"What was that?" Standish asked.

"He said we're moving too slow."

"How do you know what he was saying?"

"We used to date," she said.

Standish fumbled his welder and caught hold of it before it could tumble into space.

****

Durand lowered her Eagle against the underside of the luxury liner's hull. Her landing gear found purchase and she powered up the mag locks on the skids. The rest of the *Breitenfeld's* air wing was already latched to the ship.

"All pilots send me a life-support check and power down. Get comfy because we're going to be here for a bit," she said into the IR net.

This wasn't her Eagle. The seat was molded to someone much larger and it would take a few acceleration burns before the seat adapted to her frame. The last pilot had died when the *Tucson* exploded, destroying his Mule and killing most of the *Breitenfeld's* Marines.

"Marie? You there?" Hale said.

She saw a single armored figure bounding across the hull toward the Eagles and Condors attached to the ship.

"I'm on your right," she said to him.

Hale floated over her cockpit. His hand swept over the glass, the grav plating glowing as it gave friction between him and her Eagle to slow him down. He twisted in the void and sat on the fuselage next to her cockpit.

"Cute, you been practicing that?" she asked.

"I was a diver. That just makes it look easy," he chuckled.

"Where will you be in all this? Hopefully someplace better than this kamikaze rocket."

Hale looked to Ceres and put his hand on the canopy.

"We're in the last drop ship, coming in on the tail of the assault wave."

She nodded, her gaze on the star field above. The diffuse wave of the Milky Way's center rose into view beyond the liner's engines. She raised a hand and pressed it against her canopy, separated from Hale's touch by an inch.

"We never got to see Saturn," she said.

"It's still there. Don't lose hope, Marie."

She huffed. "'Hope.' If Valdar's plan turns sour, we'll need a lot more than hope."

A red light pulsed on Hale's Ubi.

"That's me. Time to go," he said.

"I wish you shit," she said.

"Wait. What?"

Durand rolled her eyes and waved him off with a flick of her wrist. "That's how you say good luck in French. Hurry, and try to come back in one piece this time. We've got a date in the cemetery when this is all over."

CHAPTER 10

The flight deck of the *America* stretched a thousand yards from stem to stern, and every foot was alive with sailors and Marines buzzing around a fleet of Mule drop ships.

Hale, in his battle armor with his helmet tucked under his arm, stood to the flank of the flight deck. The fifty drop ships packed onto the deck was a nightmare come to life for him. He'd been deviled by dreams of needing to be in an exact place at an exact time, but every place in the dream was identical to every other. The Marine colonel in charge of the assault had just reassigned him and his team to drop ship Three-Seven from the *Tarawa* and Hale didn't know where it was on the deck.

Every joke he'd ever heard about lost lieutenants played through his mind as he made his way up and down the line of drop ships hoping to see a familiar face in the mélange of naval ratings and Marines prepping for battle.

Tail numbers on the drop ships weren't helping him as most of the fleet's drop ships were on the *America* for this operation. Mule Three-Seven could be from half a dozen different ships.

"Ken!" came a voice from behind him.

His brother, Jared, clad in armor identical to his but for its dark green color and 3rd Marines patch on his shoulder, jogged over and gave Hale a quick hug.

"You look lost," Jared said. Two columns of Marines, Jared's men and women by their armor and nods they gave to him, passed by. More than one did a double take when they saw the two nearly identical twins in disparate armor speaking to each other.

"My team got stuck in a different bird a few minutes ago." Hale's voice lowered to a conspiratorial whisper. "I'm on *Tarawa* Three-Seven. You know where it is?"

Jared shook his head at his brother and looked at his forearm computer.

"Two up and three deep. The IR net is overloaded. That's probably why you didn't get...you're on VIP duty?"

"Guess so. Where are you going?" Hale asked.

"Node four. We're going in ahead as a feint, get any defenders away from your beachhead." Jared looked at his brother, a stream of thoughts and worry behind his eyes. Hale knew he had the same sheen to his countenance.

Jared choked back his emotions and his face went hard. "You've fought them. If you can take a few down, then this will be a walk in the park, right?"

Hale slapped his brother on the shoulder and flashed a false grin. "If you can shoot straight for once in your life, this would be the day to do it."

"Sir!" someone shouted from the ramp of a

326

waiting drop ship.

"That's me. You…you stay safe," Jared said.

"You too."

They clasped forearms, their grip lingering before they parted ways.

Hale didn't look back as he sidestepped through the scrum of sailors and Marines as he found his assigned drop ship. Cortaro stood on the drop ship's lowered ramp, his head bare and scanning the crowd. Cortaro caught sight of his lieutenant and helped Hale over the side of the ramp.

"Last-second changes are my favorite kind of changes, especially on a flight deck just before a drop," Cortaro said, his voice so even the implied irony was unmistakable.

The rest of their team was already buckled into their acceleration mats. Standish had his head against his chest and Hale could have sworn the Marine was sleeping.

"Why'd we get the switch, sir?" Torni

asked.

A motorized cart pulled up to the drop ship and a slight figure in battle armor got off her ride and stutter-stepped up the ramp. Battle armor took some getting used to and the new arrival looked as if this was her first time in it.

"Hey everyone," Stacey said.

"We're in for some shit, aren't we?" Franklin asked.

Stacey shrugged her shoulders in apology and went to an empty acceleration pad.

"Command decided that, given our team's vast experience in fighting the Xaros, we'd escort Ensign Ibarra to the Crucible and keep her safe until her mission is complete," Hale said.

"And what is the good ensign's mission?" Cortaro asked. "We were supposed to breach node two and gain a foothold on the station, and that's as far as our old orders took us."

"Node one," Stacey said. "That's where the control room is." She held up her right hand and the probe's light showed through her armored glove. "I need to get in there and then this will take control of the Crucible."

Hale checked over Stacey's straps and started undoing them.

"You did these wrong," Hale said to her. "Can't have you smeared against the bulkhead after the first turn. That'll get me fired."

Stacey pursed her lips, her chin quivering. Hale fastened a strap over her waist then hooked her helmet into the acceleration pad.

"I'm scared too," he said. Her eyes went wide and she looked at him, baffled. "It's good. Keeps you sharp. Courage isn't the absence of fear—it's the strength to keep going when you are scared. OK?" He tapped the side of her helmet twice, confirming that she was strapped in correctly.

"You don't know what's waiting for me—for us," she said.

"An alien space station full of genocidal robots?"

"Close enough," she said. A warning buzzer sounded and the ramp closed with a pneumatic whine.

"*I'm proud of you,*" Ibarra said to her.

"Don't be. This isn't what I want. This is what I must do," Stacey said under her breath. "And if Hale knew what was coming, I doubt he'd be so frigging heroic."

****

Valdar looked over the fleet's course plots again. *Breitenfeld's* maneuver wasn't complicated in and of itself, but trying to thread the same needle as sixty-five other warships didn't leave much room for error.

He spun his command chair around and sent it to the acceleration lock in the center of the bridge.

"All stations report ready, captain," Ericson said.

"Security teams have the pneumatic bolts?" Valdar asked.

"Aye aye, fresh from the machine shop."

"Five minutes to the release point," the

lieutenant at the conn said. The pitted, desolate surface of Ceres rolled toward them on the forward view screens.

"XO, give action stations," Valdar said. Klaxons blared and lights across the ship went red. Valdar opened his ship-wide address channel.

"*Breitenfeld*, this is Valdar. In the last…twenty-four hours, everything we know has changed. Everything we knew is gone. This battle is for a future. A future for all of us, all of what's left. *Gott mit uns*. Valdar out."

He closed the channel and pulled up the conn officer's view.

"Conn, you ready?" Valdar asked. He saw the helmsman's head bob a few times as a plot track materialized in front of him. The tracks of other vessels crept into the space around the *Breitenfeld's* projected path.

"Stand by for burn," the helmsman said. "Burn in three…two…one...fire all aft thrusters!"

The ship rattled as its engines roared to life. The fusion reactors accelerated the *Breitenfeld* through the confluence point on the opposite side of Ceres from the Crucible and its defense platforms and shot it around the dwarf planet.

Valdar's hands struggled against the press of g-forces and tapped against the holo display in front of him. Six stiletto-shaped civilian luxury liners were well ahead of his ship and the rest of the naval vessels. The civilian ships and their cargo would clear the horizon in the next few minutes, all according to plan.

I hope this works, Valdar thought.

****

"103rd squadron, stand by to release," Durand said. Her finger hovered over the pulsating green button that would free her Eagle from the cruise liner. The longer she waited, the more of a surprise she and her squadron of Eagles and Condors would have, but the longer she waited the more likely she was to get blown to hell with the rest of the doomed ship.

The release button went red and a warning buzzer sounded in her helmet. Her ride was about to maneuver.

"Release!"

She jammed the button and braced herself against her seat. The cable and mag locks holding her Eagle released and she split away from the luxury liner. Her engines came to life and she climbed into space. The rest of her truncated squadron, four Eagles and a pair of Condors, rose into formation around her.

Torpedoes streaked away from the liner and bore down on the nearest Xaros orbital, designated Alpha. Dozens of torpedoes from the other liners, their engines burning like miniature nova, joined in the assault. All the civilian liners, now free of the fighters and bombers that had hitched a ride into the battle on their hulls and their momentum, adjusted course to converge on Alpha.

The yellow beams struck out from the targeted orbital and picked off the torpedoes with an almost contemptuous ease. The Xaros platform rotated toward the closest luxury liner and a magenta blast blew through the spine of the liner, coring it from stem to stern.

The remaining liners kept their acceleration toward the same target as the light at the center of Alpha's cannon grew in intensity. With the increasing speed of the liners and the recharge time between Alpha's cannon fire, one or more of the liners would make contact with it—which was probably why the other three liners brought their cannons to bear on the encroaching kamikaze ships.

"103rd, we've got our window. Begin our attack run on Alpha, on me," Durand said.

She gunned her engines and followed the attack vector that would take them into a diving attack on Bravo. They did not want to be in the line of fire for what was about to happen.

Alpha destroyed another liner with its cannon; a second was blown to dust by Bravo.

"Fighter element, this is the *Constantine*, clearing the horizon. Stand by for broadside," came over the IR net.

Durand saw the glint of rail guns firing just over the curve of Ceres' surface. The rail gun slugs ignited a trail of fire through Ceres' pitifully thin atmosphere, erasing the distance between the rail guns and Alpha so fast it looked as though the *Constantine* fired lasers.

Yellow point defense beams blew the rail gun slugs out of space. Laser beams whirled like a swarm of fireflies as the fleet's cruisers cleared the horizon and added their rail guns to the fight. The sparks of destroyed rail gun rounds encroached closer and closer to Alpha's hull. The orbital jerked from an impact and a liner slammed into it like an uppercut against a boxer's chin.

The civilian ship broke into splinters of graphene composite steel and spun off into space.

The liner that had been Durand's ride into the battle bore down on the stricken Xaros orbital. Its point defense lasers morphed from yellow to white and *pushed* the liner off course. It flew past the orbital and continued unabated into the vast reaches of space.

While the orbital was focused on the liner, the next fusillade of rail guns readied. Half the fleet's available rail guns fired as one and hit Alpha with the massed power of a shotgun blast. Alpha convulsed as rail slugs perforated it and it burned away to nothing.

Cheers went up through the IR as the first orbital broke apart and burned into cinders.

****

Point defense lasers knocked away incoming rail gun shots screaming toward Bravo. Durand covered her eyes as another blast from the orbital seared through space. The icon for the cruiser *Paris* flickered and went deep red—ship destroyed.

"Task force Valkyrie, stand by for Q-rounds. Launch your attack once they're through," Admiral Garrett said. The pilot commanding the fighter wave acknowledged and Durand clenched her flight stick, poised to begin her attack run.

The point defense on Bravo flared to life and

an electrical storm burst between the orbital and the fleet. Tendrils of lightning struck the leading edge of the orbital and the point defense beams stopped with the suddenness of a flipped switch.

Two squadrons broke from the formation and dove toward the silent orbital. Eagles fired their rail guns, sending sparks and gouts of silver-black material from the Xaros hull like ejecta from a volcano. The Condors loosed their torpedoes and pulled up from their attack runs. The dumb fired torpedoes were released so close to their target that it would be a miracle if they missed.

"103rd, follow me." Durand inverted her Eagle and dove toward Bravo. The alien construct filled her canopy, blue swirls of electricity quivering where the fighters' rounds had hit home. Dozens of fighters and bombers flew between her and her target, her chance to finally shoot back at the enemy stifled until the shot was clear.

The torpedoes came within a hundred yards of Bravo and the orbital burst into life. Point defense lasers annihilated the incoming torpedoes and savaged the squadrons that had hurt it.

An errant yellow blast passed Durand close enough that she flinched. Screams filled the IR as pilots and machines died, victims of the orbital's point defense lasers.

"Pull up! Pull up! Abort the attack." Durand fought to keep blood in her head as she flipped her rear engines toward the orbital and fired her afterburners, skipping out of the reach of the lasers. An Eagle to her flank erupted in a fireball that lasted for a heartbeat and a wave of static filled her IR channel.

"What the hell?" said a Chinese accented voice.

"Regroup on me, hurry," Durand ordered. She flipped her Eagle over and got a look at the orbital, which had ceased firing. The surface shook like the surface of a sand dune struck by a sudden gale.

"Did we kill it?" Choi asked.

"That's not what happens when they die," Durand said.

The orbital came apart, its single mass transforming into a swarm of single drones racing toward the fleet.

Durand opened a channel to Valdar.

"*Breitenfeld*, you've got incoming."

****

Valdar's tactical plot became a mass of red target icons as Bravo orbital morphed from a single grave threat into thousands and thousands of new problems.

His hands flew through his display, plotting new positions for his flotilla.

"Get our destroyer escorts in between us and the drones. Tell the frigates to get into this fight now. We need their anti-aircraft batteries," Valdar said.

"Sir, that will leave the civilian ships defenseless," Ericson said.

"They'll be damned useless if enough of those drones get past us. Hurry!" He slammed a fist into an intercom button. "Gunnery, fire the Q-round we have loaded into the rail gun into the coordinates I send you. Stand by to fire."

Valdar watched as one of his rail batteries slewed toward the approaching mass of drones.

"Fire!"

The *Breitenfeld* shook as the rail gun fired. Drones veered away from the incoming projectile and tendrils of massed drones flew toward other capital ships on the line. The Q-round erupted and bright white electricity arced from one drone to another, snaring hundreds in a web of coherent power.

Some drones burned away but most of the affected continued on, their pre-blast angular velocity guiding their disabled bodies through space.

"Destroyers *Ogden*, *Vancouver* and *Milan* in place. They've linked their batteries through IR and are engaging," Ericson said. Approaching drones withered under the destroyers' gauss cannons but their leading edge of their advance kept coming.

"Gunnery, get effective fire on those disabled drones. They're unpowered and the more we can kill now the more—"

A sunburst of red light flared from Charlie, a wide-angled blast that cut through space like a curtain. The sheath of light sliced through the *Tarawa*, the *Breitenfeld's* sister ship at the far end of the line. The fore section tumbled into space like a popped cork.

The wall of light hinged on Charlie and swept through the line. A pair of destroyers flared into puffs of flame as the beam caught them.

"Evasive maneuvers! Get us out of its path," Valdar said.

His ship lurched downward, the wide beam approaching them with the assurance of death itself.

****

Elias felt a wave of relief as the energy wall vanished, but his respite was short-lived as warnings and cries came over the IR.

He looked up. Dozens of drones glinted in the sun's rays.

Elias aimed the Q-round launcher mounted on his forearm and fired. With only five rounds, each shot had to count. The Q-round struck a drone and tendrils of light shot out but failed to reach any of the other drones.

"They're learning. Wait until they're bunched up before using your Q-rounds," Elias said. His dual gauss cannons flashed and destroyed the disabled drone. Part of him longed for this battle to be in atmosphere. The sound of explosions, the thrum of his heavy sabatons against the Earth and the comfort of hearing his fellow soldiers and Marines firing alongside him were absent in a void battle.

A red beam struck the hull in front of him and he twisted to the side and launched himself into the void. He drew down and pelted a drone with shots, the force of the recoil pushing him back against the hull. The drone cracked in half and dissipated.

A scream in the IR cut out. He looked to a firing position that had been manned by three sailors. Two sailors floated listlessly away from the hull while a third fired useless low-powered gauss shots into the drone towering over him.

Elias snapped off a pair of shots, winging the drone. He ran toward the threatened sailor and hit the drone again. The drone dangled from a stalk embedded in the hull, stunned by the blows. Elias retracted the hand on his left arm and grabbed the drone's stalk with his right.

He swung his left arm at the drone and activated the pneumatic pump within.

The spike impaled the drone and stabbed through its back. Elias shoved it away, the gold pyrite within crackling with reddish energy. The drone blew apart with a blast from Elias' gauss cannons.

Elias plucked a spinning gauss rifle from the void and handed it back to the sailor.

"High-powered shots only. Everything else is useless," Elias said.

The sailor, his eyes wide in awe or terror—Elias couldn't tell which—nodded furiously.

A flash of red to his left caught Elias' attention. A drone shot the hull in the exact same place three times in quick succession as it flew toward the *Breitenfeld*. The drone elongated as it approached, narrowing into a cigar shape.

Elias failed to hit the drone as it plunged into the hull through the hole it made.

"Bridge, you've got a border. Deck thirty-seven just ahead of the magazines," Elias said.

"Can you get inside and help?" Ericson said, her voice reedy with panic.

Another trio of blasts hit ahead of Elias. He ran toward the hole and brought his left hand back out of the housing. He saw the approaching drone elongating and ran a projection through his hardwired ballistic computer.

His hand shot out and caught the drone, half into the hull. His iron grip pulled it free and he slammed the drone against his knee. The drone bent from the blow and Elias tossed it away like a boomerang. He blasted it with his gauss cannon and ended its threat.

Laser blasts smashed into the hull next to him, another pair of drones heading right for him.

"Bridge, I'm going to need a minute."

****

MacDougall ran through the passageway, breathing labored as he struggled with his handhold on the metal box. Three other sailors helped him carry it, each suffering as he did. They ran past the electrical shop, sick bay, the entrance to the crypt; he felt like his destination was getting farther away instead of closer.

"If I'd wanted to run fast and carry heavy things, I'd have joined the Marines and not the navy," MacDougall groused.

"Security party seven, where are you?" Ericson asked through the IR.

"Deck thirty-six, section 2-B and I don't see any damn drone," he answered.

"Thirty-seven! Get to deck thirty-seven now!"

The sound of heavy metal thumps against the ceiling marched toward MacDougall and his team. He tapped the shoulder of a sailor carrying a gauss rifle loaded with Q-rounds. The metal stomps ceased a few yards ahead of them. Muffled shouts and cracks of gauss fire echoed from the corridor above them.

MacDougall tightened his grip on the handle welded to the box. The nearest lift was twenty yards ahead. The entrance to the ship's magazine stores—and hundreds of missiles and torpedoes—was right next to them. The armor around the magazines was the thickest on the ship; that door was the easiest way in or out.

"Do we go or what?" a sailor asked. Screams mixed with the sound of metal being ripped apart.

"No laddie, we're right where we need to be," MacDougall said.

A laser blasted through the ceiling,

blackening a swath of deck plating. Fire edged the ragged hole in the ceiling and the stalks of a Xaros drone reached into the corridor with the nimbleness of a spider. The swirling, oblong body of the drone followed a heartbeat later.

"Shoot it! Shoot the damn thing!" MacDougall ordered.

The sailor aimed his gauss rifle. A crimson beam shot from the drone's stalks and hit the sailor in the center of his chest. The man faded into a puff of red smoke, gone before his face could register the shock and pain of the death blow.

His rifle clattered to the deck.

MacDougall lunged for the weapon as another burst of red death passed over his head. He scooped up the weapon, the handle slick with the powdered remnants of the last man to hold it. The drone pointed a stalk at him, a ruby-hued star twinkling at its point.

With no time to aim, MacDougall fired from the hip. The rifle shot snapped with the sound of a great oak breaking in half. The recoil shoved

MacDougall back so hard he tripped over his own feet and crashed to the deck.

He pushed himself up and saw the drone lying on the deck, stalks twitching as a line of electricity ran between them like a Jacob's ladder.

Only one other sailor remained, standing dumbstruck next to the box.

"Bloody tosser! Move yer ass!" MacDougall grabbed each handle on his side of the box and the other sailor followed suit.

Adrenaline-fueled muscles lifted the box off the deck and they ran it toward the helpless drone like it was a battering ram.

"Stunner! Activate!" MacDougall yelled and a light on the box glowed green. The box hit the side of the drone, and the pneumatic spike in the box drove into the alien machine with enough force to crack any armor ever made by mankind.

The spike cracked the drone and sent it sliding across the deck. The stunner shot back from the impact and out of the sailors' grip. The spike retracted into its housing with a click-clack sound.

The drone stirred.

"Fuck me runnin'. Again!" They lifted the stunner and ran to the drone.

A stalk speared out and hit the other sailor in the heart, stopping him dead in his tracks. The stunner smashed to the ground and MacDougall stumbled over it. The stalk retracted with a slurp and stabbed into the sailor's eye.

MacDougall braced his feet against the deck and lifted the stunner, his muscles screaming in protest.

"Get off my ship!" He swung the stunner with a roar and slammed it against the drone. The spike cracked the drone like a dropped egg and it burned away.

MacDougall fell to the deck, his chest heaving. He looked back at the dead sailor, blood pooling around his body.

"Bridge. We got it." He rolled onto his back and felt a creeping tide of pain in his lower back and shoulders.

****

Durand sent a burst of gauss rounds into a helpless drone, shattering it.

"I've got one on me! Help!" came through her IR. She looked up at the sender, one of her last Eagles.

The Eagle corkscrewed wildly, micro bursts of its maneuver thrusters fouling the pursuing drone's shots.

Durand brought her nose up and blasted toward the chase. Her first shots winged the drone, sending it end over end. Her next squeeze of the trigger blew it to bits.

"Thanks, Gall. I owe you," the pilot said. She overtook his fighter, slow enough to look it over for damage. The Charlie orbital came into view from behind the other Eagle.

"Get back in the fight and—wait," she zoomed in on Charlie, its hull scabbing over in red embers. Lumps the size of drones shed from its surface and disintegrated.

"103rd, anyone who can hear me, form up and make an attack run on Charlie, now!" Durand bellied over and hit her afterburners.

"Are you crazy? It will eat us alive," Choi said. Despite her objections, her Condor raced to Durand's target.

"It's burning apart trying to keep up that energy output. It won't have the power to hit us with point defense," Durand said.

"If you're wrong?" Choi asked.

"Then you can tell me 'I told you so' in hell." Durand fired off her rail gun, the recoil rattling her Eagle like she'd tapped the brakes in a speeding ground car. Her round hit home and the energy wall fired from the orbital faltered.

A second rail shot from Durand blew a hole in the orbital.

She banked her Eagle onto its side and pointed her nose at the Xaros mass as she passed across it, keeping her speed as she brought her gauss cannon to bear. She squeezed the trigger on her cannon and didn't let go. Her rounds stitched across the surface, gouging out lumps of material that burned away within seconds. Another Eagle followed her lead, mimicking her path of destruction.

"Torpedoes...loose!" Choi said. Durand risked a glance and saw the four torpedoes from the Chinese–piloted Condor break from the fuselage and fire their engines. The Condor hit its afterburners and streaked ahead of its ordnance.

The torpedoes slammed into Charlie. One well-placed torpedo could have destroyed the *Breitenfeld*; the combined payload of four torpedoes ripped through the Xaros like an ax though a log of wood.

Peals of laughter came from the three Chinese pilots as they flew ahead of the destruction.

"Look out!" Choi shouted.

Durand righted her fighter and almost ran into a stalk that had sprung from Charlie's hull. The stalk stabbed out at her but a barrel roll sent the stalk's strike wide by a few feet.

"Choi, watch out for that—" Durand looked

over her shoulder and saw Choi's Condor tumbling end over end through space. Charlie burned away to nothing, but it had struck a final blow.

The Condor flopped over and over, air venting from the crew compartment.

"Eject, damn you," Durand said.

Rapid-fire, incomprehensible Chinese came over the IR. An ejection seat flared from the Chinese bomber, counteracting the bomber's tumble. The bomber floated through space like a leaf falling from a tree, and two more ejection seats flew from the bomber.

"Get to Ceres. Hole up in a crater until this is over then hit your beacons," Durand said.

"*Zhen?*"

"English, damn it!"

"Yes, roger that, ma'am. Thank you," Choi said.

Durand turned her fighter around and returned to the fight.

****

Stacey felt her lips and cheeks tug against her face as the drop ship shuddered through another maneuver. Turret fire rattled through the ship, which she knew was not a good sign. If the drones were close enough to shoot at, their ship was close enough to get hit.

The temptation to turn on the drop ship's IR net nagged at her, but *not* knowing if a half-dozen drones were about to rip her to pieces struck her as a better option than exposing herself to the fear and knowledge of things she couldn't control.

Keeping her eyes shut helped too.

The drop ship bucked like an airplane in turbulence.

She opened an eye as a mess of sparks showered down from the dorsal turret.

"That's not good," she said. Hale's Marines unlocked gauss rifles from their acceleration pads and slapped fresh batteries into the weapons.

"Not good at all." She turned on the IR.

"—on top of you!" Durand's warning came

through the IR. A patch of starlight suddenly appeared on the roof and a pair of stalks wrapped around the rent hull.

Stacey slapped at the gauss pistol on her chest, struggling to remove it from its holster. She shouted a warning and pointed frantically to the drone tearing its way inside.

"*Tarawa* Three-Seven, hold your course *very* steady," Durand said.

Heavy gauss rounds ripped through the top of the drop ship, perforating the bulkhead with a dozen ragged holes. A solid hit launched the drone into space. Durand's Eagle zipped over the drop ship a moment later.

Stacey got her pistol free and fiddled with the power settings.

"*That's useless*," Ibarra said to her.

"Why don't you shut up and do something useful?" she muttered.

"Prepare to drop!" Hale shouted. The Marines unsnapped their restraints and stepped onto the deck, their boots locking tight against the metal.

Stacey looked down at her harness like it was a Gordian knot.

Torni unbuckled her with practiced ease and yanked her out of the acceleration pad. She snatched the pistol out of Stacey's hand with the shake of her head and jabbed it back into the holster.

"If that probe knew this was coming, he should have sent you into the Marines," Torni said.

"Should I tell her about the time you fainted when a squirrel snuck into your room?" Ibarra said.

"Shut up," Stacey hissed.

"What?" Torni asked. The taller woman wrapped her arm around Stacey's waist and hefted her off her feet. Torni's arm mag-locked against Stacey's armor.

"Not you. Wait. What're you doing?"

Hale stood on the open rear hatch, one hand locked to a pneumatic strut as he looked below the drop ship.

"Drop zone is hot," Hale said. "We're jumping in. Follow me!" Hale stepped off the hatch and dove headfirst into the abyss.

Torni ambled forward as Franklin, Cortaro and Standish jumped from the drop ship.

"Wait, can we talk about this?" Stacey said, wiggling against Torni's iron-clad grasp.

Torni's pace quickened to a run and Stacey fought against a scream as they skipped into the void.

Warships sparkled in space as their cannons fought against drones swarming through the void. A cruiser exploded, showering Stacey with dirty yellow light.

Torni twisted and the grav linings on her boots sent the pair into a dive.

Stacey's empty stomach lurched as their speed increased. She looked up and gasped at the Crucible's interlocked thorns, motes of golden light winking within the basalt black thorns. The Crucible was massive, each thorn a mountain peak against the backdrop of Ceres.

A half-dozen thorns converged into a dome, its shape the only differential from the surrounding basalt spikes.

As she got closer, Stacey made out white armored Marines clustered on the peak of the node. Silver muzzle flashes from gauss rifles fired at a pair of drones swooping toward the landing zone. One drone spiraled into the dome and slid over the horizon while the second danced in space, peppering the Marines with yellow laser blasts.

"Hold on tight," Torni said as the dome grew larger and larger in front of them.

Stacey's stomach lurched toward her knees as Torni swung her feet toward the dome and their view inverted. Torni slowed their descent with her gravity lining. They came to a complete stop a few yards above the dome.

"That's not right," Torni said. Her boots shifted to pull them the rest of the way in and they shot down like a slug launched from a rifle.

Torni's hold on Stacey broke as they slammed into the dome. Stacey spun away, grasping for purchase at the dome's perfectly smooth surface. Her fingers scratched against the dome as she pin wheeled across it, the precipice of the dome's edge spinning into her vision, closer with each revolution.

"Use the mags in your boots!" Torni shouted.

Stacey knocked her toes against the dome, unable to remember the very brief instructions she'd received when fitted for the suit. Her kicks managed to stop her slide along the dome and sent her floating into space.

Torni stood on the dome, her feet planted wide apart as she swung a line in her hand like a bolo.

"A little help!" Stacey's heart pounded as she looked down and saw the edge of the dome sail beneath her feet. It was a long way down to Ceres.

Something whacked into her chest and she jerked to a halt. A safety line, anchored to her chest by the electromagnet at the end of the wire, went taunt and Stacey floated back toward Torni, the line tugging at her chest with each of Torni's heaves.

"…have to babysit some VIP with the

tactical sense of a potato. Not in the recruiting video, I'll tell you that much," Torni's complaining came through the IR as the two women neared.

"How do I use my boots?" Stacey said, reaching for Torni as her feet skidded across the dome.

"You don't." Torni threw Stacey over her shoulder and ran toward the apex, Torni's magnetic linings sizzling with tiny auroras as they latched and released from the dome's surface. Once they'd passed into the perimeter of Marines, Torni took Stacey off her shoulder and sat her on the dome, Torni's hands pressing firmly against Stacey's shoulders.

A pair of combat engineers ran laser torches around a wobbly circle of sliced basalt, the path of the lasers etched in blood-red trails.

Marines knelt around her, their weapons at the ready for another drone attack.

The Crucible was a range of perfect spires around her. She caught glimpses of the artificial rings around Ceres through the peaks, flashes of light from the battle raging between the fleet and the orbitals far above her. She felt like a mouse lost in a maze of thorns.

"We're almost in," an engineer said. He cut through the final inch and the manhole-sized breach burned away like a dying drone.

"Knock knock, assholes," Standish said. He grabbed the edge of the hole and lowered his legs into the dome. His smooth descent turned into a plunge and he yelped in surprise, vanishing into the hole like something had yanked him down.

"Standish!" Hale leaned over the hole, his weapon crisscrossing the opening.

"I'm OK." Standish's voice came over the IR. Stacey dared a peek over the lip of the hole. Standish was in a hallway, a diffuse red light around him.

"There's gravity," Standish said. "That's what pulled me in. About 5 percent over standard, not too bad." He looked hard at the Ubi on his forearm. "There's atmo too. Pressure and oxygen are a bit high but it's almost to Earth standard."

"How are you standing in atmosphere with a big hole into vacuum above your head?" Cortaro asked.

"I don't know, gunny. Maybe because I'm standing in an alien space station made by an advanced civilization?" Standish replied.

The cut hull beneath Stacey's fingers pulsed. She pulled her hands back like she'd touched a snake and watched as the edge contracted inwards ever so slowly.

"Um, it's healing itself," Stacey said.

Someone, Stacey strongly suspected Torni, grabbed her and shoved her into the hole headfirst. Gravity's familiar embrace brought her down in a messy fall, where Standish caught her by her shoulders and her legs smacked into the deck.

The deck wasn't the same as the hull or the walls around her. An inch of black sand shifted against her legs. A kick moved the shallow mounds around but didn't knock any grains into the air. She tried grabbing a handful, but the sand evaded her grasp like she was trying to pick up water beneath a plastic sheet.

A hallway extended away from their breach, branching off into two parallel directions at each end. A red glow illuminated the hallway from the walls, but not from any light source she could see. The roof was a flat arch, almost ten feet high.

Hale and the rest of his team dropped down and formed a semicircle around her. She looked up and saw their entrance shrink faster and faster. An engineer watched them through the hole as it shrank from the size of a plate to the circumference of a beer can to nothing in a span of seconds.

Hale looked up at the ceiling. No trace of the hole remained.

"Sir?" Cortaro asked. The sound of the team's breathing mixed with the low hum of the station.

Hale looked at Stacey. "It took twenty minutes to cut that entrance. We can't wait for another hole while the Xaros beat the hell out of the fleet. Where do we go?"

"Put me against the wall," Ibarra's tinny

voice said over the IR.

Stacey stood up and took a tentative step toward the wall. The sand beneath her feet deformed against her steps, then tightened around her boots. She put her palm to the bulkhead and warmth like a hot stove top invaded her glove.

"Ow," she said.

A pulse of white light emanated from her hand and raced down the wall. The pulse returned less than a second later.

"We aren't that far from the control room but if we want to bring more Marines to this party, we'll need to access the air locks," Ibarra said.

"Are there any Xaros in here?" Hale asked.

"Not sure, the pulse was a hack. If I poke around too hard, they'll know I'm here and we'll have a serious problem on our hands."

The hallway shook as a low rumble of thunder rolled through the hallway.

"We can't leave them out there. Which way to the air lock?" Hale asked.

"Behind you, take a left," Ibarra said.

"Let's go." Hale turned and ran down the hallway.

Stacey followed with Torni dogging her steps and encouraging her to move faster in uniquely Marine terms.

How was that a hack? she thought.

I used your body to do it. I said you were special, think I'd lie?

Her legs felt like rubber in the heavier gravity and her lungs burned to keep up with Hale. Cardiovascular strength wasn't a perk her body could use.

You don't have much of a reputation for truthfulness. What else can I do?

Oh Stacey, Ibarra chuckled in her mind. *Just you wait.*

****

Elias stomped a foot on a stunned drone bouncing along the hull and thrust a spike into it. A ring of disintegration emanated from the entry wound and Elias looked into space for his next target. A frigate burned far above him, explosions rattling the doomed ship as its armament destroyed it from the inside out.

"Elias. Hangar. Need you," came a garbled message from Kallen.

"Hold on." Elias cut the mag locks on his boots and jumped toward the aft of the ship. The thrusters in his calf housing popped open and blasted him along the hull. He rocketed toward the bridge, all of the crew but the captain ducking into their seats as he buzzed past.

He cleared the engines' cowlings and saw a tear in the armor plates meant to protect the hangar. He cut his rockets, twisted round and reengaged his thrusters. The hole in the armor looked just big enough to accommodate him.

Elias dove toward the Xaros-made entrance and almost made it inside without a hitch. Almost.

An ankle caught against a jagged edge and turned his smooth flight into an uncontrolled oscillation. Elias smashed into the hangar deck so hard his womb couldn't compensate and his head—his true head—banged against the armored tank. Stars filled his vision. The dual input from his real eyes and his suit's sensors threw off his balance and he wobbled to his feet like a drunk.

Kallen stood over Bodel's suit, prone against the deck, wrestling with a drone. She had a pair of the drone's stalks locked in her grip as her other arm jabbed at the drone with her spike.

Elias killed his suit's sensor feed and opened his vision slat. He lined up a shot as best he could and fired.

A round sparked off the drone and shoved the alien machine against Kallen's chest. They went down in a heap of arms and stalks. The second round missed the drone, ricocheted off the forward armor plates, bounced against the deck back toward Kallen and hit the drone. The drone reared up, exposing its underside, and Kallen drove her spike into it.

Kallen recovered as the drone disintegrated. Elias brought his sensors back online and raised his gauss cannons to his suit's head mount as if to blow on the barrels.

"That was a shit shot and you know it," Kallen said.

"Bodel? He OK?"

"His motor unit took a hit. We'll need to—behind!"

Elias whirled his torso around on his hip actuators' servos and impaled a drone leaping at him. He spun around and blasted another drone trying to crawl through the hangar doors. He shot away a stalk that poked into the hole.

Red blotches grew against the door face as drones burned their way through the reinforced armor.

Elias, his gauss cannons still trained on the hole, ejected his left arm from the ball socket in his shoulder.

"Give me Bodel's arm," Elias said.

"You'll redline," Kallen said but complied with his order as she disputed it. She twisted Bodel's right arm to unfasten it then yanked it clean from his suit. She slapped it into Elias' suit and the new arm whirled in the socket.

"Doesn't matter." Elias used his skull jack to work up a firing solution as the metal of the hangar wall melted away like flowing lava.

Kallen raised her firing arm, spike at the ready.

"*Gott mit uns*," she said.

Elias cycled ammo into his twin cannons, "*Gott mit uns*."

Almost two dozen drones broke through the hangar gate. Elias fired his cannons at separate targets, his brain burning as his nervous system screamed for him to lessen the strain. Every shot sent an icy jolt of pain up his true arms in psychosomatic pain. His arms cramped and curled into a sold mass of muscle and agony as his suit took out another pair of drones.

His right arm ceased firing, the ammo counter blinking empty. His left cannons went dry a second later.

Elias' vision swam red. The snap of Kallen's

cannons were distorted and tinny.

Shut down, a distant part of his mind begged him.

A yellow beam tore into Kallen. A cry of shock and pain made it through the haze as she went down.

Elias popped his spikes and charged the four remaining drones.

He jumped in the air and fired his thrusters. The brief boost gave him enough room to dodge a crimson beam and he came down on a pair of drones, driving a spike into each one. He swung an impaled drone at another drone, its stalk burning red.

The drone's beam hit the Xaros skewered on Elias' spike and dissipated against the dying drone.

The other drone he'd stabbed burnt away and Elias punched his free spike into the third drone. The tip broke the drone's shell and it jerked against the spike like a wolf with its paw stuck in a trap.

Elias ran forward, driving the spike deeper

into the drone and bum-rushed the final drone. The last drone's stalks clattered against Elias' armor as they slammed into the hangar door, a drone disintegrating between them.

Elias brought his arms back and thrust them into the final drone, the spikes piercing the drone in an X shape. Elias raised the drone over his head and pulled his arms apart, flinging dismembered pieces of the drone into the hangar.

Blackness blurred the edges of his vision. He saw Kallen roll onto her side, then the darkness took him.

****

Hale stepped past a corner, his rifle up and ready. A pair of lines ran from the floor to the ceiling in the middle of the wall just beyond the corner, a single baleful red button between the lines at shoulder height.

"Not ones for warning signs, are they?"

Franklin said from behind Hale.

"Open it," Hale said to Ibarra.

Stacey walked up to the air lock and tried to press her hand against the red light but her arm refused to extend fully.

"If I do this, the Xaros will come running for me," Ibarra said.

"Then open all the air locks on every node. Get every Marine inside. Confuse them," Hale said.

"Fine, fine, fine," Ibarra sighed and Stacey regained control of her arm. She touched the button and the air lock didn't so much as open as it melted apart. The wall split and tiny grains flowed toward the walls like a sandcastle succumbing to the waves.

The mountain peaks of glittering basalt stood silent in the space beyond the air lock.

"I've sent a message to all the Marines on the surface along with directions to the nearest entrance. We can meet up with our shore party closer to the control room. Shall we?" Ibarra said.

Stacey's hand and arm pointed down a corridor of their own volition. She grimaced and pulled her arm back against her body.

"Stop that!" she hissed.

Hale gave her a confused look as he ran past.

The Crucible offered little insight as to the form or function of anything as they ran down the corridors. Stacey caught sight of a few tall arched lines, doors for someone or something much taller than the average human.

They came to a four-way intersection and stopped.

"Which way?" Hale asked.

"This intersection wasn't here when I scanned this place. How odd," Ibarra said. "Touch the wall again."

Stacey moved toward the wall, Franklin just behind her. She reached out for the wall.

The instant her hand touched the hot bulkhead, the floor beneath the rest of the team shot up, taking them above and beyond the lip of the ceiling. A blank wall of solid basalt cut them off from the intersection, leaving them at a dead end.

"Oh, that's not good," Franklin said.

Stacey looked to her palm where Ibarra's light shimmered through her glove.

"Unexpected," Ibarra said.

A thrum strong enough to set Stacey's teeth on edge echoed down the hallway.

"That's a drone. Come on." Franklin pulled Stacey along by the hand and ran them back to the pervious intersection.

"There's another way to the control room. Take a left," Ibarra said.

The thrum grew closer as they ran.

****

"How long until the number two battery is operational?" Valdar asked the petty officer on his holo screen. Sparks poured from severed wires behind the sailor and Valdar could see open vacuum through all the damage.

"The drone severed the gear housings. The battery is locked in place. Rounds still in the breach," the sailor said. "It won't move until we're back in dry dock. Forward battery is operational. Ventral guns have no power. It's a real mess on the gun deck, sir."

"I need the forward battery operational—otherwise we're nothing more than a target. Got it?"

"Aye aye, sir."

"Captain!" the astrometrics officer yelled. "The last orbital is moving toward Crucible."

Speed and heading vectors popped up next to the Crucible on the tactical plot. The orbital would reach the Crucible in less than ten minutes.

"The boarding teams must have found something," Valdar said. He hailed Admiral Garrett and the man's taciturn face came up on his holo.

"Sir, orbital is—"

"Yes, I see that. I'm dealing with borders on ten different ships. Make this fast."

"We can't let it reach the Crucible. If it breaks up like Bravo, there's no way the landing party can fight them off. And the only thing that matters in this whole offensive is what's on

Crucible," Valdar said. His hands flew around the tactical display, adding waypoints and attack vectors for what remained of the fleet.

"If we get any closer to that orbital, it'll eat us alive," Garrett said.

"I don't think we have a choice, sir." Valdar sent the plots to Garrett. The admiral looked over the plan and nodded wearily.

"All ships," Garrett said, his feed on the fleet-wide address channel, "all ships full speed to orbital Delta. Hit with everything you've got." Garrett cut out.

"Conn, lay in an intercept course for the orbital," Valdar said.

"Already on it, captain."

Valdar focused on the fleet's position. Fewer than half the navy ships that started the battle remained for this assault.

He panned over to the *Charlemagne's* icon. The carrier hung motionless in space as the rest of the fleet moved toward the orbital. The icon blinked rapidly, then a red "X" covered it.

"Oh no…." Valdar saw a second sun burst in space where the *Charlemagne* had been. As the carrier's death flare faded out, the bridge crew paused for a moment, then returned to their duties.

"Guns, fire on the orbital as soon as the *London* and *Prague* are within range. Give the enemy more targets than they can handle."

A painfully slow minute ticked away and the *Breitenfeld's* forward battery fired. Rail gun rounds from the surviving cruisers peppered the orbital, each shot knocked away by its point defense lasers.

A crimson lance fired from the orbital and the *London* blew apart.

The fleet closed in on Delta and the *America* flew into effective range. The carrier's six rail batteries fired as one, and one rail shot hit the outer edge of the orbital. An ugly hole appeared on the orbital, its edges simmering with fire.

A tiny red star coalesced in the center of the orbital.

"Conn, bring us to one-two-eight mark nine-one. Gun deck, fire battery two on my order,"

Valdar said.

"Sir, the guns can't aim!" the gunnery officer said.

"I'm aiming the ship for the guns," Valdar said. "Make ready."

The Xaros orbital fired. The lance of energy pierced the *America's* hull and burst out the other side of the carrier. Admiral Garrett's flagship listed on its side and went dark.

Valdar's jaw clenched. Thousands of sailors were aboard the stricken ship and there was little to nothing he could do to help them.

"Guns, fire on my mark....Fire!"   ·

Breitenfeld's damaged rail gun battery crackled with electricity and two rail gun slugs shot away, a trail of burning space dust in their wake.

The orbital swatted aside one of the rounds. The other impacted and spun the orbital slowly like a wind chime in a slight breeze. The orbital flipped over and brought its cannon to bear on the *Breitenfeld.*

"Guns?"

"We've nothing, sir."

"Conn, evasive maneuvers," Valdar said. His ship skewed away from the orbital slightly—his spaceship did not turn on a dime.

The cannon flared, red forks of lightning snapping from the power source.

"All hands, brace for impact!"

The orbital jerked as a rail gun shot lucked past the defenses, deflecting its cannon shot ever so slightly.

The orbital's beam sliced through space and ripped across the *Breitenfeld's* outer hull. The hit gouged the armor and continued on into space. Damage alerts flooded the bridge, a chorus of panicked voices and klaxons swirling around Valdar as his ship rolled over.

"Engineering! Get attitude control back before we slam into Ceres," Valdar said. He tried to pull up a damage report on his screens, but his screen was locked in solid blue.

"Decks nine to forty are open to vacuum. Main engines offline," Ericson said.

Valdar's screens came back to life. The damage was bad, but not fatal to the ship or what remained of the crew.

His tactical plot was gone but Valdar could see the orbital dead ahead of them. A dozen Union ships closed in on the orbital, pounding it with rail gun shots and their anti-fighter gauss cannons.

The orbital's point defense lasers raged against the incoming fire, annihilating thousands of rounds before they could make a dent in the thing, a feat impossible for any human mind or computer ever developed by man or woman. A rail shot hit the flank of the enemy station and the point defense ceased.

The *Gettysburg* fired a full broadside into Delta and it broke apart like a shattered plate. The pieces burned away and the bridge erupted in cheers.

Valdar sat against his chair and let out a slow breath.

Victory wasn't theirs yet. Not until Crucible was under their control.

****

"Go right. We're almost there," Ibarra said.

Franklin quickened his pace, leaving Stacey a few steps behind. He ran past the corner and raised his rifle as a shout barely escaped his lips.

A stalk shot out and struck him in the chest, flicking him away like an errant insect. Franklin smashed into the bulkhead and careened to the ground with a sickening crunch.

Stacey's feet skidded to a halt. The drone crept toward Franklin like a spider, stalks digging into the sand with each step.

A red ember grew from the stalk tip reaching toward Franklin.

Stacey pulled her pistol from her holster and fired off two rounds. Both bounced off the drone.

The drone swung around toward her. The ember on the stalk died away and it moved toward her with a sense of purpose.

"Run," Ibarra said.

Stacey did as advised. The thump of stalks against the floor bore down on her faster than her worst nightmare.

A stalk swept against her ankles and she fell to the floor face-first. She tried to crawl forward but a stalk speared into the ground just ahead of her shoulder. The stalk whipped her onto her back and pressed against her chest. The stalk was ice cold, leaching heat from her entire body as the central mass of the drone loomed over her.

A stalk tip hovered over her face. It snapped apart into eight digits and grabbed her right forearm. She struggled against the hold but she was a mouse against a python.

The drone brought her hand closer to the body, Ibarra's light reflecting off the geodesic patterns swirling over its surface.

"Hey! Leave her alone," Franklin shouted, his voice burbling through a punctured lung.

The drone flipped a stalk toward Franklin and a red light grew from the tip.

Stacey heard the crack of a gauss rifle and

an electrical storm broke over the drone.

The Q-round Franklin fired sent thin bolts of lightning through her body. Her muscles convulsed and a scream fought to get past her locked jaw. The reek of ozone filled the air as the drone collapsed to the ground.

Stacey fought to breathe and pushed the stalk off her chest. She scrambled away from the drone and got to her feet.

"Franklin?" she asked. Franklin, propped against the bulkhead, his head hanging on his chest and rifle smoking at his side, didn't answer.

"Can you do something to the drone?" she asked.

Ibarra didn't answer either.

"Grandpa?" she looked at her palm. His light was gone. She shook her hand. "Grandpa, can you hear me?"

A stalk twitched. Another scratched at the ground.

With the bulk of the waking drone between her and Franklin, she turned and ran, hating herself for it.

****

The snap of a single gauss shot echoed around Hale. Even with his helmet off, the acoustics of the Crucible played hell with locating where the shot came from.

They stood at a confluence of three hallways, each leading a different direction from which they'd come. After the station had rearranged itself to cut them off from Stacey and Franklin, Hale and his team had run through the station, trying to double back on the air lock and reunite.

With no map and racing through hallways with no discernable features among them, Hale was pretty sure they were lost. The only beacon for finding Stacey and Franklin was the sound of a few cracks from a pistol and the gauss rifle shot.

He wiped sweat from his brow. The air was just over a hundred degrees and so dry that it leached moisture from him with every breath.

"I think…right," Cortaro said.

"Maybe we should split up," Standish said.

The *crack-crack* of pistol shots flit through the air.

"Straight," Hale said. He donned his helmet and ran down the center hallway, holding his rifle at waist level as they ran, the weight pulling his upper body forward and low. His head jutted ahead of the rest of him, leading him face-first into whatever danger the Crucible held. He never wanted to lead Marines into a fight this way, blind and grasping toward the enemy.

The flash of pistol fire lit up around a corner. Stacey turned the corner, her head down, blind firing her pistol behind her.

"Drop!" Hale shouted. He braced himself against the black sand and raised his rifle against his shoulder.

Stacey looked up, her face awash in terror, and fell forward.

The drone was a second behind her, its stalks pushing against the floor and rounded walls.

Hale fired and the rifle mule-kicked his shoulder. The round sheared off a stalk and the drone stumbled. Hits from Cortaro and Torni to the drone's body knocked it back like punches against a heavy bag.

Time slowed as Hale waited for his rifle to power up the next shot. His weapon trembled as the capacitor charged, an eternity as the drone sprung forward on its stalks.

Standish hit it dead center. Cracks spider-webbed from the impact but the drone didn't slow as it lunged for Stacey.

His capacitor went green and Hale squeezed his trigger.

The drone burst in half, the two pieces falling to either side of Stacey and burning away. The smell of smoldering coal filled the air.

Stacey sat up, her chest heaving on the edge of hyperventilation. Torni ran up to her and pulled Stacey's helmet free. Her face was awash in sweat, her hair matted against her head. She pushed aside Torni's proffered hand and tried to run back the way she'd come.

"Where's Franklin?" Hale asked.

"Back…there…" Stacey said, struggling for breath between words.

"Is he all right?"

"No." Stacey swallowed hard and pointed ahead.

****

Hale knelt next to Franklin's body, still sitting against the bulkhead. Franklin's chest plate was cracked and blood dripped from the damage and seeped into the black sand. The drone's blow had driven broken ribs into his lungs—mortally wounding him. That he managed to fire his sole Q-round and hit the drone was a testament to his will.

Hale slipped the ID chit from Franklin's shoulder armor and closed his fist around it, then he pressed a button on the temple of Franklin's helmet and the visor popped loose. Hale moved the visor aside and touched Franklin's eyes, half-open and staring into nothing, and closed them with his fingertips.

"The control room. Zzzzt—close," Ibarra said.

"You OK?" Hale stood up and walked to Stacey. She held her right hand palm up, the light within sputtering.

"Think he had to do a hard reset, but he's getting better fast. That Q-round screwed him up pretty bad," she said. Her head cocked to the side and she said, "Go, go, go—stop that!"

Her hand jerked away from her and practically dragged her down the hallway, an invisible force pulling her along.

The hallway, which led to a distant red blur, suddenly bent downwards just ahead of Stacey. The Marines huddled around her, not wanting to be separated again. They stepped over the bend and the hallway spilled into an amphitheater.

Stairs, too tall for easy steps, led down into the center of the control room. Pale blue light wavered against rings of black stone emanating from a plinth in the middle of the room.

"I really don't like this place," Torni said.

"Get me to the center-target bull's-eye…,"
Ibarra said, trailing into static.

They hustled forward through a gap in the
rings. Standish ran his hand over a ring and gold
speckles shimmered in the wake of his touch.

"How do they control anything if there are
no buttons? And why do drones need stairs?" he
asked.

"Think-think-think this is for drones?
Stacey, touch the altar," Ibarra said, his voice
modulating out of tune.

She stopped a few feet from the center of the
room, then took a step back.

"What will happen?" she asked.

"I told you. Transmutation—chrysalis—
something wonderful." Ibarra's voice snapped into
normal with the last word.

She closed her hand and brought it to her
chest.

"Stacey, Marines and sailors are dying to

buy you time. Please," Hale said.

She looked at Hale and nodded quickly.

"We've lost so much for this. What's one more sacrifice?" She held her hand over the plinth and Ibarra's light grew so bright Hale had to look away. When the light subsided, he saw a single sliver of light hovering over the plinth.

Stacey backed away, rubbing her palm.

"My, this is more than I expected," Ibarra said. Lines of energy burst from the plinth and into the control room. Standish danced away from where the lines shot beneath his feet.

Holograms wavered over the rings and molded into focus. Alien script wrapped rings around holos of the Earth, individual ships of the fleet, and depictions of the solar system.

"So much more."

The sliver of light that was Ibarra deformed and snapped into a crown of thorns model of the Crucible. Red specks of light in the model, some in the spikes connecting the station together but most concentrated in the nodes, moved slowly.

"Let's take care of the drones," Ibarra said. A pulse of light emanated from the plinth, through the floor and into the walls of the Crucible. The red dots on the model ceased moving and blinked out.

The pulse of light returned and filled the plinth with burning white light, which then faded, leaving the altar as a cylinder of golden light.

"I can use their energy to open the portal. Are you ready, Stacey?"

Stacey looked up at the altar as it floated toward the ceiling. Golden light bathed her face and a tear rolled down her cheek.

"Hurry, before I change my mind," she said.

Hale grabbed Stacey by the shoulder.

"Wait, what is this?" he demanded.

"Nothing that concerns you. Now be silent. This part is tricky," Ibarra said.

The golden light swirled faster and faster, motes of stars pulled into a black hole so fast they nearly burnt away before they could be consumed. The swirl accelerated until there was nothing but a solid plane of gold light, then it dimmed to an unblemished oval of white the size of a door.

"Go," Ibarra said. The portal lowered to the ground without a sound.

Stacey pushed Hale's hand away.

"It's all right. I'll come back," she said. She reached out and touched a fingertip to the portal. Her hand held still for a moment, then her fingers slipped into the portal. The white field crackled with blue-white energy where she broke the plane. She pulled her hand back, all fingers still attached.

"It tingles," she said.

She stepped a foot into the portal, looked over her shoulder at Hale, and went through.

The portal blinked out of existence, leaving Ibarra's sliver of light in its place.

"Admiral Garrett? Where are you?" Ibarra said. Hale heard the echo of the words in his helmet IR.

A holo display reset to show the *America*, venting gasses and listing in space.

"This is Garrett. I'm in a life pod on my way down to Ceres after I had a carrier shot out from under me. How's it going in there?" the admiral's gruff voice responded.

"Mission accomplished. The Crucible is secure and our ambassador is away. I'm reading a few drones still functioning outside the Crucible. I'll relay their location to the fighters and this fight will be over," Ibarra said.

"Get a fix on lifeboats while you're at it. I'm going to have plenty of company on this rock and our air will only last so long," Garrett said.

"As you wish," Ibarra said.

Hale looked at his three Marines, each tired, banged up and overheating.

"What now? What about us?" Hale asked Ibarra.

Ibarra's light flickered.

"This battle is won, but the war is far from over," Ibarra said.

****

"I want the oxygen lines cut to deck nineteen cut *now* and that fire contained. We've got casualties crew in the aft compartments and we can't open the deck to vacuum," Valdar said to the exhausted crewman on the holoscreen.

"The passageway is blocked, sir, we can't get to the environmental controls," the crewman said, pleading.

Valdar swiped a schematic of the ship next to the holo and looked it over. Red damage icons cut a path along his ship's hull like a bleeding wound.

"One of the drones cut through the decks across from the magazines. Climb up through it and then take the service lift next to the armor storage. Can you do that?"

The crewman nodded and cut the feed.

"Engineering, damage report." Valdar swung his chair away from the holo table.

"We've got engines two and four back online. We can keep orbit around Ceres but I don't think we can get back to Earth anytime soon."

"That's progress," Valdar said.

"Sir, we've got a priority fleet transmission…from Admiral Garrett," the communication's officer said.

"Put it up," Valdar leaned against his chair and watched as active fire icons went from red, to amber, to green on his damage control screens. The *Breitenfeld* had fought through the worst of the damage, but making her whole again would take time.

Admiral Garrett, in an emergency space suit with the barren Ceres landscape behind him, looked into the camera with stern determination.

"To the fleet, to all that is left of us…we've won. The Crucible is ours. The Xaros are destroyed. Our planet is free once more." Garrett looked up. "I can see our ships, some burning in space. Some still fighting to survive. All with battle scars. We're hurt, but we're alive. We are few, and we are all that remains. But we are embers, and we will reignite humanity.

"My orders are to save every ship we still can,

care for the wounded, get the civilians back to Earth immediately. And would someone get down here and pick me up?"

CHAPTER 11

Her universe was an abyss of white. She felt her arms and legs moving; whatever ether she was in offered no resistance, nothing to push against. Her armor was gone, replaced by a violet jumpsuit that had no feeling to it. She opened and closed her eyes, but the white light didn't change. It was all.

She clicked her teeth together—no sound.

Ibarra wasn't in her mind anymore. The only way she knew to count the time was to sing songs in her head over and over again and keep count.

Hours, probably more, passed.

How long until I lose my mind? she thought.

Eventually, a grid pattern formed in the

distance. Her attempts to swim toward the black lines were fruitless; they didn't get any closer or farther away. Was her mind, starved of stimulus, creating something for her to see? Was this the first step toward insanity? She lashed out, clawing at the air, and screamed in silence.

She swung her arms again and again, then her foot touched something.

She looked at her feet. Three foot-long squares rimmed in black were just beneath her feet. Her toes scraped at the ground, then her body lowered to the floor. She fell to the ground, hugging the cold floor and breathing in the smell of dusty linoleum.

"Finally," she said. She sat up with a snap, shocked at the sound of her own voice.

The walls and ceiling of the room she occupied were just like the floor, a black grid of lines on a white background. She stood up and walked toward the wall, just a few feet away from her, but the wall stayed the same few feet away without moving.

She ran forward, but she couldn't tell if she moved ahead or stayed in the exact same place—the perspective remained the same.

"Hello? Anyone there?" she said.

A handful of grid lines on the wall ahead of her faded from black to white, a rectangle big enough for a person to walk through swung open, and white light flooded the room. Stacey put her hands up to her face and tried to peek through her fingers.

A dark humanoid silhouette stood in the white light. The door closed behind it.

It was shaped like a man. A maroon jumpsuit hung over shoulders so thin it looked like it was made of pipes instead of flesh and blood. Its head was a mask of iron, with dark pits for eyes and slight mounds in the metal passing for features.

It stepped toward her, achingly smooth in its motions for something that looked almost primitive in design.

"Greetings," the word was toneless, mechanical. "I am your integration assistant. Please follow me. We have much to discuss." Its hand—made of exposed metal joints—gestured toward the door with the grace of a ballerina.

"Wait, where am I? Where's Ibarra?"

It held still as a sculpture.

"The assessment AI remained behind, standard procedure. I do not know where we are in relation to your home world. Your hosts refer to this facility as—human equivalent—Rendezvous."

Stacey looked around its shoulder toward the open door. Darkness awaited.

"You cannot remain here," it said.

"No, guess not. Do you have a name?"

"I am purpose built and do not require a designation."

"Then your name is Chuck. My commander wants me to meet with whoever sent the probe to our solar system. We deserve some answers after what we've been through."

Chuck's head spun around and his feet and hands followed suit, changing his direction without moving.

"You will have your answers. Come with me," Chuck said.

CHAPTER 12

Driving a car felt natural to Hale. With his brother, Jared, in the passenger seat, Hale could almost imagine the world before the Xaros came. Driving through the neighborhood they grew up in brought back memories of bike crashes against walls, baseball games on overgrown fields and useless childhood brawls with local bullies on more than one corner.

That the neighborhood was devoid of other people ruined his memories. Only the emptiness remained.

"When is this scheduled for demolition?" Jared asked.

"Next month. Automated farms for produce and beans will go in, I think," Hale said. He turned their car into their old subdivision, one- and two-story homes built near the turn of the century.

"We could put in a request with the board, keep the house," Jared said.

"Let's take a look at it first."

Their parents' house was there, on the corner across the street from a crumpled playground overgrown with weeds, same as it ever was. He parked across the street, on the curb of the house where his first girlfriend lived.

The brothers got out of the car, hands on their holstered pistols. There was no threat from the Xaros; every one of them had been destroyed in the battle for the Crucible. No bandits to worry about, the Xaros had left none alive. But there were plenty of coyotes and packs of feral dogs around them. With a few generations to forget humans, the animals saw them as prey.

The mesquite tree in front of the porch had grown out of control. Branches hung over the front door and swept against the roof in the breeze. Weeds poked through an exposed fault line of the solar panel driveway. Faded, cracked paint covered the house like a lake bed baked in the sun.

"You first?" Jared asked.

"Let's get this over with," Hale said. He pushed past the mesquite branches and grabbed the knob, which was rusted shut. A swift kick to the door knocked it loose and it swung open with a creak.

A sheen of dust and pollen covered the mahogany floors, real wood that his mother had dreamed about for years after their family moved into the house. Hale shifted his foot over the floor, exposing the dark wood. Their father had the new floors put in during a family trip to the beach. He remembered how happy his mother had been, dancing across the floor in her bare feet.

A layer of dust covered the furniture in the living room. A bloom of mold stained the ceiling like a stormy sky. An old-fashioned picture on the wall of the brothers—both in dress uniforms from their commissioning ceremony—and their proud parents had rotted in its frame, victim of the water that had invaded their roof.

"I knew it wouldn't be pretty, but…," Jared said.

"You think they were here?" Hale asked.

Jared shrugged his shoulders and pushed past Hale. They went past a decayed kitchen and into the hallways leading to the bedrooms. Each had had his own room, but they'd been converted into a man cave for their father and an art studio for their mother after they'd left for college.

A door at the end of the hall led to the master bedroom. Black mold covered it like soot from a long-ago fire.

Hale pushed the door open with his fingertips. The room stank of mildew. Closed shutters had robbed the room of light for years. Hale poked his finger into the wooden slats and let in the sun.

The bed was unkempt. He looked to the ceiling, no distinctive Xaros disintegration holes there. His father was a stickler for hospital corners and bed sheets so tight he could bounce a quarter off them. He wouldn't have left the bed like that.

"Closet," Jared said.

The closet door was ajar, light spilling around the crack and under the sill.

Hale stepped slowly to the closet, his footfalls like moving through clay. He could rationalize what was beyond that door. His parents were dead, murdered by the Xaros like every other human being that wasn't in the fleet. His mind knew this, accepted it, but his heart hadn't. Not yet.

The closet door opened with a squeal of rusted hinges. Light shone through two unnatural holes in the ceiling. Dust motes danced in the rays pointing to where their parents had died. Deep red dust on the floor and wall crudely outlined where they'd spent their final moments.

"They were holding each other," Jared said.

Hale nodded. He wiped a tear away on his sleeve and knelt down. He reached out to touch the red dust, but couldn't.

The scrape of metal against rotting wood came from above him. Jared had pulled a lockbox off a shelf.

"This should be it," he said. Jared took the box into the bedroom and put it on top of a dresser. He un-holstered his pistol and slammed the butt against the rusted lock. The box popped open. Jared took an oblong wooden box the size of his palm out and looked it over in the feeble light.

"Held together well," he said. He opened the wooden box, and gold glinted from within.

Jared held up a ring, thick and wide at the top, intricate crests on either side, a crown of sparkling diamonds and rubies on top.

"Granddad's academy ring," Jared said. The elder Hale had fought in the Iraq War and worn that ring every day he'd been in combat. Their father would take it out and share stories about Granddad on the anniversary of his death, tales of valor meant to guide the boys into becoming good men.

Jared held it out to Hale.

"Here, you take it," Jared said.

"You always wanted it."

"Yeah, well, you're the one that fought through Euskal Tower, got the probe back to the fleet, killed who knows how many drones when you singlehandedly took the Crucible, etc., etc. I landed on node four as part of the feint, shot at one drone and then the battle ended. You deserve it more than I do. Granddad would agree."

Hale took the ring, tested its weight and slid it on. It fit snug, but it fit.

"But these are mine." Jared held up a pair of brass spurs, another relic of their grandfather. Family lore had it that the spurs were from the melted down bust of the dictator toppled in the Iraq War.

Hale looked back in the closet, ice filling his heart.

"Let's go."

They stood in the driveway, swapping stories each knew by heart as they waited to finally say goodbye to the home.

"Look, there's Titan Station," Jared said,

pointing to the horizon.

The space station, originally designed as the hub for the Saturn colonies meant for orbit around Titan, crested over the horizon. It had grown from scaffolding to a dome surrounded by spokes in the month since the battle for the Crucible. The robot construction crews had built it in record time and more than one ship was already in dry dock for repairs. If Hale had his helmet on, he could have zoomed in to see the *Breitenfeld* docked against the station.

Hale looked to the other side of the sky, where a new moon orbited far beyond Titan Station. Ceres had arrived last week and nestled into the Lagrange point like it had always belonged there. The alien rings around the dwarf planet sometimes refracted light from the sun, an infrequent reminder to those on Earth that something new and terrifying was in the sky above them.

"Let's get back to Phoenix. War hero or not, there's a curfew," Jared said.

"You going to miss this place?" Hale asked,

climbing into the car.

"No. This isn't our home anymore," Jared said. He tapped the unit patch on his shoulder, then his brother's shoulder. "This is all we have left. All we are."

"For now. We've got our world back and we're going to rebuild it."

****

Bodel and Kallen made their way through the long-term care ward. Most rooms were filled with Marines and sailors still recovering from injuries sustained in the Battle of the Crucible, skin grafts over burns and limb regrowth that needed more therapy and time to heal.

Kallen, pushed along by Bodel, nodded to patients as they went past rooms. They'd gotten to know most of the ward during their daily visits. She smiled as they passed an empty room; Johanna was finally discharged after her body accepted the cloned organs.

The windows surrounding Elias' room were opaque for his privacy, a favor he'd appreciate when he finally awoke. The door slid to the side as Bodel and Kallen got close and she saw Dr. Yanish, a diminutive bald man with a hawk nose and round glasses, before Elias' tank.

Elias remained in his armored tank, catatonic after he'd redlined during the fight on the *Breitenfeld's* hangar. The trauma to his nervous system was severe enough that Dr. Yanish and the rest of the doctors and engineers dedicated to the armor program wouldn't risk removing Elias from the tank. Elias hadn't made a move or a sound since the battle ended.

"Doctor, nice to see you," Kallen said.

"Is it?" Yanish asked. "When have we ever seen each other for something positive? It's always 'He's bleeding to death' or 'Does this look infected?' never 'Come to this bar often?'" Yanish ran a finger down a display on Elias' tank and grunted.

"Bad news?" Bodel asked.

"His cognitive state remains unchanged, still catatonic. I don't believe he's lost higher brain functions. Still, the longer he stays in the tank, the better chance he has of developing an infection and then everything will go south. His body is withering, but we can't risk stimulating his muscles remotely for fear of what it'll do to his system."

"My offer still stands," Kallen said. "Let me link with him, see if I can coax him out."

"And my very firm 'no' remains. No. What you propose has no basis in medicine and would certainly be dangerous to you both."

"We're the ones with plugs. We are armor. Let us try," she said.

"No," Yanish said with a slight shake of his head. "If you'll excuse me." He left the room with a huff.

"I hate crunchies," Bodel said. He tapped on Elias' tank and a view slot opened. Elias hung in the amniotic fluid, eyes half-open.

"Hello, Elias," Kallen said. "We found someone with a copy of that old Japanese Anime series you were always talking about. Want to watch it?"

Elias hung in his tank, unresponsive as ever.

Bodel tapped at his Ubi and a holo screen playing a 2-D cartoon popped up between the three Iron Hearts.

Inside the tank, hidden from Kallen and Bodel's eyes, Elias' fingers twitched.

****

Admiral Garrett crossed his arms over his chest and sighed loudly. Every time he had to visit the Crucible's command center he ended up losing hours as Ibarra yakked incessantly over every detail of maintaining the Crucible.

The control center had been converted for easier human use—the control rings lowered, seats installed and the temperature brought down to cool and crisp, just how Garrett liked it—although the Crucible remained unmanned most of the time. Ibarra could handle the station with minimal effort and the crew of the fleet was better utilized repairing the fleet and rebuilding Phoenix into something habitable.

Now, Garrett's bridge crew—the few that survived the damage to the *America* and an amalgam of sailors from other ships—took up duty stations around the plinth where Ibarra had remained since he took over the station.

"The amount of omnium recovered from Mars and the mines within Ceres is in the tens of thousands of tons, more than I'd projected," Ibarra said. A hologram over the plinth displayed the Crucible as time projections and mass numbers pinged from the incomplete edges of the ring of thorns.

"We can't *use* omnium. Why are we wasting time with this?" Garrett asked.

"We can't use it yet, as I've told you every time you whine about the most amazing substance my intelligence has ever come across. Once we know how to convert it, we'll be able to complete this station and access the Xaros jump gate network," Ibarra said.

"And the Xaros will have access to this gate too. I'm in no hurry to open the door for more drones," Garrett said.

Captain Valdar entered the control room and stopped to gawk at the alien construct.

"Isaac, come over here," Garrett said to Valdar.

The captain of the *Breitenfeld* tromped down the steps, marveling at the holo display.

"I'd heard rumors, but this is incredible," Valdar said.

"We've kept this classified for as long as we can," Garrett said. "Some of the civilians are already trying to worship the Crucible, calling the Xaros decimation the rapture and claiming the probe here is a prophet."

"They send the nicest letters," Ibarra said.

"We'll man this station once we have the need and personnel available. Let the civvies come up and talk to this joker for a bit. His attitude should convince just about everyone that he's the same sanctimonious jerk he was in human form as he is in…electrons. Whatever you are."

"What is this place supposed to be?" Valdar asked. "There are stairs, atmosphere, and gravity. The drones need none of that."

"Correct," Ibarra said. The holo collapsed back into a sliver of light. "We've seen the drones build gates identical to this one in systems with Earth-like planets. Some systems have been rearranged: planets moved into the Goldilocks' Zone where liquid water can exist on a planet's surface, and terraformed. Thus far, none of the planets have ever been colonized."

"Someone is coming," Garrett said. "Whoever sent the drones to clear-cut intelligent life from the galaxy isn't interested in sharing the neighborhood."

"OK, but what does that have to do with me? I've been neck deep in repairing the *Breitenfeld* since the battle ended," Valdar said.

"The Xaros display an interesting foible," Ibarra said. "When they come across an intelligent species, they wipe it out. When they come across a planet once inhabited by an extinct civilization, they preserve what remains." The holo morphed into a planet covered in lush jungles, shallow and small seas and tiny ice caps.

"This is Anthalas, colony world of a spacefaring race that vanished almost fifty thousand years ago. Anthalas is just within range of our solar system," Ibarra said.

"Range? How? I thought this gate was incomplete," Valdar said. "And why should we care about some rock when the Xaros will almost certainly come back here?"

"Captain Valdar, there is more than one way to travel. As for your concerns, we believe Anthalas may have technology capable of helping us win this fight with the Xaros."

"And this involves me…how?" Valdar said.

"As soon as my wayward—ah, here we go," Ibarra rose from the plinth and a column of gold light coalesced around him. Golden points of light swirled into a perfectly white portal and lowered to the ground.

Stacey stepped through the portal wearing her battle armor. She moved clear of the portal and pressed her hands against her temples.

"Ugh, that got old fast," she said. She looked at her hands, then furrowed her brow at the armor covering her body. She tapped at the armor, like it wasn't meant to be there.

"That's funny," she said.

"Ensign Ibarra," Garrett said, "do you have it?"

Stacey's head shook quickly, like she'd been woken from a deep sleep.

"Sir! So nice to see another actual human being," she said and blanched as she looked around the room.

"Where is the DNA interface?" She jogged around the nearest ring of workstations and pointed at a naval rating.

"Move." The rating jumped from his seat and scurried away. Stacey stripped a glove off and pressed her hand against the black rock. The rock glowed with a pale blue light and the holo display above it went wild with incoming data.

"It took the Qa'Resh days to come up with the equations, but it should work," she said.

"Ensign, what are you talking about?" Valdar said.

"Grandpa, we have to adjust the gravity field for the station. Move the spikes into the configuration after I leave," Stacey said. She removed her hand and put her glove back on. "No time to explain, I'll foul the wormhole if I stay too long. Ibarra will fill in the details." She took a deep breath and jumped into the portal, which shrank to a pinprick and winked out.

"We're sending the *Breitenfeld* to Anthalas, Captain Valdar. First, we need the means to get there, and someone to show us the way," Garrett said.

****

From his perch on a Mule's open rear hatch,

Standish watched the thorns comprising the Crucible shift like a sea urchin fighting against the tide. Torni ducked down next to him, watching the spectacle over his shoulder.

"That is just freaky, isn't it?" Standish asked.

"You're worried about what the Crucible is doing, but not why we're sitting in the center of it while it...moves?"

Standish stiffened.

"Hey, why *are* we sitting out here? Sergeant Cortaro?"

Cortaro and Lieutenant Durand floated out of the cockpit, pulling themselves toward the open hatch via handrails running along the cargo hold.

"Captain Valdar said something small is coming through the gate," Durand said. "We're supposed to pick it up."

Standish did a double take at the lieutenant.

"Do we need our rifles? We haven't had a lot of luck with sudden alien encounters," Standish said.

"You keep talking and your big mouth will catch whatever's coming through," Cortaro said. He pushed a lifeline harpoon to Standish, who put the harpoon to his shoulder. The device would shoot a magnetic plate connected to a carbon fiber line and the internal winch would reel in whatever the plate attached to. Torni got one too.

Durand spoke to the other pilot through the IR, sending minor course corrections.

A point in space ahead of them twisted, distorting the light around it. A black circle grew from the point and a white lump of metal shaped like a rounded squash burst forth. The disk vanished and the metal, which looked like a life pod to Standish, rolled in the void.

"Ready harpoons," Cortaro said. "Keep your lines slack until you anchor."

The spinning pod slowed and the two Marines hit it with their harpoons. They bolted the winches to either side of the cargo hold and the winches pulled the pod closer.

"Adjust Y-axis by six degrees, slow relative

speeds to zero on my mark," Durand said. She backed away as the pod floated into the drop ship. The white metal was pitted and scarred. Four blisters, evenly spaced across the surface, looked like they were glass, encrusted with ice on the inside.

The pod cleared the hatch and the Marines detached the harpoon lines.

"Mark," Durand said. The pod hung steady.

"Latch it down, hurry," Cortaro said.

Standish hooked flat yellow fabric line into the hull and tossed the slack over the pod. It bent against the pod as it crossed. Standish moved to the other end of the hull and caught the hook from another line that Torni sent over, crisscrossing the other line. Standish hooked the new line to the floor and the cargo straps tightened over the pod, squeezing it to the deck.

Standish stood up and peered into the icy blister.

"I wonder what's inside." He tapped the blister with his knuckles.

A hand slammed against the inside of the pod, a hand twice the size of a man's with four reptilian fingers.

THE END

ABOUT THE AUTHOR

Richard Fox is the author of The Ember War Saga, and several other military history, thriller and space opera novels.

He lives in Las Vegas with his incredible wife and two boys, amazing children bent on anarchy.

He graduated from the United States Military Academy (West Point) much to his surprise and spent ten years on active duty in the United States Army. He deployed on two combat tours to Iraq and received the Combat Action Badge, Bronze Star and Presidential Unit Citation.

Sign up for his mailing list over at www.richardfoxauthor.com to stay up to date on new releases and get an exclusive Ember War short story.

The Ember War Saga:

1.) The Ember War
2.) The Ruins of Anthalas
3.) Blood of Heroes
4.) Earth Defiant
5.) The Gardens of Nibiru
6.) The Battle of the Void
7.) The Siege of Earth
8.) The Crucible
9.) The Xaros Reckoning

Made in the USA
San Bernardino, CA
23 May 2020

72051376R00237